I0593054

Fleur Blüm is a Melbourne-based writer, performer and musician.

Her blog can be found at https://fleurblum.com/blog

Also by Fleur Blüm:

Sophie's Path: A choose your own romance adventure

Discovering the Franklins

The characters and incidents portrayed herein are fictitious. Any similarity to a name, character or history of any actual person, living or dead, is entirely coincidental.

All rights reserved. No part of this publication may be reproduced without prior written permission of the publisher.

First edition 2020

Copyright © 2020 Fleur Blüm
ISBN 978-0-6483654-2-6

Editor: Annie Seaton
Cover Design: Charmaine Ross

Published by Fleur Blüm, Melbourne, Australia

My Mother's Secret

Fleur Blüm

To my mother, who has always supported me and my writing, I love you.

Chapter 1

Early on Thursday evening, Cassandra Morton was counting up the cash takings in the office above the restaurant where she worked. Even now, when so many people were using their cards, they took several thousand dollars cash each day. They were open for breakfast, lunch and dinner every weekday, and till five in the afternoon on weekends. At a push, it could seat about sixty people when it was busy.

Cassie was coming down the narrow stairs to the dining area when she saw someone she hoped she'd never see again: her ex-boyfriend, Tony. He was dishevelled as he stumbled into the middle of the dining room. He'd stopped and was leaning on the shoulder of a customer.

Obviously drunk, he looked like he'd had a rough couple of weeks. The man he was leaning on was in his mid-thirties, having dinner with two kids, both aged about ten. So far, the kids didn't seem to be worried by the stranger who was suddenly joining them but their father was leaning his body as far away as he could without having to get up from the table.

'Where is she?' Tony straightened. 'Cassie!'

Cassie hurried across and put her hand on Tony's shoulder. 'I'm here, there's no need to raise your voice,' she said quietly.

He was wearing a business shirt and tie, but the shirt was unbuttoned at the top and the tie was loosened and askew. He was a broad-shouldered man, not much taller than Cassie. His normally clean-shaven cheeks were covered with straggly stubble and his short, black hair was tousled.

'Where have you been? Baby, I've missed you so much!' He tried to plant a kiss on her. She took a half-step back out of range.

'I know you have.' Cassie's mind worked quickly, trying to figure out the best way to get Tony out of the dining room and away from the customers. His breath stank of booze, rum by the tang of Christmas pudding. Her skin crawled to be so close to him again, but she needed to hold herself together.

'Why don't you come out the back and we can talk without all these people hearing us, wouldn't that be nice?' Cassie voice faltered a little, she hoped he wouldn't notice.

'Why can't we talk here?'

Cassie's neck and shoulders started to ache from the force of tensing them, Tony was swaying a little. She flicked her eyes down at the children; the younger one was starting to cry. She took Tony's hand, it was hot and sweaty, and tried to pull him towards the kitchen.

Through the kitchen, at the back of the restaurant, there was a small courtyard where the bins were, and a couple of beaten up folding chairs where staff could sit on breaks. It had always felt like a sanctuary for Cassie, somewhere she could retreat. Now she led her drunken, volatile ex there, into her safe space.

She had seen the look that Emma had flashed at her as they went through the kitchen to get to the courtyard. Emma knew who Tony was and their history. She said nothing as they came through, but she'd looked angry and worried. It wasn't the best idea in the world, but it was the only one she had.

'What are we doing out here?' Tony asked.

'It's okay... babe,' Cassie tried not to choke on the word. 'We're just getting some quiet time. It's too hard to talk with all those people out there, looking at us.'

'Fuck 'em.' He wobbled and sat down heavily on a black folding chair.

There was a light on in the courtyard, but its beam was pointed at the bins, the chairs were in shadow. The night sky was heavy with rain clouds that hadn't yet burst.

'What did you want to talk to me about?' Cassie asked, resting her back against the cold brick wall. She tried to look casual while being ready to run.

'I don't hear from you for weeks. Then I hear your mum died. I wanted to be there for you. But of course, you don't answer my calls anymore. You forced me to come find you at work.'

Cassie had changed her phone number so that she could get away from Tony. She had blocked him online and had asked her friends to stop seeing him. Those who wouldn't, she didn't see anymore.

'I'm sorry. I should have told you about Mum,' Cassie said. She didn't believe it, but she knew she couldn't argue with him in this state. The best she could hope for was to get him to leave, or wait until he fell asleep, neither seemed very likely. He kicked a can on the ground by his feet, it was loud in the small space.

'You don't talk to me anymore. I know I could get you back.' His voice was soft. 'I did the wrong thing. I treated you real bad, I know that. I've been working on myself since you left, babe, and I know I can do better if you'll just give me a chance.'

She was silent. She'd heard it all before.

'You have to give me a chance, I deserve that! I'm not some fucking puppy you can just leave in a dumpster, you know.'

Cassie shuddered at the violent image. 'We don't work, Tony. It's just going to hurt us both if we try

again. Some people are just not meant to be together.'
She chose her words carefully. Now was not the time to
bring up the constant cheating or alcoholism. It wouldn't
ever be the right time to talk about the threats and
coercion.

'How can you say we don't work? I love you more
than anything I've ever loved in my life. You haven't
even given us a chance. You've never put in the effort to
make us work. You're a lazy, lying, selfish bitch.' Tony
stared at her across the courtyard. His voice was still low,
it had an edge.

'Tony, babe. We shouldn't be doing this now. Why
don't we talk another time? I have to go back to work.
You don't want to do this here, do you?' She swept her
arm over the wheelie bins and cardboard boxes.

'Fuck you. You can't just get rid of me.' He stood. 'I
deserve to be heard, you whore, and you have to stay
here and listen to me.'

'I don't have to stay here.' Cassie's whole body was
vibrating with fear. 'If you don't leave, I'm going to call
the police. You don't want that do you? Go home, get
some sleep. We'll talk tomorrow.' She put her hand on
his forearm and gave it a squeeze. She hoped it would
seem affectionate.

He had never hit her, even with all of their troubles.
The closest he'd come was punching a hole through the
wall directly next to her head. He'd had to go to hospital
and have stitches for the gash he'd torn along the side of

his hand. It had taken her nearly a year after that to leave him.

'Cassie, we need you back on the floor,' Emma said, popping her head out the back door.

There was a tense silence between the three of them; the sound of customers laughing, and clanking plates and cutlery thundered in Cassie's ears.

'Alright, alright,' Tony said, he seemed deflated, his shoulders hunched and exhausted. 'I'm going okay, you got what you wanted. We had some good times; you owe it to us to try to fix this.' He leaned forward and kissed her on the mouth. She stood rigid as he tried to force his tongue between her tightly closed lips.

He straightened and wobbled his way back through the kitchen. Cassie wiped the back of her hand over her mouth and followed him silently to the door of the restaurant. The man and his children had left. She watched Tony walk away down the street before she let out her breath and went back to the kitchen.

'What the actual fuck, babe?' Emma said, her words quiet but her face was full of thunder.

'I don't know. It's not my fault.'

'I never said it was your fault.' Emma rested her head on Cassie's shoulder briefly.

'Someone told him Mum died. He's been trying to call my old phone, and obviously I didn't answer. I think he's been driving himself crazy convincing himself we should be back together.'

'And after not hearing from you for weeks, he just decided to show up at your work?' Emma glared at her.

'I guess so. I thought it was clear that we were over, but he doesn't seem to understand.'

'You need an intervention order or something. This isn't normal. You can't just ignore him and hope he goes away.'

Cassie looked down at her shoes and was silent. How could she call the police on someone who was in so much pain? It's really not his fault he acts this way.

'If he comes here again, I'll call the police,' Emma added.

'I know. I'm sorry. I'll talk to him, when he's not so drunk.'

'Do you think talking to him will make any difference? He's completely ignored your request not to see him again.'

'I haven't *actually* told him that I don't want to see him. I told him I needed space when we broke up. I changed my number, but I didn't tell him because that would have meant telling him the new number. He's still my friend on Facebook, but I've put him on restricted, so he can't see anything I post, and he can't contact me.'

Emma's hands were busy with dressing a plate. She put the plate on the pass, ready for one of the wait staff to take it to the table. Then she looked at Cassie.

'You haven't told him he's not welcome? That he needs to leave you alone to move on? I mean, have you even told him you broke up, coz it sounds like you're being a big fucking coward.'

'I don't want to hurt him.'

'It's not hurtful to let him keep trying to contact you on that other phone number? So, he turns up at your place of work and frightens the customers, and me, and everyone else? You need to take a look at yourself, Cassie and see you're making life harder than it needs to be.'

Cassie's eyes stung with tears. She looked up at the ceiling, trying to hold them back, but it didn't work. They spilled over her lashes and down her cheeks.

'But it's so hard. My mum is dead. Penny insists her drug use isn't a problem and then ends up in hospital unconscious. Why can't I have five minutes where I deal with one crisis at a time?' Her voice cracked.

'I know it's not fair, hun. That's why you shouldn't have come back to work so soon. Give yourself some breathing space.' Emma reached out and wrapped Cassie firmly in her strong arms.

'Now wipe your face, go tell Simone that you have to go home, and ask her to get the others to cover your shifts for a week. I don't want to see you back here until you've sorted through some stuff: your mum, your sister and your ex. Alright? We'll be fine here.'

Cassie accepted the hug but didn't have the strength to return it. She felt safe for one tiny moment until Emma moved away again.

The other staff seemed relieved when she said she needed to take some time off.

'You're not superhuman, go easy on yourself, okay?' Simone said as she left for the night.

It was easy for them to say but the thought of being at home alone all day without anything to do was terrifying. What if she fell apart completely?

Chapter 2

Cassie sat rigid in the uncomfortable hard leather chairs, both feet on the floor and her hands clenched so tightly in her lap her knuckles were white. Her sister, Penny, scrolled through pictures on her phone, as though everything was fine. They sat at opposite ends of the large sofa and neither of them spoke.

'Beechworth?' A man a little past his middle years walked into the reception area and looked at them as he spoke.

Cassie only vaguely registered her mother's surname and stared when he called it again.

'Sorry, that's us.' She stood, wiped her sweaty hand on her jeans, and went forward to shake his hand.

'I'm Mr Pierce. My condolences for your loss. If you'll follow me into my office.' He gestured to the door.

The probate lawyers' office would have been the height of sophistication in the nineteen-eighties but was now tired and dated. The building, at the top of Collins St, the exclusive 'Paris-end' in Melbourne's CBD, was old and despite its a grand façade the lifts had stopped with an alarming grinding sound.

'It'll be fine,' Cassie said to her sister, sitting down in a stiff chair.

'I know,' Penny replied.

Cassie tapped her fingernails against one another and looked around the room. The vast mahogany desk was almost empty and had no computer on it.

'I have a copy of your mother's last will and testament. There are a few things that we'll have to go through. Funeral arrangements?'

'Yeah, we've done all that. Mum made her own arrangements. I think it's a bit morbid myself, but y'know,' Penny said.

'When you know you're dying, maybe you want to feel like you're doing something useful,' Cassie replied. They'd had this same conversation with everyone who had asked about the funeral arrangements.

'I still think it's creepy.' Penny folded her arms across her chest, twitching her left foot restlessly.

'So how do these things usually work? Do you have to get everyone around and read out the will?' she asked. Mr Pierce turned his eyes back to Cassie.

'Usually we present the content to the next of kin, which is yourselves in this case. We try to ascertain who the other parties to the will are and contact them. If there are any parties who wish to challenge the content, which is rather common, I'm sorry to say, then that will happen at this stage. A magistrate will have to rule whether or not the challenge is accepted. Only once that's all settled can the estate be released.' Mr Pierce's voice droned on, as though he could give this speech in his sleep.

'That sounds relatively straightforward, I guess,' Cassie said.

Penny still sat with her arms and legs crossed and said nothing.

'Shall we begin?' Mr Pierce asked.

'Let's get this over with.' Penny uncrossed and recrossed her legs.

'She's left much of her estate to you, her children. The distribution of her assets is listed here.' He handed an A4 page to Cassie, and then a second copy to Penny. She ignored it, so he placed it back on his desk.

'Mum's left you her car, Pen.' Cassie turned the page towards Penny.

'Yeah, fine.'

Their mother, Eleanor Beechworth, had not been rich. She had never owned the house she'd lived in, but she had been comfortable and had built up a few things of value. Cassie would inherit her mother's shares, such as they were, her books and music collection. Penny got the car, kitchen stuff and furniture.

There were a few items on the list that went to other people, a necklace to Cassie's aunt, Tessa, a fine China dinner setting to her mother's best friend, Nora. Nothing to Cassie's father, the will had been updated after the divorce.

Cassie frowned as she reached the end of the list.

'Kerry Strickland? Do you know who that is?' she asked Penny as she pointed to the name.

'Nope.'

'You didn't even look. Here, Kerry Strickland. Do you know her?'

Penny grabbed the list. 'Could be a man...'

'That's not helpful. Do you know the name?'

Penny scrunched up her face and sighed. 'Nuh.'

'Do I take it that neither of you recognise this person?' Mr Pierce broke in.

'No, I don't. Do you have any other information?' Cassie said.

Mr Pierce looked through the papers on his desk, blowing little puffs of breath through his pale lips. After some time, he looked up to Cassie.

'There doesn't seem to be any further mention at any point. Usually I have something to go on, an address or date of birth, to help make sure we get the right Kerry Strickland, but there's nothing here,' he said.

'He gets all of Mum's good jewellery,' Cassie said, as disbelief filled her.

'I thought you said I got all her stuff!' Penny interjected.

'Read the list, since you snatched it off me. You get the car and house stuff, Aunt Tessa gets a couple of rings, Kerry Strickland, whoever that is, gets all the rest.'

Cassie stopped herself before she went on. Immediately irritated with her sister it was hard to resist devolving into the usual bickering. She took a deep breath.

Penny read over the list, muttering to herself.

'We don't need to get upset about anyone listed here just at the moment,' Mr Pierce said. 'If you feel, once we have established who this Strickland is, that he does not have a valid claim you can contest it later.'

His voice was soft and calm, as though he were trying to smooth things over, but Cassie sensed a tone of dismissal. He barely looked at her, and when he did, his eyes were on her cleavage more often than her face.

'Get fucked. He doesn't deserve Mum's stuff. I do. I'm her daughter, and you're getting way more than me anyway.' Penny stood up and flung the list at the lawyer. The page wafted to the floor. She grabbed her handbag and stormed from the room, slamming the door behind her.

'I'm sorry,' Cassie said.

'Some people express their grief in a rather histrionic way.'

Cassie's skin crawled, the way it had with the funeral director a few days before. It was such an unpleasant way to characterise Penny's reaction. Mr Pierce didn't even try to hide his ogling now.

'Is there anything else I need to do today? I really should go...'

'Today was just a formality to show you the will.'

Cassie stood up, slinging her bag over her shoulder. 'Thank you for your time, Mr Pierce.'

'You're welcome, of course. If there is anything I can do, please let me know.'

'Thank you.' She shook his hand and this time his skin was dry and papery.

'Oh, and take a copy of the list. It's yours.' He handed her the copy from his desk.

'Thank you,' Cassie said again, wiping her hand against her jeans. The solicitor stayed behind his desk as she made her way back to the reception area.

'Did you see where my sister went?' she asked the young man standing there. Cassie was caught off guard as he looked at her, even through her grief and disgust with Mr Pierce, she was struck by his looks. A lock of golden-brown hair fell over his forehead as he looked at her.

'Just now? No, I'm sorry. I can't see much from my desk,' he gestured to an office just off the reception area where there were four desks closely packed together.

'I thought you were the receptionist.'

'No. I'm one of the junior associates, we're all in that office together.' He leaned closer to her and lowered his voice. 'The reception desk is just for show. You don't get a big fancy office until you're a partner. We live to serve the partners.' The corner of his mouth tugged up in a grin.

Cassie smiled, her grief forgotten as she stared into his grey eyes. She folded the list and placed it neatly into her bag to give herself a moment.

'Do I call you to make another appointment? Penny seems to have cut this one short somewhat.' Cassie kept her eyes down this time, she needed to keep her mind clear.

'We all take turns answering the phone when it rings.' He hesitated then and took a small step back, he looked very serious. 'I'm very sorry for your loss,' he said. There was not a trace of his earlier playfulness. Cassie looked at him and he was no less distracting when he was being earnest.

'Thank you,' she said, her throat strangely dry.

He put his hand on her shoulder, the warmth of his fingers reminded her how long it had been since she had been touched like that. Despite the difficulties with Tony, she believed in love, and longed for someone to come home to.

How can you be flirting when your mother has just died?

All the sadness she'd pushed down over the last few days threatened to come back up and she turned and rushed out without a backward glance.

The lift was empty. Cassie ran her hands over her face and through her hair as she descended.

Penny was waiting in front of the building, smoking and playing with her phone.

'Thanks for waiting,' Cassie said.

'Sorry. When it comes to Mum, it's all still pretty, y'know, new and stuff.'

'I know. Let's go home.'

The sisters were quiet on the tram back to Penny's rundown rental in Brunswick West. Cassie was stuck in her own mind, trying to process what the lawyer had said. She wondered if death always brought out the worst in people.

'Isn't this our stop?' Cassie said.

'Hmm? Yeah.' Penny stood up with a wobble and made her way down the steep steps to the road.

'Are you feeling alright?' Cassie reached out and took Penny's arm.

'Yeah, why? Whaddyou mean?' she said.

'You can't even walk straight. Are you sick or something?'

'Lay off.' Penny wrenched her arm away from her sister. 'I had a couple of Valium while I was waiting for you to come out of the fucking lawyer's office. I just need a little rest.'

Cassie sighed and said nothing. The walk took no more than five minutes usually, but Penny kept stopping to stare vaguely at the sky. She flinched each time Cassie tried to shepherd her forward.

It was only mid-afternoon, but the winter air in Melbourne had a bite to it. Penny was shivering but didn't seem to be bothered by it.

'Is Kev going to be home when we get there?' Cassie said.

'I dunno. Probably.'

'I might not stay long. I should drop in to work and check they don't need anything.'

'They will cope without you, you know. It's not like you're the god of shitty hipster cafés.' Penny dug around in her bag. 'You don't have to come in.'

The street was quiet, the afternoon school run had finished but the workers were still not on the way home. The quiet made Cassie think of her mother.

It had been only three weeks since she had been rushed to the hospital with difficulty breathing. Eleanor had always suffered from severe asthma. Throughout their lives she had been hospitalised at least once a year, given oxygen and the strong steroids she wasn't supposed to use for long periods of time.

For the six months leading up to her death, Eleanor had been straightening things out. She'd rewritten her will and consolidated her assets. Cassie had tried not to think about what it meant, but when she got the call from the hospital, she knew Eleanor was dying.

'Are you coming in or what?' Penny asked. They'd reached the shabby orange-brick veneer unit while Cassie was lost in her thoughts.

'Yeah, I'll have a cup of tea or something.'

'We haven't got any milk... no, we have milk, but it's off.' Penny laughed.

'Maybe I'll just head off then.'

'Whatever.' Penny went inside. Cassie heard her complaining to Kev as she hovered in the doorway.

'Babe, it was so shit, the lawyer was a massive creeper and Cass has been super morbid all the way back.'

'She's not coming in then?' Kev said. He was never called Kevin; he said it sounded like a P.E. teacher who shouldn't be left alone with children. Kev sounded like a man who meant business.

Cassie turned away before she heard any more. She walked to her car and plonked herself in the driver's seat, she'd driven over so they could go to the city together. She pulled the door closed behind her and when she looked out through the windscreen her vision was blurred with unshed tears. In that office she'd wanted the attractive young man to fold her into his arms and comfort her while she sobbed. Hardly an appropriate fantasy; they didn't even know each other.

She hated fighting with Penny, but they were very good at it. As the older sister, Cassie felt protective and Penny baulked at having any help.

She wiped her eyes. It wasn't time yet to allow her grief out. Penny and Kev might leave the house and see her sitting there. It was just the sort of thing that they'd tease her about.

The restaurant where she worked was about halfway between her sister's place and her apartment in

Northcote. She started the car and decided to head over for something for dinner.

The Fat Chef was two shops that had been joined together by knocking out the middle wall. The kitchen out the back was tiny and Cassie never understood how they managed to get all the food out in time.

'Hey, babe!' Emma called as she stepped into the kitchen. 'I thought I told you not to come in for a while?'

'I'm not here to work. I've had a tough day and I need some comfort food.' Cassie gave Emma a one-armed hug, careful not to get in the way of the several dishes she had going.

'Comfort food. Lemme have a think,' Emma brushed her hair off her face with the back of her forearm.

'That smells amazing,' Cassie said, pointing to a mushroom sauce she assumed was for pasta.

'You want that? I'll do it up special for you. Ten minutes max.'

Cassie moved away from the kitchen and loitered behind the counter. She knew from years of experience that trying to talk to the chef while she was busy never went well.

The front of house was busy, the food was good, but not great, the service was reliable, but never fine-dining. The clients were mostly locals.

The walls were exposed brick and the ceilings still had their cream pressed tin covers. The owners had furnished it with oddly matched tables and chairs, while it should have looked like junk, the aesthetic somehow worked.

'You're back in tomorrow, right? We've had a hell of day without you.' Simone, the assistant manager, had snuck up from the other side of the venue and caught Cassie off guard. She took over running the place when Cassie wasn't in.

'I'm sorry, I… you know I've had family stuff.'

'I'm kidding! We've managed just fine without you. We love you, and of course we want you here, but your mum died, for God's sake. You don't have to drag your misery guts in here because you think we need you.'

Cassie was stunned, she tried to reply but her throat was parched.

'Relax.' Simone put one arm around Cassie. 'You're an important part of the family, but you need to take care of yourself. We'll manage. That's all I'm saying.'

'Order up.' Emma called from the kitchen.

Simone dropped her hand from Cassie's shoulder.

'I've had a rough day,' Cassie said, her words finally returning to her as the hot mushroom-garlic-cream smell drifted up from the bag Simone collected and put into her hands.

'Of course, you have.'

Simone nodded her head, her eyes sad and gentle. They'd worked together for a couple of years, Simone had started about six months after Cassie. It was meant to be only a temporary break from her Social Work degree, but the pace of the work, the closeness of her team, and the ready access to excellent comfort food meant that five years later she was still there and her uni days were behind her.

At home Cassie opened the bag and saw that Emma had given her an enormous serving. She'd also included a smaller container of chocolate brownies, and a note.

'Eat all of this. Doctor's orders.'

Cassie curled up on her couch, opened her laptop and played a movie on Netflix. It was a rom-com that she'd seen before, she just wanted something to distract her from her mother, from the niggling anxiety of who Kerry Strickland was, and from the cute lawyer who made her feel guilty every time he popped into her head.

As soon as the first piece of tortellini reached her tongue Cassie remembered she was starving. She had scoffed down the pasta and half the brownies before she the holes in her belly, and her heart, were full.

Chapter 3

Jason Harding walked home from the train station. He was restless, almost jittery, in a way he couldn't quite pinpoint. It was an average day in the office, most of the work the firm handled was probate which meant the office was often filled with grief and high drama; a competing version of a will, or someone cut out who didn't like it.

Jason's boss, Mr Pierce, first name Leonard, but Jason couldn't think of him as anything other than Pierce, had a client meeting that had gone awry. It was straight after lunch and he'd returned barely minutes before the client turned up. Two sisters, both in their twenties, by Jason's estimation, and clearly still distressed by their bereavement.

The younger sister, thin frame, big hair and worried-looking, had stormed off and was out the door before he could do anything. He'd stood and waited, and it wasn't long before the other sister had walked out. He'd noticed her as she was waiting for Pierce earlier, her features were severe and dark, the opposite of her sister. She looked distant when she came through.

He'd tried to take her mind off her grief and anger by making a joke at his own expense, he wanted to see her face lighten with a smile, sure she would look even more beautiful.

She was so easy to watch. Her long, straight brown hair moved over her back like water when she walked. He wanted to touch it. To stroke it while she let out the grief that was barely contained below the surface.

She smiled a little at his joke, but even as it left his mouth, he worried he'd overstepped. *Don't flirt with the clients*.

'I'm very sorry for your loss.' His voice had become mechanical as he tried to get back to a professional demeanour.

When he'd touched her shoulder and she flinched away, he wasn't surprised. He watched until she disappeared into the lift before turning back to his desk.

What a disaster! He thought, *all it takes is one pretty woman and I turn into a perve.*

He put his head around the solid wooden door into Pierce's office. His boss was sitting at the desk stacking papers as though nothing had happened.

'Why did they leave so quickly?'

'Who knows.' Pierce didn't look up. 'Someone listed as a beneficiary neither of them has heard of. Women can be very unreasonable when they're emotional.'

Jason clenched his teeth. 'Did you manage to sort anything out about proceeding?'

'No, not really. I just gave them the list of bequests and then they had a hissy fit and stormed off. I didn't even get to explain the executors' duties.'

'I'll call tomorrow and follow up with them,' Jason said.

'Good idea, son.' Pierce had collected the papers together and handed Jason the file.

Not only sexist but supremely patronising, as always, Jason thought as he stalked back to his desk. He couldn't understand why anyone still used Pierce to handle their affairs.

There was another partner, who was slightly better but still objectionable. Evelyn Thomson was his name, a snob who spent a lot of time complaining about his health. Both partners drank much more than was appropriate, especially during lunch. Jason and the other junior staff had agreed Pierce was the worst, but only by a narrow margin.

Settling at his desk, Jason read over the client's file. He wished he'd asked Pierce who the interloper was, but he probably hadn't even noticed. At four o'clock both Pierce and Thomson decided it was time to go home; that was a long day for them.

'See you tomorrow, boys,' Thomson said on his way out. The junior lawyers were all men in their twenties.

'You've got a ten o'clock appointment, Mr Thomson,' Daniel, one of the juniors, called after him.

'Yes, yes, I know. Just have the file ready for me when I get in.' Thomson waved away the reminder.

'As if you would have remembered on your own,' Daniel muttered as the bell from the lift sounded. He shook his head and caught Jason's eye.

'We should just let them forget,' Jason said.

'They'd still manage to make it our fault.'

'True.' Jason put his head down and went back to his work.

***

Back at his apartment, Jason reflected on his part in the whinge sessions. His mother had always told him that negativity breeds negativity. He sighed and stepped inside.

Guitar, dinner, gym, sleep, he thought as he dropped his bag onto his bed.

Jason lived in a two-bedroom apartment on the top floor of an art-deco duplex in Hawthorn with his best mate, Lucas. Brown bricks and stained cream plaster covered the sweeping curves of the building. The lounge held a strange mixture of items from each of them: a couch, coffee table, television, Xbox and drumkit from Lucas. Jason had contributed another couch, an armchair, an absurdly bright rug from his mother, and several guitars. Lucas wasn't home, he would be at his bar job by now, so Jason picked up his battered acoustic guitar and started to play. He was no lead guitarist, but he had a good grasp of the chords and could sing along most of the time.

He got lost in the music and as soon as he looked up, his belly rumbled loudly, it was after eight. He sighed, stood and wandered over to the kitchen. The fridge was mostly empty, but he looked through the cupboards and found a can of baked beans and some bread for toast.

After eating, Jason felt weary. *The gym will have to wait till another night.* His track-suit lay in a pile on his bedroom floor. A pang of guilt struck him even as he told himself a walk would do him good.

'Pa pa pa poker face, pa pa poker face!' Jason caught himself singing along with Lady Gaga as he walked. He smiled to himself already feeling better.

***

The next morning, as Daniel had predicted, Thomson was late for his first meeting.

'I'm so sorry, Mrs Park, he's with another client out of the office. I'm sure he won't be long.'

Daniel and Jason exchanged a glance as the elderly Mrs Park sat in the reception area, waiting. Daniel had called Thomson just before ten; typically, he was still at home in Caulfield. He was unlikely to get to the office before eleven but had given them strict instructions to do whatever it took to keep Mrs Park there until he arrived.

'Can I get you a cup of tea?' Jason asked at twenty-five past the hour. He was ready for one.

'No, thank you. I don't expect I'll be waiting too much longer.' Mrs Park looked much smaller sitting on the enormous hard leather couch she had settled in.

'Are you sure?' Jason said.

'If you insist,' she said.

Once he'd made the tea, Jason pulled out the Beechworth file. Cassandra Morton, the elder daughter was an executor, and Tessa Beechworth, the deceased's sister was named as a co-executor. He wondered if either woman had had the role explained to them; he was sure Pierce wouldn't have done it.

He dialled her number.

'You've reached Cassie, I'm not able to come to the phone right now…'

'Hi Cassandra, my name's Jason Harding, I'm a lawyer working on your mother's estate. We met yesterday in the offices of Pierce & Thomson. There are a couple more things we need to discuss. If you can give me a call back when you have a moment.' Jason left his contact number and ended the call.

Thomson turned up just before eleven, his shirt wrinkled under his suit jacket. Jason hoped Mrs Park wouldn't notice.

'Well, you won that bet, mate,' Daniel said after they'd disappeared into Thomson's office.

'What's that?'

'I said not before eleven and you said, 'even he's not that bad', so you won.'

'Oh. It's not a very good way to do business. At some point they'll run into someone who has a real problem being stood up by an hour.'

'Almost an hour,' Daniel corrected.

It wasn't until well into the afternoon that Jason's phone rang.

'It's Cassie Morton, you called about my mother's estate?' she sounded hassled and there was a lot of noise in the background.

'Yes, I know you were in here yesterday, but I noticed – ah well, the meeting was cut a little short, and there are a few things we need you to do as the executor.'

'I'm the executor?' she asked.

'I'm surprised this hasn't been explained,' Jason said, hating himself for lying.

'No, I haven't been told anything. After the funeral arrangements this is the first I've heard of the will. Mum lodged it with you and, to be honest, I assumed you guys were the executors.'

'A solicitor is not usually an executor.'

'Look, I can't really talk now.'

'Perhaps it's best if I make an appointment with Mr Pierce on Monday, but you might want to do a bit of research on the role of the executor-'

'Great, something else I have to fucking deal with.' She stopped speaking suddenly. 'I'm sorry. What time?

Earlier is better for me, I start work at noon. Is there anything else?'

'Well, the other executor listed is Tessa Beechworth, your aunt. Do you know if she's been told?'

'There are two now? Fine. I'll tell her. Can you email me with confirmation?'

'Of course, I'll send it now,' Jason said.

'Thanks. At least you're looking after me,' Cassie laughed mirthlessly. 'See you then,' she said.

'If there's anything else, please call.'

Jason was used to dealing with people who had lost loved ones, but seeing Cassie jerked around by the partners was more upsetting than usual.

'I'm going for a walk,' he said picking up his jacket.

***

On Saturday morning Jason went around to his dad's place to pick up his younger brother, Knox. His father had remarried a woman twenty-two years younger than him. She didn't work, or at least had given it up after the wedding. Knox had come along within a year.

'Hey mate, you ready to go?' Jason said, clapping Knox on the shoulder. His footsteps echoed through the vaulted foyer of his father's house.

His brother was ten, but small for his age, his head just reached Jason's chest. He had delicate features, dusty brown hair and the same grey eyes as Jason and their father.

'Yeah, cool. Mum's out the back, you wanna say hi?'

'Alright.' Jason found it difficult to understand what anyone saw in Becca – she always had the right shade of tanned skin, blonde highlights in her golden-brown hair, and brightly-coloured false fingernails. They were green today. She ticked all the boxes to be considered pretty, but he had never been the least bit attracted to her.

'Jason! Baby! How are you?' She waved from the lounge chair next to the pool. Jason zipped up his hoody and thrust his hands into his pockets against the chilly morning. Becca sat reading a magazine in the weak sunshine wearing an oversized grey cardigan.

'I'm okay. Just taking little mate out for the day. When do you need him back?'

'You can keep him.'

'Thanks.' Jason shivered as a frigid gust of wind whipped around his neck.

'Does he have homework or anything we need do remember to do?'

'Oh, I don't know, babe, I'm sure it'll be fine.' Becca waved her long talons in dismissal.

'We'll be back tomorrow sometime,' he said. 'Come on, mate.'

Knox talked most of the way on the drive from Brighton to Hawthorn. Jason often worried he was just another accessory to Becca.

Their father, David, was a stockbroker—a very rich, self-made man. He spent long days at the office and most of his weekends away from the house. It had been the same when Jason was little.

Knox's small hands demonstrated the size of the turtle that he'd seen at the aquarium. 'It was so cool, you should have been there.'

'I wish I'd been there, then I'd've seen it too, hey?' Jason looked back to the road. 'I thought we could play some Frisbee in the park near my house while the sun is out, then you can help me make some lunch, and then we can play Xbox.'

'Can't we play Xbox before lunch?' Knox asked.

'Nope. Gotta be active before we're sedentary.'

'What's sedentary?'

'It's when you do things sitting down, like Xbox or watching a movie. You need to have variety.'

Jason had had a little sister to keep him company growing up in a big, empty, expensive house, but Knox had no one. Becca showed no interest in having any more children. Every month or so Jason had Knox over to stay. It wasn't much, but at least it was consistent.

'Can you ask Dad why I can't have a dog?' Knox said after they'd spent an hour throwing the Frisbee.

'Sure mate, I'll see what I can do. I wasn't allowed to have one either.'

Dad was too worried about it breaking stuff or pissing on the carpet.

'Oh.' Knox looked down.

'Do you have any friends at school who have a dog? You could go visit. That's almost like having one of your own.'

'No, it's not.' He stabbed at the ground with his shoe, in a full sulk now.

'We can't have everything we want. That's part of growing up. Sometimes things don't go our way, but we have to make the best of what we have, right?' Jason hoped Knox didn't notice he sounded patronising.

'I don't want everything. I just want a puppy.'

'I know. Let's go get some lunch. I'm making burritos. You like those right?' Jason put his hand on Knox's shoulder in a half-hug and kept it there as they walked back to the car.

A dog would make it less lonely in that house, Jason thought as he watched Knox buckle himself in.

***

When they got back to the apartment Lucas was home. He'd been trying to get Knox into drumming.

'It'll annoy your dad no end if he has to buy the kid a kit!' he'd said after the last visit, tapping on the table with his long fingers. He looked like a surfer with his longish hair and stubble. 'You been practicing those games we played last time?'

'Yeah, a bit.' Knox chewed his burrito.

Jason looked over at Lucas and raised his shoulders in an exaggerated shrug. Lucas did the same in return.

'Are you okay?' Jason asked Knox quietly, after Lucas stood up to wash the plates.

'What's a gold-digging whore?' His little brother frowned.

'Who said that, mate?' Anger roiled in Jason's gut. *The poor kid.*

'Dad said it to Mum. They thought I was in bed, but I wasn't.'

'Uh, it's a mean thing to say. I think maybe Dad just got a bit angry with your mum. I'm sure he didn't mean it.'

'Maybe.' Knox chewed on his bottom lip. 'If Mum and Dad get a divorce, will you still come and visit me?'

'Of course, you'll always be my brother.' Jason's heart was pounding so hard he couldn't think straight.

'But I mean just because they had one fight...' he added.

'They fight all the time. Johnno at school said they were going to break up and it was my fault.'

'Grownups fight sometimes. I'm sure they'll sort it out.' The platitudes felt false coming from his mouth, but what else could he say.

Jason's parents had split up when he was eight. His sister, Tamara, had only been five. All the feelings Jason had thought he'd bottled up came back as he watched the trembling bottom lip of the little boy sitting at his kitchen table.

'I'll talk to Dad. It'll be okay.' He wanted to promise it would be, but he couldn't lie to Knox. His jaw had started to ache as he clenched it.

He pulled his brother into a bear-hug. Knox endured the hug for a long time before protesting. 'Get off. You're strangling me.'

Jason let his brother go and gave his hair a tousle. He put on a movie, and Knox snuggled down on the couch with a yawn.

All the fighting must be keeping him awake.

It would be no good to call his father now, he'd be out with his golf buddies. He could call Becca, but he never knew what to say to her. Maybe he could catch Dad tomorrow when he dropped Knox back.

'Shit,' he muttered. He'd forgotten to email Cassie Morton with a time for the meeting on Monday. He had been about to press send when Pierce had needed him to get to the bank before it closed. He'd thought about Cassie a hundred times since then, but only realised now he'd never sent the confirmation.

There was nothing he could do about it now; they couldn't access work email from home, and he didn't have a key to the office for the weekend.

If I call her first thing on Monday, that should be enough time. Pierce has already jerked her around and now I'm adding to it. I hope she isn't really angry, Jason thought, pacing the kitchen.

'Come have a cheeky cone with me, you seem tense,' Lucas spoke quietly.

'Man, not with the kid here.'

'Okay, good point. What about a beer on the balcony? He won't know and you need to chill out a bit, bro.'

'Alright.' Jason stretched his mouth wide open, trying to loosen his jaw.

Chapter 4

Late on Sunday night Cassie realised the lawyer had not confirmed their appointment. She still had to invite Tessa to accompany her.

Nothing to be done about it, she thought, pulling out her phone.

'Tess here,' her aunt answered.

'Hi, it's Cassie.'

'Ah, darling! How are you holding up? Did you see the lawyers last week?'

'Yes. That's what I'm calling about.' She picked at a piece of dirt on her trousers. 'We had a meeting with the lawyer last week and Penny stormed out—'

'Typical! Trying to get out of her responsibilities again.'

Penny didn't have a job most of the time which made her lazy in Tessa's opinion. Tessa hated laziness.

'It's been a pretty tough time for everybody. Penny was upset because of someone in the will—' She broke off; she didn't need to defend her sister. 'What I was saying before is the meeting last week was cut short, so I have to go back tomorrow. One of the juniors rang to say I was named executor of the will.'

'That makes sense I suppose. Did they explain what you have to do?' The noise of the TV had faded, Tessa must have walked into another room leaving Uncle Ian to the football.

'No, not really. But they said you were the co-executor.'

'I didn't know you could have two.'

'Can you come with me tomorrow? I—'

'I have to work, but I can make some time for this.'

'I'll ring them first thing and let you know what time.'

'You alright, love?' her aunt asked after a long moment.

'Do you know who Kerry Strickland is?'

'Who? I don't think so.'

'The name was in Mum's will. I didn't know who it was. You don't know either?'

'It doesn't ring any bells.'

'Okay.' Cassie sighed. She didn't want to ask her father about Kerry Strickland. That would open a wound she wasn't ready to deal with.

'Are you alright?'

'I don't know,' she hesitated. 'I haven't been to work for a few days, but I don't want to be at home. I kept forgetting things and I nearly burst into tears all the time.' She took a deep breath. 'I keep waiting to feel better and I just don't.'

'It's only been a couple of weeks,' Tess said, her tone gruff. 'You've been running around like a blue-arsed fly getting the funeral sorted. I wish I'd been able to help you with that, but it hit me harder than I thought it would—' She sniffed loudly, her breath hitching as though she had started to cry.

'It wasn't that much work, really.' Cassie lied, but it was comforting.

'Nonsense. Now that I've come back to the real world, I'll be able to pull my weight.' Tessa's voice broke into a sob.

Cassie was so shocked her brusque, stoic aunt was crying she couldn't say anything. Tessa hadn't even cried at the funeral.

Perhaps it's only now starting to feel real, Cassie thought, trying to keep her emotion under control.

'It'll be okay. At least she's not in pain anymore,' Cassie said.

'You're right. No sense blubbering about it.'

'So, I'll let you know the details and then we'll sort it out from there.'

'Right you are.' Tess made a sound that might have been a laugh.

When she ended the call, Cassie was surprised to feel a new tenderness toward her aunt. A woman who had lost her only sister, she seemed to be caught out of time,

Cassie thought she belonged on a sheep station in the fifties.

Growing up, Cassie and Penny had both been terrified of their mother's older sister, a tall, stout woman with broad shoulders and muscular legs. She'd been single for most of their lives and Penny had insisted that it was because she was a closet lesbian. Cassie refused to admit the lack of a boyfriend or husband proved anything.

About two years ago, however, Tessa had started seeing Ian. He was a man out of time too; a country boy with a rough vocabulary and generous spirit. It was under the influence of Ian that Tessa had started to soften around the edges. She'd finally found a place to belong.

***

The next morning, Cassie's phone rang one minute before nine.

'Cassie Morton?'

'Yes, hello. Who's this?' she asked, although knew who it was.

'It's Jason, from Pierce & Thomson. Again.'

'I remember. You were going to let me know what time my appointment was today. I don't know if I'll be able to make it now, with only a couple of hours' notice.'

'I know I was supposed to email you, but I've managed to get a spot in Mr Pierce's diary for eleven. I hope you can still make it.'

'Hmm,' Cassie pretended to think it over. She shuffled some pages on her desk. 'That should be fine.'

'Great,' he said, Cassie thought she heard him sigh. 'Did you manage to get some information on the role of the executor?'

She'd meant to research the duties as soon as she'd heard about it on Friday, but every time she sat down to do it, it had seemed so overwhelming she'd put it off. 'No, I haven't had the chance.'

'Right. If you were able to get to the office about ten minutes early, I could go through what the executor does before you go through to see Mr Pierce. It's not very difficult, all common-sense stuff really.'

Cassie was only half listening. She didn't want to be the executor. Even with her very limited understanding of what the job was, it seemed like it would take a lot of time. Her mother's death was still fresh, and Cassie thought it would be a lot of heartache and not much reward.

'I'll see what I can do. As I said it's very late notice.' Cassie was happy to come into the office a little early to see Jason; he was so much more pleasant to deal with than Pierce.

'Of course, we really are very sorry.' His voice was definitely strained now.

She sent a message to Tessa after she disconnected. 10:45a.m. apparently. They just confirmed. Do you need the address?

Having her no-nonsense aunt with her would certainly help keep her emotions in check and hopefully Mr Pierce's condescension to a minimum.

***

Tessa met her outside the building where the lawyer's suite was. Cassie gave her a hug and was surprised that Tessa lingered.

The lift was jerky and her aunt pressed her hands to her thighs while they waited for the doors to open.

Jason greeted them at the door of the suite. 'Good morning. Can I offer you tea or coffee?'

When he smiled Cassie remembered how handsome he was. Now that she wasn't crying, she could appreciate his fine, straight nose. On the dark wood coffee table were two printed sheets of information on the role of the executor.

She watched him move to the kitchenette to make tea for her and Tessa. Her eyes drifted to his firm, round bottom. She shook her head and told herself to behave.

Jason handed both of them a cup of tea and perched himself on the edge of the coffee table. Cassie and Tessa were sitting together on the hard leather sofa.

'Is that mahogany?' Tessa asked, taking a sip of her tea.

'I don't know. I suppose so. It looks expensive, so that would make sense,' Jason said.

Cassie put her tea on the frosted glass coaster and picked up the document.

Jason turned his attention to her. 'The role of the executor of the will, in a nutshell, is to ensure that the wishes of the deceased are followed. It's up to the executor, or executors in this case, to find the named parties in the will and deliver the bequests. They also dispose of the deceased's possessions as per their wishes, as well as repay any debts. It includes administrative details such as closing bank accounts, redirecting mail, notifying utilities etc. You can nominate to have someone from this office take on the actual work, charged at our usual rate of course.'

'Mmm. Most of the work has been done already.' Cassie scanned over the documents, she was unwilling to pay these lawyers any more than was strictly necessary.

'It doesn't seem like too much bother then, really. I think Ian did it for his uncle,' Tessa said.

Cassie turned to her aunt. 'Following up everyone named in her will, going through all her stuff...'

Jason stood up and went back to his office, Cassie glanced up as he left. She wasn't sure whether to be thankful for the privacy, or annoyed that he'd slunk away.

'Nonsense. It won't take long, and besides, who better to do it than you and me?'

Cassie tossed the paper back onto the coffee table.

'I know it's exhausting but do it for her sake.' Tessa reached over to put her hand on Cassie's knee. Cassie looked at her watch, it was nearly twenty minutes past eleven.

'Is Mr Pierce running late?' she asked Jason when he sat at his desk in the adjoining room.

'He's at a meeting in another office. He won't be long.'

'I did mention to you that I have to be at work by noon...'

'Yes, you did. He'll be here soon.'

Mr Pierce swept into the office at half past and gave no apology for his lateness.

'Come through,' he said without looking at them.

He sat behind his big empty desk and tapped his fingers on it. When he tried to rush through their appointment Tessa was having none of it.

'It's your job to take us through this, given the rate you're charging us, you will stay here and explain it until we understand,' she said.

'Usually the juniors do it, they're perfectly capable. Surely Jason has been through it already. I did ask him to do it as soon as we were notified of Ms Beechworth's death.'

Cassie was inclined to believe Jason's earlier assertion that this was Pierce's job; he seemed the more sincere of the two. Though forgetting to confirm the appointment did make her wonder if Jason was competent.

'That is beside the point, it wasn't done, and you will go through it with us now.' Tessa had puffed herself up. She was quite an intimidating figure when riled, even seated. Her dark hair was swept back into a neat bun at the base of her neck, she wore no make-up and had dressed in a severely cut navy suit.

'Alright,' Mr Pierce relented.

After spending fifteen minutes watching the lawyer being interrogated by Aunt Tessa, Cassie started to fidget, every moment was making her later for work.

'Well. We must be going. It's very disappointing to have had to wait half an hour for an appointment, Mr Pierce.' Tessa stood and marched out without a backward glance.

As Cassie trailed through the reception area behind her, she looked for Jason. She was hoping she might be rewarded with one of his smiles after having sat through another meeting with Pierce. When Jason wasn't there, she felt a disappointment much stronger than was sensible.

'I still don't have any idea what I'm supposed to be doing,' Cassie said as they walked through the foyer, her voiced echoing strangely against the domed ceiling and the polished stone walls.

'Let's have a coffee and we can talk it through.'

'I'm supposed to be at work in five minutes,' Cassie said.

'Well, you're not going to make it.'

'I'll have to call them. It's only a short shift over lunch, I'm sure they won't mind if I cancel just this once.'

While Cassie made the call, Tessa selected a small kiosk style coffee shop at the top of Collins Street. Its façade was open to the wind and three stools were lined up along in front of the window. Cassie suspected it catered primarily to the takeaway caffeine boost.

'Simone said it was fine to have the day off,' Cassie said as she entered the cafe. Simone had sounded almost eager for Cassie not to come in again, but maybe she was imagining it.

'Good.' Tessa seemed unconcerned by the cold and uncomfortable seating. 'What's all this really about then? I can't believe you don't understand what's expected of you.'

Cassie wriggled herself onto one of the stools. 'I don't want to do it. I thought with the funeral over I'd be able to get back to my life. I don't want to think about Mum anymore. I want to go back to how things were.'

'We all have to find our way forward, but grief is a slow process. It will never be the way it was. Sorting through your mother's things needs to be done, and it'll give you an opportunity to say goodbye.'

Cassie leaned her elbows on the narrow wooden bench top and hid her face with her hands. 'I can't. I have stuff I need to get on with.'

'Like what?' Tessa's tone had taken on a hard edge.

'Like getting back to work. They've been good about it so far, but I know it's hard. Shit just isn't done properly without me.'

'Work is not a good enough excuse. What else is so pressing that you can't spend time on mourning the death of your own mother? You don't even have a boyfriend to distract you anymore, not that that would be an excuse either.'

It was all Cassie could do to hold back the wave of tears building in her throat. She'd never confided in her aunt the real reasons for her most recent breakup, only her mother.

'I can't devote my whole life to cleaning up after Mum. It's not fair.' Cassie lifted her head and glared at her aunt.

Tessa took a sip of her coffee and returned her gaze steadily. 'No one is asking you to sit on a rock wailing and tearing your hair out, but you need to accept that being Eleanor's daughter means taking care of the business of death.'

'So why don't you make Penny do it?' Even as she said it, Cassie knew she sounded childish. She turned her face towards the street. A steady stream of people passed by the coffee shop, many of them were wearing black and carrying scowls on their faces. When she turned back her aunt's face had softened.

'You know why your mother couldn't ask Penny to do it. With all the… well, you know what she's like.'

'I know. But it's too hard.' Cassie wiped away a tear.

'It is hard, hopefully it will be the hardest thing you'll ever have to do. I'll be there to help.'

'I guess so.'

'Plus, Mister Pierce said that trying to get out of being an executor is a total nightmare, so that seems hardly worth it in the end. And you don't want to pay that lot to do it, do you?'

Cassie tried to smile, but it felt very weak. She looked at her coffee, now cold and unappealing. She supposed she would need to get Mum's house cleaned out soon or she'd have to keep paying the rent on it. Mr Pierce said that it could take up to twelve months for the inheritance to come through, so she would have to pay it herself. With all the time she'd taken off work, she couldn't afford that too.

'I'll find some time.' Cassie pushed away her untouched coffee.

'Alright, you just let me know and I'll make sure I make time to help.'

Cassie rubbed her hands over her face then remembered that she'd put make-up on that morning. Her hands came away smeared with foundation and black mascara.

'Fantastic,' she said.

'Go to the bathroom and fix yourself up.'

The toilet looked as though it might have been converted from some sort of storeroom. Cassie bumped both of her elbows against the walls trying to get in around the sink. She looked at the floor; the lino was torn and stained.

Clearly, they don't get much call from customers to use the facilities, she thought as she looked in the mirror.

Her face was blotchy. Her eye make-up had migrated to the tops of her cheeks and her eyes were bloodshot. She fixed herself up as best she could. Taking one last look, Cassie went back to where Tessa was waiting.

'Alright, we can go now. I should be fine if you want to just head off.' Cassie wanted her aunt to stay with her, but she didn't want to ask.

'Nonsense. It won't be a long wait this time of day and the stop is right there.' Tess clapped her hand on Cassie's shoulder roughly.

Tessa hugged her niece as the tram approached. Again, Cassie was struck by how tender the moment was. She climbed onto the tram and took a seat facing backwards so she could watch the robust figure of her aunt recede.

Chapter 5

Jason was even more intolerant of the partners'
behaviour that day. He had watched Cassie and her aunt
walk into the meeting and, through the partially closed
door, he could hear the dismissive tone Mr Pierce had
used. The older woman had managed to wrest
information from Pierce, and he was glad Cassie had her
by her side.

Not for the first time, Jason thought he should find
another job. He'd been there for five years ever since
he'd left university. At first, he'd stayed because he
wanted a decent length of employment on his résumé,
but now it felt like inertia.

The last time he'd looked, before Christmas, he'd had
an interview at one of the large firms. They'd told him
the hours expected were 8 a.m. to 6 p.m., five days per
week, plus overtime and work taken home, and he'd
decided to withdraw his interest. Since then he'd avoided
the job websites.

My Mother's Secret

On Monday evening he sat on the couch in his lounge room, with his computer on his lap.

God this is boring, he thought as he scrolled through ads on the job website. Graduates, junior lawyers, solicitors, even legal secretary positions scrolled past but none of them grabbed him. He didn't have the motivation to find a new job, but he had to get out of his current one. He leaned his head against the back of the couch and closed his eyes.

'You still up?' Lucas said, walking through the front door of the apartment, his hair tied in a messy bun.

'What? I must have fallen asleep.' Jason rubbed the back of his neck. 'Have you got food?' The smell of lamb and garlic sauce had followed Lucas into the room.

'Yeah, that's my dinner! Didn't you eat before you passed out?'

'I meant to have a quick look before getting something proper. It's soooooo boring!' He tipped his head back to emphasise his point and his neck twinged painfully. Jason glanced at his watch and got up. 'Well g'night.'

***

Come to this warehouse party with us tomorrow bro. Good times to be had. His sister, Tamara, had texted him on Friday afternoon.

Who's going? he'd replied.

Usual crew; Gem, Ant, Steve. Bring Lucas. Steve's got pills if you want.

He sighed. Sure, I'll meet you there. Send the deets.
We'll meet at yours. I told mum I'd crash with you.

Great, she'll come in at sunrise and crash out on the couch. It's better than going home with someone she's just met.

The last time he'd gone out on a big night with Gemma and Tam they had ended up in the emergency department trying to work out what they'd taken. Gemma had collapsed on the dance floor, but Tam had refused to call the ambulance.

'They're in with cops, we'll get done for sure.' She said.

'She's really not well, we have to take her to the hospital. They won't arrest you. It'll be fine.' He'd stroked Tam's hair and she'd relented.

Jason had a sick feeling in his stomach when he read that there would be pills. He had to go, make sure she was alright. Lucas would provide some backup, but he tried not to get involved.

Warehouse party with me and Tams tomorrow? They're getting shitfaced. He texted Lucas as he got on the tram to come home.

Can't. I'm working, six nights in a row. Sorry.

Lucas always encouraged him to look out for Tamara, whose penchant for drugs and wild parties tended to get her into trouble.

It's not like him to be so dismissive, he knows the score.

My Mother's Secret

***

On Saturday night Tamara and her friends came on the train to Jason's place. Tamara still lived with their mother in the eastern suburb of Blackburn and most of her friends were from down that way too.

'We've got some pre-drinkies and some pills to get us on the way.' Tam tottered into the apartment and perched on the arm of Lucas's couch.

'What are they?' Jason asked, leaning down to speak to her in a quiet voice.

'I dunno, probably MDMA and some other stuff. Steve says they're the shit.'

Tam had always been a solidly built girl who didn't exercise much. She and her friend, Gem, had lost a lot of weight recently on a lemon cleanse diet. Tam had been so pleased with her new look she'd bought an entirely new wardrobe and dyed her hair pale blue. Jason worried she would attract the wrong type of attention.

She was wearing beige high heels which were not quite the same shade as her legs, now slightly orange with fake tan. Her dress was a sleeveless stretchy black number with fringing around the bottom. The dress ended at the top of her thighs and the fringe extended it to mid-thigh.

'Has Steve tried them?' he asked.

'Nah, his supplier said they were dope though.'

'Aren't you going to be cold?'

'I've got a coat.' She held up a waist-length, zip-up, bomber style jacket covered in silver sequins. It didn't look like it would be much use at keeping out winter in Melbourne.

He downed his second beer and gave up trying to tell Tam to be sensible. He'd hoped by twenty-five she would have outgrown the wild party phase.

'Is Lucas coming?' Gem asked from the other couch where she was trying to fix the strap on her shoe. She pulled at it and raised her foot into the air, giving everyone in the room a view up her dress.

Jason looked away. 'Nah, he's working tonight.'

'That's a shame. He's fun for an old guy.' She giggled.

Lucas was exactly four months younger than Jason—they'd been friends since high school—but looked older. He'd spent a lot more time in the sun and he smoked.

'You having one of these, or what?' Tam waved a baggie with pills in it.

'I'll stick with beer.'

Tam screwed her nose up at him. 'Weak,' she said, and popped a pale-yellow tablet into her mouth. 'We need to get into the party before these kick in. Can you call us a taxi, darling brother?'

***

Within an hour they were all standing in front of a converted factory in Kensington. The line into the venue wasn't long and the other patrons were drunk, but not yet rowdy. The poorly-lit street didn't sit comfortably with Jason.

They entered through a door cut out of a much bigger roller shutter, the lip across the bottom of the door meant they all had to step over it. That would cause more than a few tumbles before the night was over. Inside was the smoking area, an open courtyard, and beyond that a set of steps up into a narrow corridor where the music was coming from. The ticket booth and cloakroom were in an alcove off the corridor.

Tam and her friends already had tickets, they went through ahead of him and were quickly out of sight.

'Fuck it,' he muttered to himself, passing the woman in the booth his money.

The main room was a low-ceilinged sprawling space. It was difficult to see the colour of the walls, possibly rust-coloured paint over the steelwork and girders. The room was dark, except for blinding strobing from the side of the stage and the sweeping beam of the green laser. The music was so loud Jason felt it through his chest more than he heard it.

The room looked about half-full. Jason decided he'd have better luck looking with a drink in his hand. The only beer they had was served in disposable plastic cups.

'Gee, thanks,' he said as the bartender gave him his meagre change. From the bar he spotted the back of Steve's head and he wove through the crowd towards him.

The pills had kicked in; Tam, Gem and the rest were standing close to the speaker stacks dancing wildly. He wished he'd brought earplugs.

***

The headline DJ started his set at three in the morning. Since he'd arrived the warehouse had filled up and was cramped with hot, sweaty bodies. He was bumped and jostled constantly. The group had been joined by a few others including one woman with a stack of wild, curly hair who looked familiar.

'Who's that?' he asked Tamara, shouting into her ear.

'Pen? Penny. From school.' Her lips were moving but he couldn't hear her over the throb of the music. His sister's best friend in high school had been Penny. Something had happened between them. He vaguely recalled a boy being involved. She didn't look much like the girl he remembered.

Steve went to each of the group and dropped another pill into their mouths. There was something erotic in it, and as his fingers lingered on Tamara's lips Jason's brain brought up vivid images of the two of them fucking— fast, messy intoxicated sex.

When Steve got to Penny, he watched her swallow the tablet and then he kissed her. She didn't seem to mind, although she didn't seem into it either.

Tamara turned her head to see Steve pulling away from Penny, and immediately planted a long kiss on him. His hand was still cupping Penny's hair. Tam pulled away and went back to dancing, her eyes closed in rapture.

Jason made his way back to the bar for his fourth over-priced beer, and when he returned Steve, Penny and Tam had all left.

'Where'd they go?' he asked Gem.

She looked at him, her eyes swimming in and out of focus. Eventually she shrugged.

'Shit,' he said. He scanned the crowd, but all he saw were indistinct shapes.

He walked back through the narrow corridor to the smokers' section where he saw Tam sitting in Steve's lap, straddling him. Penny was slumped in a tatty armchair next to them.

The courtyard didn't have music playing directly into it, although the DJ playing inside could still be clearly heard. In the relative quiet Jason felt the fuzzy cotton balls in his ears that would turn into ringing later on.

'Fuck off, will you!' Tam broke from kissing Steve to look around and saw him approaching.

'I was just checking where you got to.'

'I'm busy.'

Jason's eyes went to Penny, whose skin had turned waxy and pale. 'Is your friend alright?' he asked.

'I dunno, she came out with us for a smoke, I thought maybe we'd be able to get her in on the action later, but she's done her dash.'

Jason gently shook Penny's shoulder. 'Are you alright?'

She fluttered her eyes open for a moment before slumping back onto the chair. Jason felt for her pulse at her neck; it was fast for someone who looked like they were sleeping.

'What did she take?' He pulled Tam away from Steve and realised that his hard cock was sticking out the top of his pants. He took his time moving it back inside them.

'I gave her one of mine. Who knows what she had before she came out?' Steve reached out to pull Tam back onto his lap. 'She'll be fine. Just leave her.'

'I can't just leave her here. I think I should take her home. Do you know where she lives?' Jason watched Penny's shallow breathing, her skin was cold and covered in sweat.

'I have no idea. Call her sister to come get her. In her bag.' Tam pointed to it, as it lay beside the armchair.

'She's called Cathy, or something.'

Jason opened the tiny bag and pulled out the smart phone. He opened the recent calls list and scrolled down to the first name beginning with a C: Cassie.

That's where I know her from, Jason thought, remembering she had stormed out of his boss's office just over a week ago. His thumb hovered above the call button.

She'll think I'm some sort of stalker if I call her now, but what's the alternative? Leave Penny here to overdose? Call an ambulance?

He pressed his thumb to the screen and made the call.

'Do you know what time it is?' a croaky, angry voice answered after six rings.

'I've found Penny's phone. I uh…' he hesitated. 'I'm with her at a party and I think she's taken something.'

'What the fuck? Who is this?'

'Jason,' he said.

'Jason from the lawyers?' Her voice suddenly sharp.

'Yeah.'

'Why are you with her? What did you give her?'

'I didn't give her anything. She's hanging out with my sister and her friends. They don't seem worried but…'

'God dammit.' There was a rustling sound and Jason thought she must be getting out of bed.

'God dammit,' she said again. 'She promised me she wouldn't do this shit anymore. Where are you?'

Jason told her the address.

'Stay there, I'm coming. If she gets any worse, call the ambos,' she said.

Tam had her hand back down Steve's pants, and didn't appear to be listening.

After a few minutes Gem and Ant appeared from inside the warehouse.

'Set's finished. Afterparty?' Gem said.

'Can we just wait two minutes for Penny's sister to get here? We can't just leave her here,' he said.

'She's fine. Are you coming or not?' Tam pursed her lips.

I told myself I'd look after Tam, what use is that if I let her go off to some random's house when she's this wasted? Jason thought. The group had already started working towards the street; Tam and Gem were both swaying in their heels.

He looked at Penny. *I can't leave her alone either*. He picked up her bag from the ground and put it under her leg, hoping that would make it less likely to be stolen. He considered pulling her top up to hide some of her exposed cleavage, but he would have had to touch her breasts to do it.

'Hey, are you sticking around out here?' he addressed a woman and her friend having a cigarette on the next couch.

'Huh? I guess so. Why?' asked a woman wearing a baby pink vinyl dress.

'I have to go, can you watch her? Her sister will be here in two minutes to get her.'

'What's wrong with her? She looks awful,' said the other woman who was wearing a romper suit which barely covered her ample bottom.

'I don't know, just wait with her, will you? I have to go.'

'Yeah, alright. We'll keep an eye on her.'

He ran towards to the exit.

Chapter 6

Cassie felt around for the light switch. Penny was in trouble. Again. She struggled out of bed, squinting against the unwelcome brightness of the lamp.

She threw on some clothes and jumped into the car. Part of her brain was still asleep. As she drove, she kept asking herself what Jason was doing there with her sister. Did he get her into this mess? It certainly wasn't the first time Penny had been in one. Usually it was her boyfriend, Kev, who called when he couldn't think of anything else to do.

Penny had been in trouble before Kev came on the scene, but it was Kev who had introduced ice to her life. He had a party habit; he would smoke a bit in preparation for a big night out and it never seemed to really get him hooked. He held down a job—retail in a building supplies store. As soon as Penny had tried smoking ice she was hooked.

Cassie hadn't found out until it had already cost Penny her job. Kev and Penny would have a smoke on Saturday night, go out to party, stay up all night, then Kev would crash and Penny would keep partying, unable to sleep or stop. She'd last until Monday morning usually, and then she'd pass out when Kev went to work. She wouldn't wake for days. Kev didn't seem too worried about it; said it was an "occupational hazard".

Then Kev had called her one Wednesday morning. 'She won't wake up!'

'Who is this?' Cassie had asked.

'It's fucking Kev! I can't wake your sister up and you have to fix it.'

'What do you mean you can't wake her up?'

'Oh fuck…' There was a very long pause on the phone.

'What? What's happened?'

'She hasn't told you. Shit. I don't wanna do this!'

Cassie wasn't sure he was still talking to her.

'Penny has been partying pretty hard. I think she's in a coma or something,' Kev went on.

'I don't know what you're on about.' Cassie's heart was racing.

'Ice. Okay? We smoke on weekends for a bit of fun. Fuckin' narc… so uh… you have to come.'

Cassie had turned up at their old place, a tragic looking place in Carlton—the façade was crumbling away, and inside the ceilings were covered in black mould—to find Penny in bed.

'Penny! Wake up. You have to go to work,' she said. There was no response.

'Penny!' Cassie shook her. 'Wake up!' she shouted.

Penny groaned but did not open her eyes. That was the first time Cassie had called the ambulance for her.

Cassie arrived at the warehouse in Kensington fifteen minutes after the call from Jason. She'd sped there, ignoring the risks. The bouncer moved to block her path as she approached.

'We're sold out. Can't let you in.'

'My sister is in there.'

'I'm sure she is, but we're at capacity. I can't let anyone else in for any reason.'

'No, you don't understand. I had a call from someone, one of her friends, and he said that she was passed out. I've come to get her. I need to know if she needs an ambulance or what.'

'Why didn't he call an ambulance?'

'I don't fucking know!' Cassie said. He put his hands on her upper arms and moved her back.

'We have two options. You can call the friend and have them bring her out here, or I can have a colleague of mine look for your sister. If she needs medical attention, we'll sort it out.'

'I don't have his number. He called me on her phone. I don't even know why he's there with her, she doesn't know him.' Cassie strained to see over the bouncer's shoulder.

'I'll call my colleague. It'll be okay. It's not the first time someone has got a bit too drunk.'

'She has an ice problem.'

He stood up straighter. 'You think she's ODed?'

'It's happened before.'

'Shit. Right. Robbo.' He called to another security guard using the radio and earpiece he was wearing. 'You need to come man the door. I gotta go inside.' He didn't wait for a response.

'Where is she?' he said to Cassie.

'I don't know.'

Cassie stepped through the tiny doorway into the warehouse and scanned the courtyard. There were couches and tattered armchairs strewn around the space. About forty people were there, mostly smoking. There was definitely marijuana too; she smelled it immediately.

Cassie made her way toward the inner door where loud dance music thumped in the space. The other security guard hurried towards them.

She ran up the seven steps leading up to the door out of the smokers' area and turned back for one last scan of the area.

'Oh God, there she is.' Penny was slumped in an armchair. Cassie didn't recognise any of the people around her; one of them had his hand up her skirt.

Running across the room, she pointed to Penny to let the bouncer know she'd found her.

'You mother fucker. Get your hands off her.' Cassie slapped the man's hand away.

The bouncer placed himself between her and the unknown man. 'Fuck off, mate.' The bouncer turned back to Cassie. 'Let's focus on her, yeah?'

'But he's a piece of shit preying on someone who can't say no.'

'You're right. But she doesn't look great to me.'

Cassie looked back to Penny and registered how unwell her sister looked.

'We're gonna need that ambulance, I reckon.' The bouncer pulled out his mobile and had started dialling as Cassie reached out to take her sister's hand. She was cold and clammy, and her pulse was wild. Cassie barely heard the bouncer as he described the situation.

'You said she had an ice problem? So, meth yeah?' he said.

'Yes. She smokes ice. But sometimes other stuff too. Always uppers though, no heroin or anything.'

Cassie looked around for Jason in the crowd but couldn't see him. He'd left her sister alone after he promised he'd wait. She stood up and took a few steps towards the doors inside but stopped herself.

The ambulance arrived within minutes; she heard the sirens wailing as they approached.

'I'm Joel, and this is Charles. We're here to help. What did you say she's taken?' one of the ambulance officers said, resting a hand on Cassie's shoulder as his colleague looked in Penny's eyes with a tiny torch and attached leads to her for a heart monitor.

'Uh, well, I don't actually know. She's got a problem with ice. One of her friends called me, I only just got here.'

'Okay. Does she take anything else? Maybe some ecstasy or something like that?' He glanced over to his colleague. 'Her heart is having a pretty tough time. We need to try to settle it down. Is she allergic to anything?'

'I don't think so.' Cassie's mouth was dry.

'Okay. That's good. We're going to put her on the stretcher and take her to hospital now. Do you want to come with us? Or meet us there?' Joel and his partner manoeuvred Penny onto the narrow trolley and started to wheel her back out to the street.

'Where are you going?'

'We'll go to the Royal Melbourne. It's not far.'

'I'll come with you.'

The drive took less than five minutes, but it felt like a long time. This time the sirens were only on periodically to get through red lights.

'We're giving her some dexmedetomidine, which should bring her heart rate down.' Joel spent the journey checking on Penny's pupils and heart rate.

Cassie knew she should feel reassured, but her mind kept returning to the last time she was in the hospital. She and Penny had been there, and Tessa. Ian had waited out in the corridor. Her mother lay there, emaciated and pale. They all knew she was dying. Cassie had hated seeing her mother like that, it felt like she'd given up.

'I'm going out for a smoke,' Penny had said. She'd barely spoken a word all day.

'Don't be too long.' Tessa looked up from the chair beside the bed.

Penny rolled her eyes.

It was difficult to hear her mother breathing as she took tiny shallow breaths beneath the oxygen mask. Cassie held her mum's hand; it had seemed so small.

By the time Penny had come back from having a cigarette, their mother was gone. Cassie had stood by the window, looking out without seeing, tears rolling over her cheeks.

'She dead yet?' Penny asked.

Cassie's chest tightened, anger and sadness bound together.

'Yes, she's gone. Come say goodbye.' Tessa's voice was strained and very quiet.

Cassie turned around, Tessa had laid her head on the bed next to her sister. Penny stood in the middle of the room, her hands dangled limply by her sides and she had looked to Cassie for reassurance.

As the ambulance officers wheeled Penny into emergency Cassie took a deep breath; she should have kept a better eye on her sister. Penny didn't deal well with emotional stuff; she'd never really learned how. It hadn't occurred to Cassie that an overdose was coming but it seemed a stupid oversight to her now.

The air smelled of bleach and disinfectant, but she could also smell something rotten. Cassie turned. A crumpled man in a baggy overcoat with matted grey brown hair, and a scrappy beard clutched his left hand to his chest, it was wrapped in a red-smeared cloth. She took shallow breaths to block the smell coming from the obviously homeless man.

'Has she been in for this sort of thing before?' a nurse asked as she hurried across to them.

'Yes, once or twice. I thought she'd stopped but—'

'I'm sure I don't need to tell you it would be best if she could lay off for a while. Next time she might not make it.'

Cassie was surprised the nurse could be so unsympathetic to the mechanisms of addiction. Then again, if she had to spend her days watching junkies dying, perhaps she wouldn't have much sympathy either.

She pulled out Penny's tiny clutch bag from where she'd shoved it inside her own larger handbag. Cassie went through it, hoping to find something that might be helpful to the doctors.

Penny's wallet was there, but it had no cash in it, she didn't often carry a lot of money around. There was a lipstick, and a small makeup compact, chewing gum and a tiny plastic bag.

The phone wasn't in there. There were two possibilities; someone had been through Penny's bag and stolen her phone or Jason still had it for some reason.

Cassie dialled her sister's number. It rang out. It was just after four in the morning.

Penny's ODed. We're at the Royal Melbourne. Come when you get this. Cassie sent a text message to Kev, but she didn't expect him to come.

She sat in the chair next to the bed in the emergency cubicle; the privacy curtain was pulled closed, but it didn't offer much of a barrier. Cassie was sure she wouldn't sleep.

***

A couple of nurses came in at 7a.m., doing handover, and checked Penny's pulse and looked in her eyes. Cassie was pretending to be asleep when she heard familiar music coming from her handbag; her phone was ringing. The caller ID said 'Penny'.

'Hello?' she said.

'Hi, Cassie, it's Jason again.'

'You've taken to stealing phones now as well as abandoning overdosers?' She was furious now her anxiety had something to focus on.

'What? No, I didn't mean to keep the phone. I just … it's been a messed-up night.'

'You can say that again. I'm stuck in the fucking hospital waiting to see if my sister will wake up this time. No thanks to you.'

She heard Jason breathing down the phone, but he didn't say anything.

'Are you going to keep the phone? Or what?'

'We'll have to sort something out. I have to go, but umm, I'll try to get it back to you tomorrow. Sorry.'

Cassie stared at the handset and felt an urge to throw it at the wall.

It was light outside, and she needed fresh air. As she stepped outside, the early morning air was crisp and the sky was an oppressive grey, with flat, featureless cloud hanging low over the city. She wanted to call her mother to fix it. To ask what she should do about her sister, and about going through the stuff left in the house.

But she couldn't. The idea was so large and heavy she couldn't breathe.

She needed to talk to someone. Pulling out her phone, she dialled her aunt's number.

'Hello?' Aunt Tess answered after only three rings.

'It's Cassie. Can I ... talk to you about something?'

'Of course, Ian and I are just about to get some coffee on, we're spending the day in the garden.'

Cassie wasn't sure how to begin. 'I'm at the Royal Melbourne. Penny's in the emergency department—' she broke off, no one had ever told Tessa about Penny's drug problems.

'That sounds serious,' her aunt said, wary but not yet alarmed.

'It is. I guess the short version is Penny's overdosed.' Cassie choked up.

'I'm coming now.'

'Thank you.' Cassie trudged back into the emergency department relieved she would have company soon.

Chapter 7

In the street outside the warehouse the group had been trying to flag down a taxi when Jason caught up with them. It only took four passengers.

'We'll have to go in two groups,' Steve said.

'Fuck that, we'll all fit. Tam can sit in your lap. The driver doesn't care, do you mate?' Ant was leaning on the open passenger side door.

'There is a small surcharge for additional passengers. Cash only,' the driver said.

'If you just give us the address Ant, I'll bring Steve and Tam with me,' Jason said. 'I'll pay.'

'Don't be a pussy. You can have the front.' He stepped away from the door to let Jason get into the cab.

Gem and Steve were already in the taxi, Tamara was climbing in on top of Steve. If he didn't go with them now, he wouldn't know where they had gone. He ignored the lurching dread in his stomach and climbed in.

My Mother's Secret

The five of them made it to a beaten-up looking share house in Footscray without incident. The trip didn't take long, and Jason had to ask the driver to turn up the music so he didn't have to listen to the wet sound of his sister kissing Steve. She had every right to be with whoever she wanted, but he didn't need to hear it.

The house was dark and empty when they arrived.

'It's cool. I know where the spare key is,' Ant said, he jumped the side fence and went around the back. A minute or two later, he was standing on the other side of the door, letting them in.

'My mate said it was all good for us to use his pad. He'll be back later on,' Ant said.

'Is there any more to drink?' Gem stretched her neck trying to see into the kitchen.

'Dunno. Have a look. Take that into one of the bedrooms, would you?' he said to Steve and Tam who were now rubbing themselves against one another on one of the low couches. Steve stood up, pulling Tam behind him and into the nearest room. He closed the door and Jason heard his sister giggle.

Ant and Gem were in the lounge room watching video clips on *Rage*. Jason now stood in the kitchen, his backside resting against the sink as he nursed a glass of water.

He'd trusted Penny's safety to strangers. Tam was fine and she had needed his help. Anything could happen and it would be his fault.

He looked at his phone, it didn't have much battery left, maybe enough to call a taxi to take him home. He turned towards the dark sky.

He finished the glass and refilled it with frigid water from the tap. The garden beyond the window was black, except for the small yellow patch directly in front of him where the dull overhead bulb reached.

Jason wandered over to one of the couches and rested his head back. *I'll go when it's light, I'll walk to the tram.*

When he woke up the sky was grey; it looked like it might rain. He looked for his phone in his pocket where it should have been but couldn't find it. He checked the other pockets in his pants, but they were empty too.

Gem and Ant were asleep on the other couch, Ant had curled up in Gem's lap, and she had fallen asleep with her head back and her mouth gaping open. She was making a soft snoring sound.

Jason got up and felt the pockets of his jacket, which he'd discarded on the floor when they'd come inside. He found his wallet, his phone, and another phone in the pockets.

'Shit,' he said. It was Penny's. *I should call. I should check whether she's okay.*

When Cassie answered he could barely talk. His brain seemed to stop in its tracks.

'… no thanks to you,' she said.

He hadn't been listening. What had she said? Clearly Cassie had found her sister alright. He let the silence drag out.

She said something else, something about the phone. He heard himself say he'd get it back to her.

'I gotta go.' He hung up. His couldn't think straight, she was so angry with him, he was angry at himself.

Steve and Tam hadn't surfaced and he couldn't hear anything; they must be sleeping too. He didn't need to be there anymore.

Walking out of the house, Jason wondered who lived there. Ant didn't have a key, he'd said it was a friend's place, but what it if wasn't. What if he'd just broken in?

Jason's mind ran over the night again as he plodded through the chilly streets. He didn't really know Ant, but he didn't seem the type to just break into a house. And he'd known the address before they got there. Maybe it was just a mate who wasn't around.

The tram stop was a lot further away than he'd thought. The Sunday morning timetable was had only two or three services per hour. He glanced at the time on Penny's phone, his had gone dead, and his belly contracted. He thought he might be sick, but it passed when he finally got on the tram.

Jason grabbed breakfast in the city when he changed trams. He stared at his reflection in the tram window. *How pathetic is it to see a grown man clutching McDonald's this early on a Sunday?*

As he walked home from the tram stop, the streets were empty, and that suited him. He didn't want to run into anyone he knew.

The door of his apartment slammed behind him and he jumped.

'That you Jason?' Lucas called from behind his closed bedroom door.

'Yes. Go back to sleep.'

***

Jason knew he should have stayed with Penny, but he'd chosen Tam. From the moment the taxi had pulled away he'd known he made the wrong choice.

He was staring into space. He knew Cassie didn't want to hear from him but needed to explain himself. If she understood why he did it, maybe she wouldn't be so angry. He doubted it; he wouldn't forgive him if he were in her place, but he had to try.

'How was last night?' Lucas, his housemate had asked when he finally surfaced at about four the next day.

'Man, it was a pretty big one. I should have just come home after the party.' Jason was still tired.

'You're gonna have fun getting up for work tomorrow,' Lucas said.

'Yeah. I'm getting too old for this.'

That night he turned to the small stash of Stilnox he'd been prescribed. Jason had taken them a couple of years ago at a party with Tam. Apparently if you pushed through the sleepiness you tripped out, but Jason had ended up sleeping jammed into the corner of a lounge room, music blaring, his arse hanging half off the beanbag.

He'd woken up to find his wallet had been emptied of cash and credit cards, at least they'd left his licence. That night had certainly been worse for him but he couldn't stop berating himself for choosing Tam, who was fine, over Penny who had needed his help.

Chapter 8

'Hi.' Cassie said as her aunt swept aside the privacy curtain around the hospital bed.

'What happened?' Tessa folded her arms across her chest.

'I got a call Penny was unconscious at a warehouse party. I couldn't wake her, so I called the ambulance.'

'You weren't surprised were you.' It was not a question.

'It's happened before.'

'Why didn't you tell me about her addiction?' Tessa sounded calm.

'I don't know. Mum knew. More or less.'

'How long has it been going on?'

'Two years I guess, so I told her at first. Once Penny lost her job. But when it looked like Mum would—' she broke off, she couldn't say the words aloud, 'like Mum wasn't going to recover, she was using much more heavily.'

'I knew something was up. Your mum never told me what it was, but I knew it was something. Penny was so thin… what needs to happen to get her to stop?'

'I don't know.' The silence hung between them for a moment. 'She doesn't know it's a problem. Not really. I don't think she knows what else to do.'

'Do you think she'll be able to stop while she's still with the boyfriend?'

'He's too in love with the drugs to give them up. They're not a problem for him, he's still able to work. And if he does it, Penny'll do it.'

'Hmmm.' Tessa paused. 'How would you feel if there was nothing you could do?'

'She's my baby sister. Our mum is gone and it's my job to look after her. I can't do nothing. I can't let her die.'

'You might have to. There's nothing helpful you can do, and plenty you could do that won't help at all.' Tessa sighed. 'You could condemn her, and she'd cut you off. You could tell her Kev is no good for her, or try to break them up, but again, she'd probably stop contact. You could try to stop her from making another stupid mistake by babysitting her, and then two things would happen: one, she'd do something stupid anyway; and two, you'd hate her for taking up all your time.'

'How can you say that? How can there be nothing I can do?' Cassie couldn't believe that was the best course of action.

'You remember my friend Jenny?'

'Vaguely... Mum didn't like her.' Cassie didn't like where this was going.

'She didn't. I never told you this, but Jenny was a heroin addict. She started out small, and then she got further and further into the drugs, she started stealing, first from me, I didn't mind so much, but she stole your mum's purse once.'

'No wonder she hated her.'

'Yes. Well, my point is, an addict has to want to change for themselves. Without that, everything else is fruitless. It's no good letting Penny take you down with her, my love.'

'But I promised I'd look after her.'

'There are some things even you can't fix,' Tessa said.

'What happened to Jenny?'

'I tried to make her go to rehab. She didn't like that, we lost contact. I heard she'd died about a year later. Such a waste.'

Cassie took a few shaky breaths to calm herself down. 'I'm sorry. What would Mum think of me, if I let Penny kill herself?'

'Your mother was proud of you, Cassie. She loved you. I want you to accept this is out of your hands. All you can do it be there to help rebuild her life when Penny finally decides it's time to stop.'

She knew her aunt was right. Cassie's opinions were often strongly expressed and quite different to Penny's. They'd had fights over boys they both liked, and over their father. But she was still her sister.

'I'll try to be strong, for Penny. I don't want her to push me away. Thank you,' she said softly.

'I know I'm not your mother, and I can never replace her, but please know you can call and ask me anything. I —' Tessa broke off, 'I love you, Cassie.'

She'd said it before, but this time Cassie felt as though she meant it in a way she hadn't before.

'I love you too.'

***

Since the night in the hospital Cassie had tried to Penny call a couple of times, but there was no answer. She kept herself busy by taking as many shifts as she could at work.

Cassie threw her tea towel on top of the others in a pile behind the walk-in fridge and picked up her bag after a long shift. She walked out to her car and her belly rumbled.

She'd been so caught up in her emotions that she hadn't had time to eat or get anything to bring home with her.

Cassie decided to check in on Penny. She hadn't spoken to her since leaving the hospital. Maybe they could all have takeaway.

I'm coming 'round with food. What do you want? Is Kev there to eat too? I'll be about half an hour. Cassie texted her sister.

If she doesn't let me in, I'll just eat all the food myself, she thought as she started the car and headed to a Middle Eastern place she knew on the way to Penny's place in Brunswick West.

She was hungry and sad, so she went completely over the top ordering a plate full of meat, Turkish bread, labneh, salad, dips, and sweet pastries for dessert. The woman behind the counter nodded approvingly at the volume of food.

'You won't go hungry tonight,' she said with a smile.

'No, we certainly won't!' Cassie smiled back, the smell of the fresh bread and spiced meats had lifted her spirits.

Kev's here, but he's eaten already, Penny had replied as Cassie was paying for the meal, and she smiled again.

Even though Kev said he'd eaten, when Cassie set out the food on their chipped Formica kitchen table, he sat down and tucked into the bread and dips. Penny and Kev used to have a housemate, but it had just been the two of them for a while now. The kitchen had seen better days, the pile of dishes next to the sink was huge, the bin was overflowing and there were fruit flies buzzing around it. The house smelled of socks and overripe fruit.

'How's work?' Cassie asked Kev.

'It's the same as always, y'know. People are fucking idiots most of the time, but that's what they pay me for.'

'Mmm,' she said. She didn't really have the energy to carry the conversation. Kev was pretty easy-going, as much as she resented him for introducing her sister to ice, she could see he was pretty chilled out. It was also this chilled-out attitude that meant he didn't seem bothered when Penny was in trouble.

They ate in silence with the TV on in the other room.

'What's on tele?' Cassie asked when she'd eaten enough.

'Not much, there's one with blind dates, later, I wouldn't mind watching. It's always good for a laugh.' Kev moved his head to look over her shoulder to see what time it was. He wandered back to the lounge.

Cassie turned back to her sister, who had been sitting with them, but seemed too tired to talk, she'd sat with her eyelids drooping and had hardly eaten anything.

'You can go now. I'm not high and I'm not dead, so bugger off, will you?'

'I'm not checking up on you. I wanted to see you. We used to hang out—'

'Before the drugs,' Penny finished the sentence.

'I was going to say before Mum got sick. I just don't want to… I dunno, I want us to be friends.'

'I don't need you to be my friend,' Penny said, her bottom lip sticking out like a child's.

They sat in silence for a while, then Cassie started to pack up the food that was left over.

'Did you get your phone back by the way?' Cassie realised she'd texted Penny assuming she had her phone back.

'Yeah, Jason dropped it round.'

'What? He came here?'

'Yeah, he said he found my address on the file at his work. It was quite sweet actually. Although when I asked what he was doing at the party he was very vague.'

'How did you end up there with him?' Cassie hadn't been game to bring the topic up herself.

'I ran into Tam, you remember, from school? Turns out Jason is her brother. He must have gone to a different school to us, coz I think I would have remembered him before if I'd met him.'

It sounded like an innocent reason, but doubt lingered in Cassie's mind. She was sure it was unethical to use his position to get Penny's address.

Jason seemed to be turning up in places where he shouldn't, and Cassie felt like it was too close for comfort. And like he'd arranged to avoid her.

That's fine, why would I want to speak to him anyway, she thought.

The food was packed up, and Penny drifted back into the loungeroom with Kev. They sat together on the couch, side by side, casually snuggled into each other. Cassie felt as though she were intruding on their moment. The last time she had had a moment like that was years ago when she and Tony had been new. A niggle of jealousy and loneliness formed in her belly.

Even cleaning out her mother's house didn't seem like such a tough task in comparison to having the conversation with Tony. To tell him he couldn't see her, that she felt threatened by him and would call the police if necessary.

It had been hard enough to pull herself out of the relationship. She hoped once she was out it would all be okay, but it seemed that was not the last hurdle.

'I'm pretty tired, I'm gonna head off.' Cassie wanted to cry.

'You only just got here,' Kev said. Penny was silent next to him.

'Yeah, I just thought I'd pop in on my way home from work. I'm going to have a couple of days off to get this stuff sorted out at Mum's.'

'I'm glad I don't have to be involved,' Penny said.

'You could help out if you wanted to.' Cassie didn't want her sister to help, but she would have liked the company none the less.

'Nah, fuck that.'

Remembering Tessa's words, Cassie bit her tongue and said nothing.

'Okay, well, if you change your mind—'

'I won't.' Penny cut her off.

'Do you want me to leave you the rest of the food?'

'Yeah, that'd be great. I'll take it to work and save on buying something tomorrow,' Kev said.

Cassie had wanted them to say no so she could keep the leftovers. When she swung open the fridge door there was almost nothing in there and she felt a pang of guilt.

How difficult must it have been to wake up in hospital, again? Penny had woken up while Cassie was out of the room and she felt guilty that her sister had had to wake up alone. Cassie had driven her home after her release but hadn't thought to check in with her since.

'I'm not working tomorrow, do you want me to grab you a few things from the shop? Bread, milk, biscuits, whatever?' Cassie said, as she walked back to the lounge.

Penny picked at her tracksuit pants and said nothing.

'Yes, thanks Cassie. We've been a bit slack lately, but it'd be appreciated.' It was more than she'd ever heard Kev say in one go.

'Cool. I'll see you tomorrow then. Text me with what you need.'

Kev waved as she left, Penny looked up briefly before turning back to the TV. Cassie knew she and her sister would have to fight it out. Penny really held a grudge. Cassie had learned when they were still in their teens she had to be the one to apologise. Overdosing and ending up in hospital would have been enough to set her sister's self-esteem plummeting.

Chapter 9

The next morning it was almost ten before Cassie pulled herself out of bed. She sat in her sunny lounge room with a bowl of porridge with stewed fruit.

Her mother's place was in Malvern, a richer suburb on the other side of the city. Eleanor had lived alone in the two-bedroom apartment since her marriage had broken down. Cassie sometimes wondered how she had been able to afford the rent but had never asked. Eleanor had been very private, especially about her money, and the idea of trawling through her personal papers to clean out her house felt wrong.

Tessa would be at work, but she texted her anyway. I'm going to Mum's today. Come join me later if you like.

When she left her apartment, she went to the supermarket for supplies for Penny and dropped them over. Penny was just as frosty as the night before. She didn't stay long.

The car trip to Malvern was about thirty-five minutes, on a good day, and all the way Cassie stoked her anger at her sister.

She walked up to her mother's front door. Her hands trembled as she tried to push the key into the lock, and she dropped the bunch of keys onto the grey carpeted floor. She took a shaky breath.

You've been in the house since she died, pull yourself together.

Inside the apartment was dark, the curtains were all drawn, and silent apart from the dull hum of the fridge. It smelled ripe and rotten; one look at the fruit bowl told her why.

Garbage bags were in a cupboard under the sink. There wasn't much food, but what was left had become foul. Her mother had died three weeks ago. There were two cups on the drying rack from the last time they'd had a cup of tea. A blanket was draped over the back of the couch, where it had always been in winter. Her mum had always liked the comfort of a blanket to watch TV even before she got sick.

The granite-look laminate bench tops her mum had insisted on installing were dreary.

Once Cassie had been through the fridge and cupboard for food, separating it into rubbish and donations, she checked her phone. Tessa hadn't responded.

As she stared at it, she thought of Jason and dialled the number for the probate lawyers' office.

'Good afternoon, Pierce & Thomson, can I help you?'

'Yes, could I speak to Jason please?'

'This is Jason speaking.'

'It's Cassie Morton.'

'Oh... how can I help?' he said.

'You returned my sister's phone.'

'I did.'

'How did you get her address?'

'I looked on your file. I thought she wouldn't mind. I mean, I couldn't call you, her phone was dead, and I didn't have the right charger.'

'You just found it in the file and went to her house? You didn't see any problem with that?'

'I, uh, didn't mean any harm.'

'I should report you to... someone! The ombudsman or... it's a breach of her privacy. You follow her to a party, drug her and leave her for dead and then—'

'Now, hang on a minute. I didn't know she'd be there, I didn't. I'm sorry you feel I acted inappropriately. I did what I thought was right. If that isn't good enough then, I promise you won't see me when you come in.'

'I hope you're proud of yourself, leaving her like that!'

'I'm not proud of myself,' he muttered. 'I had no choice.'

'Everyone has a choice. You chose to leave. No one in my family ever wants to see your face again.' She hung up.

'What a fucking creep,' Cassie said. As she took the bags of rubbish out into the hallway and dropped them. She was furious and sweating.

After splashing water onto her face and neck, she patted her skin with paper towel. It was almost five o'clock. She bent down and put her head on the faux-granite benchtop exhausted.

Her phone bleated.

'Yes?'

'Cassie, it's Tess.'

Cassie let out a long sigh. 'Hi.'

'I'm just leaving work. You want a hand?'

'Yes, please. It's really lonely.'

'It's like there's an Eleanor-shaped hole in the house now,' Tessa said.

Cassie stifled a sob, but a squeak still escaped from her throat.

'I know. It's okay. I'll be there in about half an hour. Maybe you can have a little sit down 'till I get there. I'll bring wine.'

'That would be good.' Cassie sniffed.

She shook off her shoes and curled into a ball on the couch pulling the blanket over her. It smelled like the perfume her mother always wore.

***

The door buzzed, it took Cassie a while to register what it was as the buzzer sounded again.

She scrambled over to the button to let her aunt into the building. About a minute later there was a knock on the door. When Cassie swung it open, Tessa was there with a bottle of red wine in one hand and a huge bunch of red, pink and yellow flowers in the other.

'I thought you might need cheering up. I always like gerberas for a bit of cheer.'

Cassie could see that she wasn't the only one who needed a bit of joy.

Tessa found a couple of wine glasses and they both sat on the couch.

'What have you managed so far?' Tessa spoke softly, the apartment still felt quiet, but no longer oppressively so.

'All I got done was clearing out the food. Everything else feels too personal.'

'We have to look after her things for her.'

'But what happens when it's all packed up? Won't we forget her?' Her throat was dry, and her words sounded thick with emotion.

'No. We'll never forget her. We'll see a tile with a chicken on it and think of her, or we'll have a curry and think of how she could never handle chilli. We'll think of her constantly. For a while it will be hard not to cry every time, but later it will be easier.'

'I don't want to forget her.' Cassie sniffed.

'I know. Let's put some music on. Why don't you start on her clothes and I'll start on her papers? I'd be very surprised if there was anything exciting.'

Tessa smiled and went into the study which had been Penny's bedroom for a time.

In the loungeroom were her mother's CDs. Cassie ran her fingers over them; Michael Bublé's Christmas album, popular classical groups, and others she didn't recognise flipped past until she came upon a best of the Beatles.

'Ah, lovely,' Tessa said, her voice coming around the corner to the lounge.

Cassie walked into her mother's bedroom; the bed was made, her mother's nightie was folded neatly and placed on the pillow on the left-hand side. On the bedside table was a lamp, four books, all with bookmarks part way through, an eye mask, several used tissues and a mug. The mug was stained with a pale brown ring around the bottom.

Cassie hadn't thought to bring boxes. She pulled out her mother's underwear, socks, bras, and stockings, items she couldn't imagine anyone would want and put them into a black garbage bag. She smiled as she dug further into the drawer, she found knickers whose colours were faded, odd socks, and pantihose with holes in them. Her mother had always had trouble letting go of things, 'you never know when it might come in handy' she would say.

As she emptied the last of the sock drawer, Cassie's fingers scraped over the wooden bottom, and something wobbled. She put down the garbage bag and pushed on a corner. The wood panel tipped up in the opposite corner to reveal a narrow space, only about two centimetres deep all the way across the bottom of the drawer. Inside were several small bundles, each one bound carefully with ribbon. Some were letters, others were journals.

'Tessa. I think you had better come have a look at this.' Her words were oddly robotic.

Her aunt strolled into the room, her wine glass in one hand and the bottle in the other. 'What have you found?'

'I don't know yet.' Cassie pointed to the papers.

'Cheeky sod! She's been keeping secret mementoes without anyone knowing! Aren't you just dying to see what they are?' Her aunt's cheeks were flushed.

'We can't read her private letters.'

'Pish tosh! She knew she was dying, it's not as though it was a surprise. She had plenty of time to destroy anything she didn't want us to see.'

Cassie was shocked at the glee in her aunt's voice.

'It all seems so out of character for her. She wasn't a secretive person, was she?'

'How would we know? If she kept her secrets well.' Tessa laughed and put down her wine on the top of the chest of drawers and reached in for one of the journals. The leather-bound volume looked handmade and quite new; its cover still soft and pliable as Tessa unwound the ribbon binding it.

Cassie chose a packet of letters from the collection. They looked like the oldest ones. It seemed sensible to start at the beginning. If the letters were from before she was born, then that was probably alright, she thought.

The bundle held seven letters, all airmail, with delicate, old-fashioned cursive writing for the address. Cassie unwrapped the ribbon and turned over the first letter. She slid out the contents, and the paper was so thin and worn she thought it might rip. Very carefully, she opened out the four pages.

'My most darling Eleanor,' it began. She turned the letter over and saw the name, Kerry Strickland. The name in the will. Perhaps now she would get some answers as to why this person was so important.

'I feel as though I'll die if I don't see you again, but my mother insists that I stay on at the college here until my degree is finished. She won't pay the airfare back until I graduate. You know I've been working a little job in a coffee shop, but with my studies and expenses I haven't been able to save much.'

Cassie turned the pages over in her hands looking for a date; the post mark was February 1981. Her mother would have been 19. She looked over to Tessa, who was engrossed in the journal, having made herself comfortable on the bed.

'I'm afraid that by the time I see you again you will have fallen in love with someone else. It was my parents' spiteful intention to separate us by sending me to study at Brown, instead of one of the perfectly good universities in Melbourne. They think the tyranny of distance will cure me of you, that you're a phase, but they couldn't be more wrong.'

A lover then, and a woman by the writing, Cassie thought. Could her mother have been a lesbian all this time? How could they not have known? It was as though this letter were to someone she didn't know.

She took a deep breath and read over the remainder of the letter which was a catalogue of Kerry's day-to-day life at Brown; her friends, her studies, the people who came through the coffee shop.

'You're sure you don't remember anyone called Kerry that Mum was friends with, maybe at school?' she turned to her aunt, who was grinning reading the journal.

'Hmm? A school friend you think. Not that I remember, but she's younger than me.'

'Are you sure? It seems like they were joined at the hip from this letter.'

'No, I don't remember.' Tessa continued to read the journal in her hand as Cassie opened the next letter in the batch.

This one started in the same way, apologising for being so far away, for not being able to come home. Talking about what had been happening and promising to save up as much as she could so that they could see each other. It was also from February 1981.

The other letters were from March, two in April, one in May and one in August. Cassie skipped straight to the one in August. Unless there had been some letters which didn't survive there was almost a three-month gap. It was a long time to wait for a letter from your lover even in 1981.

It started the same way as they all did. Kerry had travelled around Louisiana with her parents and couldn't write. They'd met a plantation-owning family, with two sons, Hank and Jack.

'My darling, I don't know how to tell you this, but Hank and I are getting married. It's a marriage of convenience and of companionship. He's like us; he loves men. He's now 26 and to be unmarried at that age, people have started to talk. They wanted to cast him out of the church!'

Kerry went on trying to justify her decision, saying she was not strong enough to live a life as an outcast.

'Please don't hate me, dearest Eleanor. Nothing can take away what we had together, no one will ever replace you.

'Love and kisses, your ever-devoted Kerry.'

Cassie's heart was racing and she struggled not to crush the delicate letter in her hand.

The last letter had no tear stains on it, and it was less worn than the first few.

Mum couldn't bear to read it over and over, to relive that loss. But she never let go of their love, Cassie thought. She folded up the last letter and put it back into the envelope. She gathered the letters together and rewrapped them in the ribbon.

'I know why Kerry is in the will.'

'What's that, love?' Tessa looked up at her.

'Kerry, the name on the will we didn't know, Mum was in love with her.'

'Nonsense. I never heard of this Kerry. Wait, did you say with her?'

'Yes.'

Tessa shook her head. 'I can't believe that. No, that can't be right. Ellie was never in love with anyone, especially not a woman. Even your father, she just sort of settled for him.'

She closed the journal in her hand. 'To be honest, I was surprised when they split up. I mean I never really thought she had strong enough feelings on the matter to do something like that. Something that decisive, it was almost emotional.'

Cassie's mind was filled with new ideas about her mother. When they were younger, Penny might have been about ten, and Cassie had been taking her first tentative steps towards love and relationships, her mother had been so angry. Cassie had hated her for it.

Now, she saw her adolescence in an entirely new light. Could Mum have been trying to save her from the same kind of hurt she'd experienced? They had never talked about their feelings.

The wine Cassie had put on top of the chest of drawers was still sitting there. It seemed unreal that with everything in the letters, her mother's house was still just as neat as it had ever been. It was as though the discovery of her mother's secret had made no tangible mark.

Cassie picked up the glass and walked through the lounge out onto the balcony. The door whispered shut behind her and the chill of the air was refreshing. She stood looking out over the tops of the houses. She looked at the big, green letter W on the supermarket and the bottle shop next to it.

They'd grown up in this area, and even when her parents split up, when Cassie was twenty-two and already living with her first boyfriend, Mum had moved into a smaller place in the same suburb. But something was different.

The door slid open behind her and Tessa joined her on the balcony.

'I read the letters,' she said.

Cassie took a sip of her wine and waited.

'I don't know what to say to you, I had no idea. I still don't remember who Kerry is. I thought I would have known if Ellie was in love, especially with a woman.'

'You don't remember a big fight or anything?'

'No, I don't think so,' Tessa leaned her forearms on the railing.

'There were some fights, well, heated whispers for a little while in Ellie's first year of uni. I never knew what they were about really. She would come home quite late at night, I assumed she was visiting a boy, but maybe it was Kerry. Our mum wasn't too worried, but Dad was a bit of a tyrant. I think Mum was probably on Ellie's side in those fights.'

Cassie had never really known her grandmother, she had died before Penny was born. Mum had rarely spoken about her family, so all Cassie had in mind was a small, kind-looking old lady who'd given her chocolate once when she fell down.

'And your dad? Do you think he knew?'

'He knew something, but how much, I couldn't say. He was a homophobic bastard. I mean it was a sign of the times to a certain extent, but maybe it's time to call it a night. I know we haven't got very far but it seems like a good reason to leave it for another time.'

She couldn't look at Tessa.

'Should we take the stuff with us? The letters? I guess they're mine, contents of the house. Do you think?'

'I think your mother was very deliberate in appointing you her executor. She would have had plenty of time to destroy the letters and journals if she hadn't wanted you to see them.' Tessa looked out over the houses. 'You should take them. I don't need them. I think Eleanor would want her daughter, and not her sister, to have those letters.'

She had no idea what her mother would have wanted. How different would her mother seem at the end of the journals?

She went back into the hollow house. The Beatles album had long since finished playing and she heard Tessa put the CD away and turn the system off.

She washed the two wine glasses, carefully holding them as she dried them on a tea towel with chickens on it.

'I'll have to get some boxes and go through it all. I mean, I don't have any use for most of it. Is there anything you think you want to take, I can keep it out for you,' Cassie said as she gathered up her handbag.

'Not particularly. I'll go and grab out the jewellery that Ellie wanted me to have. I know the pieces she had in mind.'

Cassie stood in the kitchen and waited. She tried to picture her mother as a lovestruck teen. Carrying that hurt with her for the rest of her life.

'Here, don't forget the papers.' Tessa handed Cassie a black plastic garbage bag with only a few items in it. Cassie looked inside. They seemed much smaller at the bottom of a bin bag.

Chapter 10

Every night since leaving Penny Jason had slept badly. He'd had nightmares about her lying on the chair in the warehouse, her throat slit, and her cleavage covered in blood. There had been so much blood. He'd woken up, his sheets wet with sweat, and had lain awake until his alarm had gone off.

By Friday afternoon he could barely concentrate on anything.

'If I don't get out of here soon, I'll quit the next time Thomson or Pierce comes out,' he muttered to himself. He closed down his computer at just before four o'clock, it wasn't even that early.

He decided to take the long way home; instead of getting the tram he walked to Richmond station. The walk was pleasant in the late afternoon, the air had the chill of winter in it, but there was no wind. The exercise warmed him up and by the time he arrived at the station he was ready to shed his jacket.

He arrived home flicked on the TV and Xbox. It still had the racing car game in it that Knox had been playing when he'd visited two weeks ago. He'd been so busy worrying about Cassie he hadn't checked in to see how his baby brother was doing.

'Yes?' Becca answered the phone.

'Hi.' Jason coughed, cleared his throat and tried again. 'Is Knox around?'

'Jason, are you alright? You're not coming down with something are you, darling?'

'Yeah, it's been a bit of a rough week. Sorry I haven't called.'

'It's fine. Hang on I'll get him for you.'

While he waited, Jason cleared his throat and wondered if his brother had a phone of his own yet. Puberty would be just around the corner and having someone to ask about girls or erections might be just what Knox needed.

He heard thundering footsteps and then a scramble as his brother picked up the handset.

'Hi, buddy. How's things?' Jason lay down on the couch, his eyes closed, resting his phone on the side of his head.

'I'm okay. How are you?'

'I'm okay.'

There was an awkward silence.

'Are you in the kitchen? Where's your mum?'

'She's here. She says we're going out for dinner soon. It's going to be super boring. Dad's work friends. Why do I have to go?'

'Because your father said so,' Becca said in the background.

'Hey mate, do you have your own phone? Maybe I can call you on that...'

'Yes.' Knox's voice dropped to a whisper. Jason wrote the number and they hung up. He waited for three minutes to give Knox time to get back to his room before calling him.

'Is that better?'

'Yeah, Mum's a pain.'

'That's not a nice thing to say. I'm sorry I didn't call you this week.'

'That's okay. Dad's been so busy he stayed over at his office two nights in a row.'

Not this again, he thought. 'That sounds fun,' he said.

'Maybe. I don't get to know anything, it's totally... bullshit.' Knox whispered the swear word.

'You swearing now, mate? Dad'll skin you if he hears that.'

'I won't tell him if you don't.'

'I won't tell, but you still shouldn't swear,' Jason said.

'Okay then.'

Jason was yawning within minutes, he hoped Knox couldn't hear him. Knox was telling him about a boy at school who was great at football.

'He can run faster than anyone else in the whole class, and he knows all these rules and stuff. It's really cool.'

'It sounds really cool. I think he has someone at home who teaches him about footy. And lots of practice. Some people pretend they don't practise. It shouldn't be uncool to practise things.'

'Come on Knox it's time to go,' Becca called, her voice muffled by the bedroom door.

'I have to go,' Knox said.

'Okay, mate. Try to be good at this dinner. I'll see you soon, yeah?'

'Yeah. Bye.'

Lucas wasn't home yet and Jason didn't feel like moving, so he ordered some Vietnamese food. He thought about ordering some beers too, but he'd had more than enough last weekend.

He watched a trashy action movie as he ate his dinner. He'd ordered enough so that there would be leftovers, but he ate all of it.

He woke up twisted into a strange shape on the couch when Lucas came home from work at 2am. The TV was still on.

'What's up, mate?' Lucas said, dropping himself onto the other couch.

'Just having a quiet one.'

'Are you alright? You seem a bit out of sorts. I thought it might have been just the weekend but… is there anything I can do?'

Jason was surprised whenever someone took an interest in him. Growing up, Dad was never around, and his mother had been too busy being miserable with his father. He sat up straight on the couch.

'You don't have to tell me. I just thought, you know, if you wanted to talk. I should warn you, I'm about four beers in.' Lucas laughed, it made Jason wonder if he had been smoking weed as well.

'It's just this woman. I—' he didn't know how to start. 'She's a client. Her sister went to school with Tam it turns out. I can't stop thinking about her. It's like she's stuck in my brain.'

'Sounds like you're in lurve.' Lucas giggled again.

'Nah, man, I… there was a thing, at that party last weekend.' He wanted to tell Lucas, but he was ashamed.

'I thought you said the party wasn't that exciting?'

'Can't you take anything seriously? Fuck. You ask what's bothering me but won't listen when I tell you what's going on.'

'Jeez. I'm sorry mate I didn't realise you were that upset.' Lucas's face was serious.

'I did a bad thing.' Jason paused. When Lucas didn't interrupt, he went on.

'Penny, the sister, she passed out, I guess she was overdosing.' He told Lucas the whole story.

Lucas grunted, but said nothing.

'And then when Cassie got to the warehouse Penny was on her own. She thinks I left her there. What if she'd died? It's my fault she was alone. And now Cassie won't speak to me.'

'Did you force her to take drugs?' Lucas said, his words slow and deliberate.

'No. She had some pills, MDMA probably, with Tam, but I think she was high before that. Cassie said that she had an ice problem.'

'So, you're blaming yourself for an addict's overdose?'

'No. I had nothing to do with it, but like, I should have stayed with her.'

'And if she'd started to, I dunno, have a seizure or something, what would you have done?'

'I don't know. I could have called an ambulance.'

'You couldn't have known that the person you asked to watch her would fuck off.'

Jason ran his hands over his face.

'It's finished, it's over. Next time you'll do things differently,' Lucas said.

'I guess. I'm wrecked.'

Lucas nodded and reached for the remote control. He'd stay up for another half an hour or so, winding down from his shift.

As soon as Jason lay down in his bed, he fell asleep. When he woke up in the morning, he couldn't remember dreaming, but he felt troubled.

Lucas was already up cooking eggs and bacon and had a plunger full of coffee already brewing.

'You want some of this? I've made plenty.' Lucas pointed to the stovetop.

'I'd love some.'

Jason sipped his coffee as Lucas finished cooking. He'd even included baked beans and toast.

'You figured out what you're gonna do about this woman then?' Lucas said, sitting down next to him at the kitchen bench.

'What do you mean? She won't speak to me.'

'But there's something there, right? You like her. You want her to like you. You want to make her understand what happened.'

'Wouldn't it be creepy if I contacted her after she said she didn't want to talk to me?' Jason took a bite of toast covered in beans.

'Yeah, maybe. Can you write her a letter? And give it to her when she comes into the office again?'

'Yeah, she's gotta see Pierce the Patronising.'

'I think it would be okay if you handed her a letter. She doesn't have to read it. But she probably will.' Lucas spoke around his food.

'I don't know.'

'I've seen relationships start from worse places than this.'

'Sure you have.'

Lucas stuck his tongue out at him and then continued to shovel food into his mouth. It was getting towards midday. Jason did the dishes, and then went through the house doing the cleaning routine. It was his turn, but the cleaning did nothing to quiet Jason's mind. He started composing the letter to her in his head as he scrubbed.

I could start with I'm really sorry your sister ended up in hospital, he thought. But she might see that and not read any further.

Perhaps I'd better start with the explanation?

When everything had been cleaned, he sat down on the couch and began to write.

At work on Monday, he looked in the calendar for her next appointment. He couldn't find one. How would he get his letter to her if she didn't come back into the office?

He couldn't call her; she'd specifically told him not to. He couldn't go to her house; he'd only make matters worse by doing that. The only option was waiting for her to turn up at the office.

It had taken him three hours to get the letter right, writing until his hand cramped up, but each time it seemed inadequate. Jason finally settled on a single page—handwritten. He placed it in the breast pocket of his suit jacket where it would stay until he saw her.

Chapter 11

Cassie put her mother's papers in a row on her coffee table and stared at them.

Her eyes lingered on the bundle of letters from Kerry. She had only read the first and the last, and the story she'd told herself of their forbidden love had been mostly filling in the gaps.

She picked up the bundle and turned it over in her hands. Kerry had probably taken Hank's name and would now be Kerry Deneuve of Louisiana. She could call the lawyers' office and ask them if they had a way of finding people, but the thought of Jason stopped her.

The other clerks would probably be able to help, but she didn't want him answering the phone. She had Pierce's direct office number too, although he was just as unpleasant.

Cassie pulled out her laptop and spent hours trying to find the right Kerry. She tried Henry and Jack and John and Hank and a few combinations of them as well but none of them seemed to be the right one. Even Facebook was no help. It was nearly three on Wednesday afternoon; almost a week away from work and she'd made little progress on packing up the house.

She put her head in her hands. I'm going to have to call the fucking lawyers, she thought.

'Hello, Pierce and Thomson.' Jason answered the phone. Her hands shook as her adrenaline kicked in.

'Yes, it's Cassandra Morton.' She paused.

'Of course, how can we help today, Ms Morton?'

He wasn't even attempting friendliness; he was infuriatingly professional.

'I'm trying to find Kerry Strickland who appears in my mother's will. We've established that she was—' she hesitated. 'I found correspondence between them when I was going through my mother's things.'

'I see.'

'I've managed to establish that she married a Henry, or Hank, Deneuve in Louisiana sometime in the early eighties. Although the letters only state her intention to marry.'

'We have people who find people. I'll get them onto it. Do you have anything else that might help?'

'No. I'll call back if I think of anything.'

'That sounds fine.'

Cassie frowned. His voice had wobbled. If he felt bad about what he'd done then she was glad, but her heart went out to him all the same. She imagined the hurt in his big grey eyes, his handsome face shadowed.

He's not a puppy, she told herself, stop thinking like that.

She picked up one of her mother's journals and opened it. It was from 1984, two years before her birth, three years after Kerry.

The journal was mostly day-to-day stuff. Eleanor was living with her parents.

'5th September 1984. I fought with Mum again today. I'm a grown woman with a job, I'm not a child. I shouldn't be treated like one. It's hardly fair for her to charge me board when she also insists that I'm still her baby. Dad's no help either, he's as cold and awful as usual. One day I'll live on my own. I'll have a beautiful garden, what they say won't touch me.'

She had only ever really known her mother as a staid, introverted middle-aged woman, never a moaning adolescent. Her own life was in such a shambles; her mother had been married with two kids by her age.

'18th October 1984. I spoke to Ben again today. I wish I felt the way about him as he does about me. I'm sure once I get to know him, my feelings will follow. I wish Mum hadn't looked so relieved when I mentioned that one of the men at work had shown an interest.'

Ben, her father's name—this was the story of how her parents had met. They had never seemed to be madly in love that she could remember. They'd appeared happy when she was a child, but as she'd grown up the relationship had shown strain.

Her phone rang. It wasn't a number she had stored, and her initial instinct was to let it go through to voicemail.

'Hello. Cassie speaking,' she said.

'Why didn't you tell me you got a new number?'

Fuck, how had Tony gotten this number? Why had she answered the phone with her name? Why had she answered it at all?

'Tony. It's over. You can't call me anymore,' she said.

'It's over when I say it's over! What about the other night at the restaurant? You said you'd listen to me. You think I was too drunk to remember but I wasn't!' He slurred his words together, he was at least five drinks in.

'It's over for me. You need to let me go.'

'You lying fucking bitch!'

'You need to calm down. If you can't talk to me civilly, I'm going to hang up.'

'I need to calm down? I wasn't the one who changed my phone number secretly. I wasn't the one who left my partner stranded and alone. Who never gave him the chance to change? No. That was all you.' He was shouting, she held the phone away from her ear.

She didn't know what to say. She focused on her breathing. There was nothing she could do to bring him down from this pitch.

'You have no heart. You're totally unlovable but I'm still prepared to make this work. You can't say the same, can you? You have nothing to give. After three years together, you just fuck off.'

She pressed the icon to end the call. It wouldn't take him long to realise, so she turned the phone off and put it in her bedroom.

She was fairly sure Tony didn't know where she lived, she'd moved out of the house they shared and never told him where she was staying. The first night was in a hotel, then on a friend's couch, then house-sitting for a month until she found this place. She hadn't told him when her mum had finally let go, she hadn't wanted him at the funeral. She knew that she wasn't strong enough to say no to him then. He'd be loving and sweet just long enough to draw her back in.

Emma had suggested getting the police involved but that seemed a bit extreme. She couldn't ask her sister. She wanted to ask her mother. She wondered how long it would be until it didn't hurt.

She stood up and paced around her living room. She needed to do something to make herself feel useful, something to keep her mind off Tony.

I'll get some packing done, maybe I can drop in on Tessa on the way home. In the week that she'd been away from work she hadn't been back to her mother's house. Soon she would run out of money and would need to go back to work.

Outside, the light was fading, and she would have more trouble being in the empty apartment at night than she would during the day. Her mood tended to spiral downwards at night.

At least she had got the packing boxes and put them into the back of her car. She shoved her feet into some old runners, picked up her jacket and walked out the front door.

When she arrived at her mother's apartment, she put the TV on to keep her company. Two hours in the loungeroom; to get the CDs, books, etc. sorted into the ones she wanted to keep and those to donate, and then she'd go.

She held one of the books she'd given her mother for Christmas and wondered if Eleanor had ever read it. She flipped through the pages and a piece of paper fell out from between them. It was a receipt for groceries. Her mother would have made thousands of trips to the supermarket over her life, buying ingredients for many thousands of meals.

Cassie had made a small pile that she wanted to keep, among the five cardboard boxes filled with donations. She put the pile in a plastic shopping bag on the kitchen counter. It was almost nine, Tessa and Ian would be curled up on their couch with a glass of wine.

***

Tessa's place was one of three units on a block, clad in brown brick veneer and built in the late eighties.

Cassie parked out the front and walked up the short path to the front door. Solar-powered lights cast eerie blue light on the path. The colours of her feet and the plants that fell under the circles of light were washed out.

Ian opened the door, his kind face was wrinkled and always tanned, with deep lines around his eyes and a mouth that spoke of smiling.

'Hi. Can I come in for a cuppa?'

'Cassie, my girl! I haven't seen you since, it must have been the funeral,' he said, lowering his gaze when he said funeral.

'Can I come in then?' Cassie prompted.

'Yes, yes, of course.' Ian smiled and stepped aside to let her in. Their unit had two bedrooms, one had been converted into a room for activities, Tessa did woodworking and Ian did embroidery. Anyone who thought it made him less manly would be swiftly corrected. Ian had spent a lifetime as a motor mechanic, getting greasy under the chassis and drinking beers with the boys. When he met Tessa, she had encouraged him to be open and proud.

'What are you doing around these parts then?' Tessa said from the kitchen. In the tiny house the kitchen and lounge room were one central room with the bedrooms, laundry and bathroom all branching off it.

'I was going through Mum's stuff.' She faltered. 'I just wanted some company before I go home.'

'Perfectly natural.' Tessa got her a glass of wine and they sat down together on the couch, Ian took the armchair.

'I've brought him up to speed on the letters. Have you found anything else in the journals?'

'I had a little look at one earlier today before I was interrupted by Tony.'

'Tony? I thought you'd given him the flick.' Tessa was frowning.

'I have. He's, well, having some trouble accepting the breakup. He turned up at work the other day.' Cassie laughed but neither Tessa nor Ian laughed with her.

'When you say turned up at work, what do you mean?' Ian asked gently.

Cassie recounted the story and they both nodded solemnly.

'It was never my place to say, when your mother was around, but, uh, Tony's not quite right is he?' Tessa said.

'He just has a bit too much to drink sometimes. It must be very hurtful to go through a breakup. Maybe I should give him an opportunity—'

'Fuck that,' Tessa interrupted. 'When a relationship is over you have to accept it. I don't believe for one moment this behaviour will have any positive outcomes for you.'

Cassie opened her mouth to reply, and her aunt held up her work-roughened hand to stop her.

'You were miserable with him. We all knew it. We watched him become more and more dismissive of you. He treated you like a possession. I had thought, foolishly, that when you broke it off you had come to see that you deserved better.'

'You can talk! You were a spinster your whole life. Ian's the only man you've ever managed to keep long enough to pin down.'

'Do you hear yourself, Cassie?' Her aunt's tone was soft. 'You have so much anger. I know you're having a tough time right now, but I won't have you speak to me like that.'

Ian sat, his head swivelling from one woman to the other.

'I can't help that Tony's obsessed with me.' Her anger had left as suddenly as it had come.

'Have you told him that he's not to contact you?'

'Sort of,' Cassie said.

'What does that mean?'

'No. It means no.'

'You have to ask him to stop. When you've done that, and he doesn't respect it, because we both know he won't, then you have to report him to the police for harassing you.'

'But he hasn't done anything wrong. He's just hurt.'

'Of course, he's hurt. What happens when he turns up to your house? He might hurt you. He might kill you. It's not uncommon.' Tessa moved to put her hand on

Cassie's knee. 'I know it seems extreme, but bad things happen.'

'Okay, okay. You're overreacting, but I'll call him tomorrow and tell him he needs to leave me alone.'

'Good. You don't owe him anything, stick to your guns.'

They sat in silence for a while, sipping their wine. Her aunt's words had given her permission to tell Tony where he could stick it.

'When Eleanor and Ben got married, were they happy?' Cassie asked.

'What do you mean?' Tessa replied.

'The stuff I read today, and the letters, makes me think that Mum wasn't ever into men. I was just wondering if they were happy. I know they were together for a long time. I just thought she might have been more open when she was younger.'

'Mmm.' Tessa drained her glass. 'More?'

'No, I've gotta drive home.'

'Of course.' She walked into the kitchen to refill her glass and brought the bottle with her.

'I'm surprised you haven't suspected before now. Have you thought about when your parents were married?'

'December 1985.'

'And when were you born?'

'May 1986.' Cassie knew immediately.

'But that only means they'd had sex. Do you think Mum loved him?'

'By the time Ellie was getting serious with Ben she'd become so withdrawn that we didn't know how she felt about anything. In hindsight it makes sense.'

'What do you mean?' Cassie prompted.

'If you've given up hope of ever being able to love someone, and believe your love is unnatural, then maybe you close down.'

'But they must have been – they must have liked each other a little for her to be pregnant.'

She watched as Tessa exchanged a look with Ian. 'Things were different then,' she started. 'When you were with a boy for a certain length of time, they expected things. It wasn't that your dad would have forced anything, but your mum probably thought she had to.'

Cassie felt queasy.

'Ben was a very nice man by all accounts, he courted your mother for nearly eighteen months before they were married, I don't think she would have gone through with it if she didn't like him at all.'

Cassie looked away. Her parents were coming apart in front of her.

'And you never knew if she loved him?'

'She wouldn't talk to me. She seemed happy enough.' Tessa took a sip of wine and looked at her hands. 'You have to understand that I was pretty self-involved back then. I was wild and I didn't really care about her.'

Tessa seemed to be ashamed, but Cassie hadn't been much better. Even now, when she knew her sister was battling with addiction, she hoped the matter would just resolve itself.

'Do you think Dad knew?'

'I don't know, hun. He might have.'

Cassie's father had thrown her mother out when she was in her early twenties. She'd already moved out of home to live with a man who sold marijuana for a living. Penny was living with them; she was seventeen and in year eleven. Penny had stayed with their father for couple of months.

Eleanor had lived with Tessa until she'd managed to get herself the little apartment, the same one she'd had when she died. Once the place was set up, Penny moved in straight away.

Their father had always had a reasonably well-paid job, when the divorce was settled, Ben paid for Penny to live with her mother. It meant Eleanor could afford to work only one job. Cassie had watched all this happening through a bong haze. After that Tony had seemed like a step up.

She wondered how many times Tony had called her since she'd turned her phone off. She dreaded the voicemail messages waiting for her. Then she thought of Jason, of whether he'd found anything about Kerry.

From the corner of her eye she saw Ian stifle a yawn.

'I'm sorry, it's probably really late.'

'It's okay love, but we're old.'

It was nearly eleven o'clock. She decided to leave the rest of her glass of wine.

As she walked out the front door she turned back to Tessa. 'Do you think I should talk to Dad?'

Tessa was silent for a moment, 'I think you'll get a version of the truth from him. It may not match Ellie's truth. Or yours.'

She hugged her aunt goodbye, the familiar smell of lavender soap and earth lingered.

***

Cassie woke as the first grey light was coming in through the slats in her venetian blinds. She'd slept soundly enough, but she couldn't get back to sleep. She lay there for hours staring at the sunlight through the blinds.

I'll get up, I have to start taking this house clean up seriously. They were already a week late with the rent, and she would have to arrange to pay the estate agent. She would give notice to vacate and arrange for the stuff she wasn't keeping to be sold or donated. The list of things she had to do seemed to be only growing longer.

She took the phone out of the drawer and turned it on. She carried the phone into the kitchen, picked up her coffee and counted the messages: there were only nine.

She had expected more.

Tony must have fallen asleep.

Eight of the messages were from him the night before. He said she was a bitch, and a cunt, and a worthless piece of shit. He told her he loved her, and he couldn't go on without her. She listened to each one in full before deleting them. She'd heard it all before.

The last message was from Jason. 'I made some enquiries about the woman you mentioned, Kerry Deneuve. I have some results that I'd like to talk through, I'll be here in the office all day, so, uh, give me a ring.'

She found his hesitation endearing. It was becoming harder to maintain her rage.

Don't let yourself be fooled by his regret. She called him back.

'You said you had information about Kerry?' she said, her voice deliberately cold and distant.

'Uh, yes, I did. I did some digging yesterday and I got some results back overnight.'

Cassie waited for him to go on.

'So, anyway, I've got a phone number and an address for someone who I think is the woman we're looking for.'

'Okay.' She would have to read the journals before she contacted Kerry, but then again, perhaps it was better not knowing.

'Are you still there?' Jason asked.

'I'm here. Is there anything else?'

'Uh...' he stopped.

'What?'

'I have a letter here for you. Is it alright if I send it on to your address? I wasn't sure given how you felt about the phone thing.' His voice was hushed.

'Why did it come to you? Is it about Mum's estate?'

'No actually. I... I wrote it. I wanted to set the record straight and I thought it might be best to send you a letter which you could read, or not read, in your own time.'

'Fine. Send it over.'

He seemed so genuinely upset she almost forgot her decision not to trust him. She was annoyed with herself; it was exactly the sort of thing Tony used to do.

Cassie checked the time in Louisiana, it was about dinner time. She didn't want to call Kerry right at that moment. She showered, dressed, and drove over to her mother's apartment. There was something that made sense about calling Kerry from Mum's house.

Cassie took a deep breath and dialled in the numbers. There was a weird delay, it sounded like the inside of a seashell, and then the phone started to ring.

'Hello, Hank speaking.' The male voice sounded far away, but it might be her imagination. He sounded like a young man, perhaps Kerry's son.

'Hi. My name's Cassandra Morton, I was looking for Kerry.'

'Sure, let me get her for you.' He put the receiver down and she heard his footsteps as they receded. His accent was strong but educated.

'Yes, hello, this is Kerry.'

'Hi. I hope I'm not disturbing you.'

'That's sweet of you, we're all done with dinner. How can I help you?' She had an odd accent, there were some words which were thick with Southern American drawl of her son, but it was still Australian.

Cassie was stalling. She didn't know if Kerry had heard about Eleanor's death.

'My name is Cassandra Morton. You don't know me. But I think you knew my mother, Eleanor Beechworth.' Cassie held her breath waiting for the response.

'Eleanor Beechworth. I haven't heard her name in a long time.' She sounded sad.

'I'm her daughter.' *You already said that, stupid.*

'I am just getting in touch with people. I'm afraid I have some bad news.'

'My God! Is she dead?' Kerry dragged the word dead out into a soft wail.

'Yes, I'm sorry to be the one to tell you, but she passed away. About three weeks ago.'

'Oh Ellie! Ellie!' Kerry had started to sob.

Cassie thought this was an intense reaction for someone she hadn't thought of for years.

'What happened? She was so young!'

'Her lungs gave up. She didn't respond to treatment. She went very quickly.' Cassie was hurrying over the words. The sound of Kerry crying over her mother threatened her control.

'Oh Ellie! My own Ellie. No, I can't believe it.' It was hard to distinguish individual words in the midst of the sobbing. Cassie found herself getting angry with Kerry, as though she didn't have a right to be upset.

'I was wondering if I could talk to you. I have some questions.'

Cassie thought she heard agreement under the sniffling and heaving.

'Maybe I'll call back another time. When you've had a chance to digest the news.'

'No. I'll be alright,' Kerry insisted between sobs. 'Hank! Hank, bring me the Kleenex, and a gin and tonic will you, honey,' she said. It sounded like she'd covered the receiver with her hand.

Cassie waited while Kerry blew her nose loudly. She wanted to get off the line, it was getting harder to talk to the woman who had broken her mother's heart.

'Alright, I'm sorry, I think I can talk now.' Kerry sniffed, and Cassie heard the clink of ice cubes against glass.

'I guess, well, there are one or two formalities. And then I have a couple of questions of a more personal nature.'

'Shoot.'

'I need to confirm that you were known as Kerry Strickland of Melbourne prior to your marriage to Henry Deneuve.'

'Yes honey, that's me. I know Ellie— I knew Ellie.'

'Okay. Great. I just needed to officially ask you. I've been named as Mum's executor. She wanted you to have some of her jewellery. In particular a gold and pearl pendant and chain, and a silver and diamond bracelet. Do you want to accept these?' Cassie felt that she was using a strangely formal tone. Her throat felt tight.

'Of course, honey, I—' Kerry sobbed loudly, and blew her nose. 'I gave her that pendant, back when we knew each other.'

Cassie's heart started racing in her chest. Her palms were sweaty.

'I came across some letters in Mum's things.' She wanted to be delicate, given Kerry's apparent emotional nature.

'Darling heart, she kept them? All this time?'

'Yes. She had them under a false bottom in her underwear drawer. None of us ever knew anything about it.'

'You've read the letters then?' Kerry dropped her voice.

'I read some of them.'

'And you've figured out the whole sorry saga.'

'Bits and pieces. But I guess I was hoping for some more from you, to help fill in the blanks.' Cassie's heart was still pounding in her ears, she held the phone with both shaking hands.

'Where do I start?' Kerry took another drink. 'We knew each other because our parents were friends. We met when we were fourteen, but we didn't realise the way we felt about each other until later, sixteen or seventeen. We had sleepovers all the time. We shared everything together. No-one suspected anything. But when we both left school to go to university, I suggested that we get a flat together, but by this stage my parents were starting to worry I hadn't had any boyfriends.'

'And then what happened?' Cassie prompted.

'Well, they went through my things and found the letters Ellie wrote to me in class. We never thought anyone would read them. They were pretty explicit.'

'Oh.'

'Yeah. My father lost his mind. He said he would never speak to me again, he called me all kinds of names. He even slapped me across the face. He was so angry and afraid,' Kerry said.

'Sounds awful.'

'It was. They said I couldn't see Ellie. I tried to tell them I was an adult, but they were supporting me, I couldn't afford to move out without their help. What could I do?'

Cassie didn't know what to say, so she just made a sound that was vaguely in agreement.

'They formulated a plan to send me over here to study. I have family up near Brown University, in Rhode Island. They kept an eye on me. I lived in a hall of residence with other girls, I don't know why my parents thought that would help.' She laughed but it was full of sadness.

'Anyway, I wrote to Ellie, but being away from her and everyone telling me it was wrong I just sort of gave up.'

'How did you end up with Henry?'

'Well I suppose I had always been a little bit more, flexible than Ellie was in her likes. I had an interest in men, not like what I felt for your mother, of course, but when I met Hank, I knew that this would be a better life.'

'And Hank, is he, does he know?'

'Oh yes, we have no secrets. Hank—'she dropped her voice to a whisper, and Cassie had to strain to hear her. 'He has his own preferences. Even now, it's hard to be this way in our area. Not like in the cities, they're very conservative here. We still have the Klan.'

'Did you keep in touch, you know, after the marriage?'

'I tried to, but the letters got further and further apart. Ellie told me she'd married Ben, she told me when she had you, and your sister. I sent her word of the important things that were happening here, usually a long letter around Christmas time, but I don't suppose she kept all those silly Christmas letters.'

'No, I don't think she did.'

'It was probably too much to ask. I kept all of hers. I always treasured the letters she sent me, but I think she was more hurt by my marriage than she let on. We were warriors together against the world, but when I got married, and chose to stay here in the States, she felt like she was alone.'

'We never knew any of it. Even her sister. Did Mum's parents know?'

'Yes, they would have known. My mum, God rest her soul, went 'round there almost as soon as she found out and told them. I would have thought Ellie's sister—what was her name again?'

'Tessa,' Cassie said.

'Yes, that's right, Tessa, well she was a fairly spoiled girl. She didn't care to notice.'

Cassie thought about this version of her aunt; they had never been particularly close growing up, but it seemed very out of character for her. The Tessa she knew now had an old-school tough-love approach.

'Did you ever know my father?' Cassie asked, after a while.

'No,' Kerry was still sniffing sporadically, but she seemed to have calmed down. 'They met at work, I think, he seemed a good egg, but I don't think Ellie loved him. I don't know if she could have ever loved anyone the way she did with me. She locked her heart away. If I could have done anything, but when you're the person who caused the pain, it's... she didn't want my advice.'

Cassie heard ice cubes jangling against the glass, as though Kerry was absently swirling its contents. Cassie didn't quite know what to say. She had never thought about why Mum was so cold.

'Is there going to be a service?' Kerry asked.

'Yes, we've had one here for family and friends. There weren't many, my father didn't show up.'

'They weren't together?' Kerry sounded surprised.

'They split up several years ago. It was quite a big deal at the time, Dad threw Mum out for reasons he never fully explained, and Mum just got on with her life. I thought she was a stone-cold bitch, but maybe she didn't feel the way you or I would.' It struck her that the loss of her mother was somehow harder now that she could never tell her she understood.

Then again, maybe Mum set it up so that she would reveal herself to us after she was gone, she couldn't bear to do it while she was alive, perhaps she was afraid, but when she was gone, she wanted us to know her properly.

'I should probably let you go,' she said, hoping Kerry would take the cue and she could end the conversation.

'Yes, of course. Thank you so much for calling. I wouldn't have ever known otherwise. I'm sorry for your loss, honey. I don't know what Ellie was like as a mother, but she was always very special to me.'

'I've got your address. I'll mail the items over to you.' Cassie hesitated; how could she say goodbye to this woman?

'I hope you do well in your life, Cassandra, and have better luck in love than your mother and me for sure. You take care now, buh-bye.'

Cassie was left with the full weight of grief pressing down on her. It came over her in waves. She lay on the couch in her mother's empty apartment and could do nothing more than breathe, in and out, for a long time.

She only moved when the pressure in her bladder was too great. By then it was mid-afternoon, she had planned to go to work that evening, but there was no chance of that now.

Don't hate me, I'm too sad to come in. She sent the text message to Emma and Simone, knowing that she was hiding from them. She enjoyed the work, and she liked the people there, but it felt like so much had happened today.

We've taken on a new person to cover your shifts. Just casual until you're ready to come back. Simone sent back after a few minutes. Neither Emma, nor Simone had been in touch to check up on her.

They had felt like her family, she'd spent enough time around them, working fifty-hour weeks for years, but it was as though when she wasn't there in front of them, they didn't remember her. Cassie's chest was tight, but still the tears didn't come.

It was dark outside when her phone rang. 'Mmm?' she said.

'Can you come 'round? I... we haven't seen you for a while.' Penny laughed, like it was no big deal.

'Sure. Tomorrow? You could help me pack up Mum's house.'

'Could you come tonight?'

'I'm so tired.' Cassie knew it was true as she said the words. The exhaustion of grief, of the stuff with Tony, of the letters and the conversation with Kerry had all drained her.

'Yeah, but can you come now?' Penny asked.

'Alright.' Cassie looked around the room, she hadn't managed to pack anything, but at least she'd found Kerry.

***

Penny and Kev were watching TV when she let herself in. They were sitting on different couches, and were purposely avoiding looking at each other, their heads rigidly turned towards the screen. Cassie stood behind them. She decided to go into the kitchen and find something to drink rather than risk choosing a side.

'How's things?' Penny walked into the kitchen behind her. The TV became louder in the other room.

'I dunno. I'm tired.' Cassie rubbed her hand across her face. 'What about you?'

'Oh, y'know. The same.'

They stood in silence.

'Is there anything to drink?' Cassie asked.

'Kev's got beers, you can have one.'

Cassie got a beer from the fridge and gulped down about a third. She hated beer.

'What did you fight about this time?' she said.

'Nothing, we didn't have a fight.'

Cassie levelled her eyes on her sister and waited.

'Kev wants me to stop, y'know, smoking. He thinks I have a problem.'

'And do you?'

'No. I can stop at any time. I just like it, y'know.'

'But what about if you stopped? Maybe you'd feel better.'

'Fuck, I thought you'd understand. With Mum and everything, like... how do I deal with that shit?' She lit a cigarette.

'It's tough. I've been finding out stuff I never knew about Mum and it changes things.'

'You reckon it's okay to keep using?' Penny used the cigarette to point at Cassie.

'I didn't say that.' Cassie closed her eyes and exhaled. 'Drugs just numb you. You'll have to feel Mum's death eventually. You nearly died last week. It might be time to stop.'

'You're taking his side? Fuck.'

'I'm tired. Why am I here?'

'So, you can tell Kev he's being a fuckstick asking me to quit now.'

Cassie looked around; the walls and ceiling were yellow with smoke, it always smelled stale in the place.

The fridge was always empty. Penny hadn't had a job in eight months.

'Your life is on hold. Kev can use just a little bit on the weekends, but for you it's your whole life. How do you even pay for the amount you use?' It was a question that Cassie had never been game to ask.

'You know what I do for money.'

'And Kev's happy with that is he?'

'It's my body. It's not like you're a virgin.'

'Would you still be doing that sort of work if you didn't have to have money for drugs?'

'I dunno, maybe I like it,' Penny said.

'Do you?'

Penny took a couple of drags on her cigarette. 'Not really. It's boring, and cold and the dudes just want to whinge. I don't wanna listen to that shit. I don't like it when it's my friends and I have to listen to, but when it's a fucking customer, it's like, fuck, get your dick out and shut up, y'know?'

How lonely people must be to resort to talking to Penny, the world's worst listener.

'But it's good money. I only do one night a week, sometimes two if it's a bad night.'

'I can't tell you what to do with your life, but I don't want you to die. I wouldn't cope if I lost you and Mum in the same year.'

Penny's cigarette dangled from her fingers. The column of ash became unstable and crumbled, the pieces fluttering to the floor.

'I don't think I know how.'

'We'll work it out together.' Cassie said. She put her hand on Penny's upper arm. She was so tired.

Chapter 12

Jason tapped his pen against his keyboard. He'd been waiting for a response from Cassie for three days and the anxiety had made it almost impossible to think of anything else. Pierce had asked him to call the Office of Births, Deaths and Marriages on behalf of an elderly client. She was investigating her daughter's fiancé, wanting a reason to exclude him from the will.

'You don't have to include him, of course, it's your will,' Pierce said. He'd had several whiskeys with his lunch and used Old Spice to cover it up.

Pierce had given the task to Jason and gone back to his office. Jason still didn't know what he did in there all day, without a computer. Perhaps he has dirty magazines stashed in the desk drawer, he thought before he forced the image away.

He'd been on hold for twenty-five minutes. He'd spoken to three people: the first had put him onto the second, who put him back onto the first, who then put him onto a third. It was the third person who was now looking into something and 'would be with him momentarily'.

The hold music was completely unobtrusive and didn't help at all with his circular thoughts about Cassie and his letter.

It was possible she hadn't yet received it. There was no reason to think that she was avoiding him. Three days was not a long time, but it certainly felt that way.

'Are you still there?' the voice of the third person on the phone asked.

'Yes, I'm still here.' Jason's tapping stopped as soon as he spoke.

'I've been able to find a couple of entries that appear to correspond to the person you're looking for. Shall I email them over?' she offered.

'That would be great,' he said, giving her his email details.

The information was not exciting; a birth certificate and a marriage certificate from about ten years ago.

No divorce record meant he would have to ask the Family Courts. That would be another long phone call.

Jason had put his mobile number on the letter, as well as the number at the office which Cassie already had. He checked his phone in case she'd tried to call him in the four minutes since the last time.

He had just looked back to his computer screen when the phone started to vibrate. The number was a landline. His hand was shaking as he answered the call.

'Hello, Jason speaking,' he said.

'Jase, it's Dad. Can you come 'round for tea tonight?'

'Hi, Dad.' Jason's voice was flat. 'Yeah, I guess.'

'Good. About seven.'

'Is it a special occasion?' It had been at least nine months since he was last invited for tea.

'Becca is having hundreds of her girlfriends over for a Tupperware lingerie party. I don't know, apparently I'm not allowed to invite anyone, but I can have a night in with my sons.'

'Okay.' Jason was relieved to hear the ulterior motive. No doubt he would be left with Knox, somewhere out of Becca's way. Dad would shut himself in his study.

'Good. See you then.' He hung up.

Jason's heart was thudding in his ears as the adrenaline in his system settled. *It gives me something to do with my night other than sitting around wanting her to call me.*

***

'Where have you been?' David said as he swung open the heavy front door.

It was six minutes past. Jason knew arguing with his father about the definition of about seven would be futile.

'I didn't check the train timetable before I left the office.' Jason sounded as though he was sorry, but carefully avoided saying the words.

'We're in the rumpus room. Knox wants to watch *Divergent* again. I told him he had to wait for you.'

Jason followed his father through the entry into the main house. The two-storey building was as much of a way to signal David's status as anything else he owned. He had a gardener come once a fortnight to ensure the lawns were manicured and the topiary trees were neat.

Muted conversation came from behind the closed doors of the formal dining room. Jason pictured the tasteful canapés being handed around. Becca would have hired caterers; she needed to be available for hostess duties. He also assumed there would be copious bottles of champagne, which, coupled with the tiny amount of food consumed would lead to some interesting scenes before the night was out.

'Right, well, I've got some stuff to attend to in the study. Order a pizza'

'Will you be eating with us?'

The face David made could have been funny if it weren't so serious. 'No. Becca's sorted out my dinner.'

Jason turned to Knox and mimed putting his fingers down his throat to induce vomiting. Knox let out a loud laugh before slapping his hand over his mouth.

'Hello, my name's Jason and I'll be your babysitter for the evening.'

144

Knox's smile faded. 'Mum and Dad are always too busy for me. I'd be fine in my room, but when there's a party I need supervision.'

'Aw, mate. I know you don't need a babysitter, but do you want some company?'

Knox's smile returned. He needed an adult influence which could counteract the neglect he got on a daily basis.

They ordered three pizzas, garlic bread and two bottles of soft drink; far too much for the two of them to possibly eat. One plain cheese, one meat lovers with pineapple, Knox's favourite, and one barbeque chicken, also with pineapple.

After the pizza arrived, they settled themselves on the floor in front of the TV.

'I've watched this movie at least a thousand times. It's definitely my favourite.' Knox said.

'Why is it your favourite?'

Knox looked down. 'Coz I like Beatrice. She's cool, and she kicks all their butts.'

Jason laughed. Knox would be an early bloomer around girls. Hopefully he'd be able to provide good advice. The sort that would have helped him avoid getting into trouble the way he did.

At fifteen, Jason had had a girlfriend, Renee, who was in the year below. The school's sex education program had been two classes in year seven which had mostly involved blowing the condoms up and batting them around the room.

He and Renee took none of the precautions they should have. They used every spare moment together for sex. They were quick, but frequent.

'I haven't had my period,' she wrote on a note which had been passed to him in the corridor.

'Fuck,' he muttered, handing his note to Lucas.

'Fuck,' Lucas said after reading it.

'What am I gonna do?'

'She'll have to get rid of it.'

'Fuck. Fuck fuck.'

'You can say that again.' Lucas put his hand on Jason's shoulder and gave it a squeeze, 'I have to go to band practice. It'll be okay.'

When Jason looked over to Knox, he saw a version of himself at that age; desperately wanting his father to notice him. David was too busy playing the big shot in front of his friends. David had grown up poor and Jason thought this must be why he was so obsessed with wealth.

'You gonna eat anymore of this pizza? We should probably clean up and put it in the fridge for tomorrow.'

'Mum'll probably throw it away. I'm not allowed pizza,' Knox said.

Jason packed up the slices of leftover pizza into one box. They didn't quite fit.

'You want any more of this?' Jason gestured with the soft drink. Knox shook his head.

He carried the leftovers into the kitchen, where the caterers were packing up.

'Do you want to try any of this before we wrap it all up?' the older woman asked.

'Oh, God, I have no room.' He raised the pizza boxes as evidence.

She smiled. 'I believe you. Can't say the same about that lot. They seem to get full on the smell of blinis. So much not eaten!'

There were mini quiches, cold cut platters, and little dumplings served on china spoons. It looked delicious.

Jason put the pizza into the fridge. It was enormous but when Jason opened it, there was hardly any room around the champagne and white wine. He moved a couple of bottles and wedged the box into the least full shelf.

As he went back towards the rumpus room, he heard squealing and giggling. He put his eye to the crack between the two sliding doors. A thin model was wearing some of the lingerie, beside her was a rack filled with frilly, skimpy nothings of lace.

Two of the women in the group had taken off all the clothes on their top half and were rifling through the racks trying things on. The others were encouraging them. When one pinched the bottom of the woman closest to her, she was met with mock outrage.

I doubt any of them have a satisfying sex life. He
wondered if Becca and his father were following the
same pattern of decline as Dad had with Mum.

Jason went back to the rumpus room where Knox was
engrossed in the movie. His father paced in his office on
the floor above. He laid his head back on the couch next
to Knox and closed his eyes.

When he woke up the movie had finished, and the
DVD end card was playing on a loop. Knox was not in
the room. Jason got up and walked out into the hallway.
The party was over, but raised voices were coming from
the lounge. He padded toward them.

'You've been cackling away with your cronies all
night and now you're fucking drunk.' His father's voice
was clear through the closed sliding doors.

'I may be drunk, but you're the one who's old and fat.
You expect me to want to fuck you?'

'When I pay for everything in this house; your
fucking dresses and hair, I'm entitled to something in
return.'

Jason put his eye up to the crack in the door and
noticed that Knox was sitting on the floor in the dark.

'What are you doing down there?' Jason whispered.

'I heard them shouting. I wanted to know what they
were saying.'

'It's not a good idea to listen to people fighting.'

'You were!'

'I was looking for you,' Jason lied. 'Let's go upstairs.'

'No, I don't wanna go.'

Jason sat beside his brother and hugged him to the side of his body. 'Grown-ups fight sometimes. There's nothing you've done to make them fight.'

'They fight about me all the time.'

'It's not your fault. It's probably just an excuse. My mum and dad fought over me and Tamara, but they would have found anything to fight about.'

In the other room the voices had become hissed whispers, and he could no longer hear what was being said.

'We can't stay out here. Come on I'll tuck you in.'

Jason stood. He couldn't see Knox's face clearly in the dark, but the boy put his arms up like a baby wanting to be carried. Jason pulled him up by the hands and flung him over his shoulder like a fireman. Knox muffled a squeal of delight, despite the heavy mood.

Jason watched Knox clean his teeth in the ensuite next to his bedroom. He had everything; expensive soaps, hair products, an electric toothbrush. His bed linen was Egyptian cotton, he had his own TV, Xbox, laptop computer and tablet device.

At least when Jason had been growing up, he'd had Tam. Knox was growing up as an only child. He sat down on the edge of the bed.

'I'll just stay here till you fall asleep.' He'd done it when Knox was little. Knox had always fought to stay awake.

'Okay.' Knox snuggled down into the blankets, Jason switched off the light.

He was still and listened while his brother's breathing slowed. In the dark, his mind returned to Renee. They had agreed an abortion was the only solution.

'My parents won't let me speak to you,' she said at school afterwards.

'Since when have you listened to them?' he asked.

'And look where it got me.' She had started to cry.

'I'm sorry. I'm sorry, don't cry.' He put his arm out to comfort her and she pulled away, out of his reach.

'Don't. I can't talk to you. I want you to go.'

'But we said we'd be together forever.'

'You believed that?' she scoffed. He'd wanted to believe her.

Knox moved in the bed beside him. Jason brushed the unexpected tears from his cheeks angrily. His father always said, 'boys don't cry'.

In the morning, Jason was still in Knox's bed. At some point during the night he'd gotten under the covers. It was a double bed, so there was plenty of room. Knox wasn't there, his pyjamas were in a crumpled pile on the carpet and he'd pulled out a lot of clothes.

It's a wonder I didn't hear him throwing all that around, Jason thought as he got up bed and stretched. The house was silent. His phone was in the rumpus room with his wallet and keys. He checked the phone, one missed call from half past nine, twenty minutes ago. There was no message.

Cassie's number; he'd dialled it enough times to recognise it. A shiver ran the length of his spine starting at the base. He closed his eyes and steadied himself, leaning against the back of the couch.

Walking into the spotless kitchen he opened the fridge door. The wine and champagne almost all gone but the pizza box remained.

He put about half of the slices in the microwave. David and Becca had probably gone out. Leaving Knox alone in the house during the day was apparently acceptable although given his wallet and stuff were still here, they might have assumed he'd look after his brother.

Sunday morning in Brighton was quiet. Knox wasn't anywhere downstairs, and he wasn't in the garden. Jason heard the microwave ping and collected the plate. He carried it upstairs, looking through all the rooms; main bedroom, guest bedroom, both looked slept in, his father's study, the exercise room, Knox's bedroom, all were empty. He took the plate back downstairs, sat at the kitchen bench and took a bite of barbeque chicken pizza.

He looked through his phone for messages since there were no notes left for him. Still chewing, he dialled his father's number.

'What?' his father answered.

'Is Knox with you?'

'No, I'm on the boat.'

'Is he with Becca?'

'He's supposed to be home. Becca had gone out to brunch before I left, and I saw you were still around, so I left him with you.'

'But did you actually see him today?' Jason's throat felt tight.

'No. I haven't seen him since last night.'

'I'll call Becca. Maybe he went with her.'

'Right.' David hung up.

Jason had always felt like an accessory his father needed to complete his illusion of being the best. A wife and two children were necessary to keep up the appearance of success, but he didn't spend any time with them.

Jason looked through his phone and realised he didn't have Becca's mobile number. The emergency contact numbers were displayed on the wall next to the kitchen phone for any real babysitters they might have.

Becca's phone rang out before going to voicemail. Jason called her back and it went to voicemail after only after three rings; she'd rejected the call.

'It's Jason, call me back,' he said.

Since he didn't have her number stored, she wouldn't have his. He picked up the house phone and dialled again.

'Hi baby, did you have a good sleep?' she answered.

'It's Jason.'

'Oh, I thought it was Knox.'

'Shit. He's not with you?'

'Why would he be with me?'

'I can't find him anywhere. I thought you or Dad had him. Fuck.'

'You'd better find him. You were in charge.' Her voice wobbled.

'He's not my son! Did you even check on him this morning?'

'No. I thought David did.'

'Well, he didn't.'

'You have to find him. I'm stuck here for a couple of hours, I can't.'

Jason didn't say what he wanted to. 'I'll look for him.'

Replacing the received on its cradle, Jason ran his fingers through his hair. He grabbed another slice of pizza and started to check through the house again.

He called Knox's name, moving from room to room starting upstairs. He noticed that the toothbrush was missing from Knox's bathroom.

Outside, Jason looked in the garage; Knox's bike and helmet were also missing.

Knox had run away.

Where would he have gone? Jason didn't know his little brother's hiding spots or hangouts. Then he remembered that Knox had his own phone. Jason's hands trembled as he dialled the number and put the phone to his ear. He listened to it ringing, then he heard breathing down the phone.

'Knox? It's Jason.'

'I know.' His voice was so faint Jason struggled to hear it.

'I was just wondering where you were? I got up this morning and couldn't find you.' Jason tried to keep his tone relaxed.

'I don't want to come home.'

'That's alright mate. I just wanted to know you're okay, that's all.'

'I'm okay.' Knox's voice was raspy.

'Where are you? Can I come hang out? I'll bring pizza if you want some. There's plenty left.'

The boy did not respond.

'I won't tell Becca and Dad where you are. I promise.'

'Can you bring the Coke too? I'm really thirsty.'

'Yeah, course. Your mum won't want it with all that sugar in it. I'll bring some water too; did you bring a water bottle with you?'

'No. I forgot. I forgot a jumper too. It's kind of cold.'

'Alright. Pizza, coke, water, jumper. Anything else you want?'

'And you promise not to tell?'

'Cross my heart. Just tell me where you are, and I'll bring all the stuff to you.'

'I'm in the park, just down the road, there's a, like, stage thing.'

Jason knew the park he meant. It was an old bandstand. It was completely open to the elements and Jason wasn't surprised his brother was miserable.

He ran inside, collected the pizza, Coke, two litre bottles of Perrier water from Becca's stash in the cupboard and some clothes. He stuffed them all into a duffle bag he found in Knox's closet and hurried off.

Within fifteen minutes he was in the bandstand watching Knox eat cold pizza. He looked so tired and miserable, Jason wanted to comfort him, but he didn't want to make him defensive.

'What time did you leave last night?'

'After we went to sleep, you were snoring, and it woke me up. I could hear Mum and Dad shouting downstairs again. I packed up some stuff and went. It was the middle of the night. It was really cold in the dark.'

Jason chewed a piece of leftover garlic bread and thought for a moment. 'What are you gonna do now then?' he asked.

'I'm not going back!' Knox shifted away.

'I know, mate, I said you didn't have to go back.'

'I guess I'll live here then.'

'You could come stay at my house. There's heating and food and stuff. You can have a holiday with me for a while.'

Knox looked at him sideways, weighing up whether he could trust him Jason expected. He chewed through a slice and a half of pizza before he said anything.

'Could we tell Mum you couldn't find me?'

'Hmmm, well I don't think we should lie to your mum. But I can tell her you're angry and you want to stay with me for a while. She needs to know you're safe.'

'My mum doesn't really care about me.'

'I think she does.'

'She doesn't even talk to me half the time.'

'Maybe she's just... not very good at showing you she cares.'

'Maybe.' Knox finished the slice he was holding and shivered. 'Can we go to your house now?'

'Sure, buddy.' Jason felt relief flood his system. They picked up all of Knox's things and carried them to the car.

When they got to Jason's flat Knox fell asleep on the couch. Jason put a blanket over his small body. It was only then that he remembered the other call he had on his phone.

She hadn't left a voicemail message, so he found her number and called her back.

'Hi,' Cassie said.

'Hi.'

There was a gap, he heard her breathing. 'You called me?'

'Yeah. I read your letter,' she said.

'Great,' he said, more loudly than he had intended.

'I'm still angry.'

'I get that.'

'You shouldn't have left.'

'I know.'

There was another long silence.

'I did try to look after her. I asked one of the girls hanging around, someone I assumed was her friend, to look out for her till you got there.'

'Did you even try to figure out if they knew each other? Why didn't you get security to look out for her? That's their job isn't it?' Each question was a little louder than the last.

'I wasn't thinking very well. I'm sorry. I failed her.'

'Yes. You did.'

'I'm sorry.'

'You said that already.' She almost sounded amused.

'I'm sorry,' he said again, his voice now lighter too.

'What do we do now?'

'I don't know. Should we have lunch? We can discuss how your mother's estate is going?' he added.

She made a sound in her throat. 'I think that can be arranged. What about Wednesday?'

It seemed very far off, but Jason agreed.

'Will I have to speak to Pierce?' she asked.

'Not if you don't want to. You don't even have to come up if you'd prefer, I could meet you somewhere.'

He wanted to say more but he thought it was better left for a face-to-face meeting.

'Right. I'd better be going then.'

'Of course, I don't want to hold you up.'

He put down the phone, grinning. He glanced over to his sleeping brother and thought he'd better call his parents.

'What is it now?' his father said when he answered the phone.

'I've found your youngest son, Dad.' Jason had stepped out onto the balcony.

'Told you he'd turn up. Is that all?'

'Fuck, Dad. He ran away. He heard you and Becca fighting and spent the night in the park. He says he won't come home.'

'And you're looking after him now, are you? Poor little Knoxy!'

'Are you drunk?' Jason spluttered against the rage he felt.

'I'm on the ocean, I have nice wine, my wife isn't here to berate me. Nothing could be better. And now I don't even have a brat to come home to. I'm winning.'

He'd never heard his father speak like that before. He had often assumed he was less interested in his children's welfare than in his expensive leather couches, but this was the first time he had said it in his presence.

'I don't want to hear from you,' David took a moment to clear his throat, 'when you're sick of him. As far as I'm concerned, he's yours now.'

'Fine.'

'Fine.'

Jason pulled the phone away from his ear and felt an urge to throw it.

He called Becca next, hoping for a better reception.

'Hi Jason,' she said, she sounded tired.

'I found Knox. He says he isn't coming home. He wants to stay with me.'

'I've been so worried, but I thought it was best not to bother you.'

'Dad says I can keep him.'

'Don't mind your father, he's a blustery old fuck when he wants sometimes, but…' she didn't finish.

'Are you and him, uh, going alright?'

'I don't know. He lost quite a lot of money recently on a risky venture that turned out flat. He thinks I'm going to ruin him, and we'll have to sell the house and cars. But he can't have been stupid enough to lose it all. He'll feel better when he gets some new deals on the table.'

'And until then? Your son is caught in the middle of your bullshit, he thinks you don't want him.'

Becca sighed deeply. 'I'm sorry Knox got dragged into it. Maybe it will be good for him to stay with you for a little while, till things settle down.'

He heard her sipping liquid, maybe some of the white wine, given the hour.

'You will try to sort it out though, won't you? I can't have Knox living with me, not long term anyway. I don't know anything about his day; what time does he have to be at school? What does he have for lunches? What's his after-school routine?' Jason was panting down the phone.

'It's okay, honey, he knows all that. It doesn't really matter anyway, it's only for this week and then it's school holidays.'

Becca seemed completely unbothered, but she was still more concerned than his father had been.

He hung up the phone and looked back to Knox lying on the couch. He wished there was more he could do but he couldn't change who his father was, and he couldn't mend his parents' marriage.

***

On Monday morning, he dropped Knox at his school in Caulfield at eight before driving into work. The traffic was a nightmare, and parking in the city was more expensive than Jason had thought was possible. He'd tried to give Knox ten dollars for lunch.

'How much do you normally get for lunch?'

'Dad sometimes gives me fifty.'

'Every day?'

'Nah, not every day. But most days.'

'I can't give you that kind of money, mate. You'll have to make do with the ten today, and we'll go to the supermarket after school and get you some stuff to take with you tomorrow.'

'Alright.' He hadn't looked happy, but he didn't argue.

Jason had no idea how a kid like Knox would go in the real world after moving out of his Daddy's house where money was no obstacle. No one else lived like that. Jason had been the same at Knox's age, but when his parents split everything changed.

He was nine, and Tam had been six when they moved. His father must have paid quite a lot of child support; whenever they wanted new things, they had them.

His mother, Melanie, had seemed sad for a while after the break-up, he'd catch her crying when she thought the two kids were in bed. Sometimes he gave her a hug, and sometimes he pretended he didn't notice.

Jason stepped out of his car and went up to the office. The partners wouldn't be in till well after ten. He started working on some correspondence with clients on their behalf; the partners would leave Dictaphone recordings of letters that needed to go out. The clerks typed them up.

Sometimes Jason was allowed to draft the letters or emails and print them for the partners' approval. It was time consuming and menial and it took up most of his day. Jason thought again about applying for a new job with more interesting work. Perhaps he'd even be able to get better pay but with the new responsibilities of caring for Knox he didn't know when he would find the time.

Knox was going home with a friend, and Jason would pick him up on his way home from work. It occurred to him that he'd become a single parent overnight. He thought about calling his father and asking for money, but that didn't seem likely given what Becca said. He could call his mother, but it seemed inappropriate. He'd text Tamara, he'd hardly spoken to her since that party.

Knox is staying with me this week. Big shitfight: Dad vs Becca. Can you pick him up from school tomorrow or Weds?

Tam had a casual job in retail, he didn't know her schedule. She agreed to pick up Knox on Wednesday, the same day he was supposed to be having lunch with Cassie. He'd come to the decision that he really liked her. It was why he'd been so devastated when she wouldn't talk to him.

***

When Wednesday lunchtime came, Jason's armpits were so damp there were wet circles under his jacket. He met her down Collins Street from his office.

'Hi,' he said, putting out his hand.

'Hi, uh.' She had leaned in for a peck on the cheek, but she changed course to take his hand.

'Where are we going then?' he asked.

'There's a pub not far. That's sort of what I feel like, pub food, if that sounds alright,' Cassie said, stuffing her hands back into her pockets.

'That sounds good.'

It wasn't far, just down the hill of Russell Street, and neither of them said anything. Being in her presence again Jason knew why he couldn't get her out of his head; she held herself with a kind of poise, straight shoulders, kind face. Her long dark hair swung down her back when she walked. The way she'd held herself together in the face of her mother's death, and her forgiveness of his role in the disaster with Penny made him admire her strength.

They sat next to each other on a large communal table in the middle of the room.

'I think I'd like a beer. You want me to get you one?' she asked, putting her bag under the table, her wallet in hand.

'I don't usually. Actually, that would be nice. Whatever you're having.'

He watched her walk away and he reminded himself this wasn't a date. His eyes lingered on her buttocks as she shifted her weight from one leg to the other.

Look away, he said to himself, but he couldn't. When she turned to come back, a golden beer in each hand, he averted his eyes so quickly he thought it must have been totally obvious.

'I got pale ale.' She placed his pint of beer in front of him.

'Great.' He took a sip; it was mild with a hint of fruitiness.

He looked over the menu and they sat in silence.

'I got in touch with Kerry Strickland. She seemed very cut up about missing the funeral.'

'Were they very close? You said you'd never heard of her.'

She looked at him over her glass and took a long sip before carefully replacing the glass on the cardboard coaster. 'I suppose you could say that.'

'You don't have to tell me, of course,' he said. It seemed like he'd overstepped an invisible boundary.

'It's okay. They were very close when they were teens, but they lost contact in more recent years. I understand why my mum had her listed in the will.'

That's doesn't feel like the whole answer. Jason dropped his eyes back to the menu. 'I'm really hungry now we're here. Maybe it's the smell of chips,' he said.

'I'm not really. My schedule's been a bit off lately and my mealtimes are out of sync.'

'Did you take time off work to deal with… things? I don't even know what you do.'

'I'm a manager in a café slash restaurant. I had some time off when Mum died, and then I tried to come back and, well I suppose it was too soon. I'm finding it really hard to go back.'

Jason didn't know what to say. 'Do you think they'll keep your job open for you if you take a little bit of time off?'

'I dunno, I hope so. I've been there for almost seven years, but in hospitality there's a culture of people being replaceable.' She sighed.

Jason leaned a little closer and dropped his voice, 'I've been thinking about looking for a new job myself.'

'You don't like where you are now?'

'Are you kidding? You've met Pierce, he's unpleasant enough to the clients, imagine what he's like to the people he has to pay. I've been there ever since I came out of uni, Pierce knows my dad. I guess I've been too lazy to change.'

'I had assumed Mr Pierce was unpleasant to us because we were female.'

'It's definitely that too. Daniel gets a lot because he's Malaysian, the partners are pretty much the bane of my existence.'

'What's keeping you there?'

'I don't know. The longer I'm there the harder it is to imagine myself anywhere else. What if I've spent years learning really bad habits from these two old timers and I can't get a job anywhere else?'

'I see what you mean. But isn't waiting only going to make that worse?' Cassie was playing with the corner of the menu.

'Shall we order?' he asked, hoping to steer the conversation away from work.

He ordered steak and chips; she ordered a calamari salad. They settled into more neutral conversation about the weather. There were a couple of long pauses. Jason's brain worked extra hard in those moments to come up with something interesting, but it felt like running up a sand dune. He hadn't been on a first date for so long he was rusty.

No one ever said it was a date.

'Is it just you and your sister then?' she said, putting the last of the rocket into her mouth.

Jason swallowed his mouthful before answering her. 'No, my father remarried, and he has another son. He stays with me sometimes, when he needs a break from them.' He regretted adding the last comment.

'That sounds nice.'

'Yeah, it can be.' He wasn't going to burden Cassie with details, but he found her so easy to talk to. 'He's staying with me at the moment, his parents are fighting a lot. It's hard coz my parents split when I was his age, and having a kid is much more expensive than I thought it would be.'

She looked at him briefly before putting her knife and fork down onto the plate.

'I guess I don't know how long he's going to be staying, I didn't really think it all the way through,' he said.

'You're very good to have him.' It looked like she was going to say more, but she didn't.

He glanced at his watch. 'I better be getting back to the office. It's been really lovely.'

'I admit I have enjoyed your company.' Her voice seemed distant, and she was looking off past his shoulder out the window.

They walked out of the restaurant together and Jason hesitated. 'I'll see you around?'

'Sure.' She put out her hand to shake his. 'I probably have some questions, things I need to tidy up.'

'You can call me at any time. I'm more than happy to help.'

'Thank you for sending me that letter. It really helped to understand what happened with Penny.' They were still holding hands, Cassie pulled away. 'See you around, then.'

'Yep. See you around.' He watched her walk down the hill towards Bourke Street and felt a sadness come over him. She'd obviously forgiven him for Penny, but it didn't seem as though she was interested in anything more. He needed to get back on track, it felt like his life was on hold. He'd never really allowed himself to get too entangled with anyone romantically. Not after Renee.

Cassie turned the corner and was out of sight before he turned and trudged back up the hill towards his office.

Chapter 13

Cassie had been so nervous about meeting Jason she had felt nauseous and had only been able to order a small salad.

She walked away from the pub without looking back. As soon as she turned the corner, out of his line of sight, she stopped and took several deep breaths.

When he'd left Penny, he'd asked someone to look after her, they'd abandoned her, but all of the anger and hurt towards him were still there. She could understand why he'd done it, and now she added guilt to her turmoil of emotions.

Cassie tried to calm her breathing. She looked towards the sky in an attempt to stop the tears from spilling over her cheeks. She inhaled through her nose and blew her breath back out through her mouth. The exhale wobbled. She found a bench and sat down, then she covered her face with her hands and wept.

She wasn't sure how long she'd been sitting there when someone tapped her gently on the shoulder. A police officer looked down at her.

'Are you alright?' he said. He was quite young, clean cut and friendly looking. There was a female officer standing slightly behind him, keeping an eye on the rest of the street.

'Yes. I just—' she sniffed and wiped her face. 'My mother passed away about a month ago and it sort of just took me by surprise. I'm sorry, I'll get going now.'

'No need to hurry. We just like to make sure everything's alright. I'm sorry to hear about your mum. That must be very hard.' He looked back at his partner briefly. 'Can we do anything to help?'

'That's very kind, but I'm sure you have better things to be doing with your time than hanging around with crying messes. I'm fine, really.' Cassie looked in her handbag for a tissue and sniffed again.

'Take one of mine,' the female officer said, holding out a wad of scrunched tissues. Cassie bit her lips to stop from crying again.

'If you're sure you're alright, we'll be on our way,' the male officer said.

'Yes, thanks.'

The two of them walked away towards Swanston Street. Cassie blew her nose and stood up. Her legs were shaky and she sat down again.

Pull yourself together, go home, it'll all be okay. She hadn't slept very well lately. Maybe getting back to work would be the cure for her insomnia.

She pulled out her phone and called the restaurant.

'Fat Chef, Simone speaking.' She sounded out of breath.

'Hey Simone, it's Cassie.'

'Hey hun, what's happening?'

'I was just wondering if I could come back to work a couple of days this week. I've been feeling a lot better and knocking around the house all day is kind of depressing.'

'Yeah, sure, I'll… hang on one tick.' Simone put her hand over the mouthpiece of the phone. Cassie heard muffled voices behind the squeaks and rattles of Simone's hand.

'We've got someone covering your shifts this week hun. It's not really fair to take them away from her. I could put you on the roster from Monday if you like?'

'Of course, you can't take shifts off the new person. That's all good.' Cassie told herself not to feel hurt, it wasn't personal.

'I'll do the roster for next week and send you a text with your shifts okay? I'll probably give you lunch or dinner covers. A couple of hours a day to start with, yeah?'

'Probably sensible. Thanks, Simone.'

Cassie tried to understand what had just happened. Before Eleanor had died Emma, the chef, was in charge of the kitchen and Cassie was in charge of front of house. That was the way it had been for three years. Cassie had hardly missed a shift.

Even the time she'd had bruised ribs from Tony shoving her down the stairs, she'd come in. She knew it had been too early to return after Mum had died, and it would have been hard on the business to try to work around her.

The more she thought about the conversation, the angrier she became. Sitting in the tram home, she played it over and over.

Was the new person better than she was? Were Simone and Emma really her friends or were they just friendly at work? Had she been fucking up and no one had ever told her? And now she'd taken some time off, they were replacing her? Her hands shook as she stepped off the tram.

Her house felt empty when she came in, the wine glass still on the coffee table where she'd left it last night; if she had a boyfriend she could have sought comfort in his arms. She wanted to talk it over with someone, normally she would have called Emma, but she didn't know if she could trust her feelings towards her.

Cassie held her phone and tried to think of someone she could talk to. Her mother was dead, her best friend might not even be her friend at all, and who would care?

The phone clattered as it slipped from her hand onto the hardwood floor. Cassie left it there and curled into a ball on the couch.

When she woke up it was dark outside. Cassie stretched and sat up.

Mon 1100-1500, Tues 1200-1400, Thurs 1700-2100. Can you reply to confirm? Thanks. Simone had texted.

That's ten hours for the week. Before Mum's death she'd frequently done fifty-hour weeks.

I can do these. There aren't any more? Cassie sent back.

Sorry. You're first on my list for sickies.

Cassie sighed. *Maybe it was best to start slowly.* People were always calling in sick or quitting, she was sure to get more hours that way.

She was tired but after napping all afternoon she probably wouldn't sleep. Getting some exercise would help, so Cassie threw on her running gear and stepped out the front door.

She put on her workout playlist. The music was fast and repetitive; thumping techno with minimal vocals. It had been a couple of weeks since she'd been for a run. Her breathing felt hard and she struggled to keep up with the pace set by the music.

Halfway around her normal circuit, she stopped to rest. She leaned her hands on her knees and panted. Every part of her body hurt. She wanted to lie down.

She bargained with herself that she would complete the rest of the circuit, but she changed the soundtrack. This time she went for a soulful pop singer; it was a good pace for jogging.

As she approached her block of flats, she noticed of a man standing across from her place. He was wearing dark jeans and a dark long-sleeved shirt. He seemed familiar.

It couldn't be him, he's not that stupid. A prickle of fear started to crawl down her spine.

She crossed to the side of the street away from the man in black and slowed to a walk. Her breathing was loud in her ears. As she got to the corner of her building, he started to move, unfolding his arms he walked across the bitumen towards her.

'What are you doing here?' she asked, pulling her headphones off.

'Why won't you talk to me?' Tony said, now on the footpath between her and the gate to the block of flats.

'We're not together. I need you to respect my space. I thought we'd had this talk.' She could hear the music still, faintly from the headphones.

'Why won't you let me make it up to you? You're being fucking unreasonable.' He was close enough to her now that she could smell him, it was mostly alcohol.

'You need to go.' She put her hands up in front of her and took a step back.

'I'm not going until you fucking listen to me, Cassie.'
He reached out to grab her wrist and she wasn't quite
quick enough to evade him. She knew where this was
going.

'You're drunk. I won't speak to you when you're
drunk,' she said, trying to pull her arm out of his grasp.
'You're hurting me.'

'I'm hurting you?' he scoffed. 'That's a good one.
You rip my heart out, refuse to speak to me and I'm
hurting you?'

He wrenched her hand, forcing her to step towards
him. Now she was close enough for him to grab her
throat.

'You listen to me, bitch. You belong to me.'

'I can't breathe. Please.' She tried to pry away the
fingers at her throat. 'Let go of me.' She said, louder this
time. She hoped someone would hear her.

'Shut your face,' Tony said.

Cassie couldn't turn her head, but from the corner of
her eye, over Tony's shoulder, she saw the shape of one
of her neighbours.

'Is everything alright here?' he said, stepping around
Tony into Cassie's line of sight.

'Let me go, Tony,' she said again.

'You stay out of it, mate. This is between me and her.'

'I think you should let the lady go. Now.' Her
neighbour was a little more than an arm's length away.

'I told you to stay out of it.' Tony dropped Cassie's wrist and punched her in the solar plexus. She couldn't inhale. Her legs felt like they were boneless, and she sank down. Tony still had hold of her throat and she didn't fall, but with her weight no longer supported by her legs he pushed her towards the footpath. Cassie felt her skull crash into the concrete and then everything went black.

***

When she opened her eyes again, she couldn't quite make sense of what she was seeing. She closed her eyes, took a breath and tried again. Her neighbour was above her, his mobile phone to his ear.

'She's opened her eyes,' he said, then nodded. 'I'm on the phone to the ambulance. He's gone, ran off when you hit the footpath.'

'I don't need an ambulance. I'm fine.' She struggled to get up off the ground, but the neighbour placed a gentle hand on her shoulder.

'They said not to let you get up.'

'I don't want an ambulance. I just want to get home.' Cassie's breathing was becoming shallow as she remembered what had happened. She was ashamed. This neighbour, whose name she didn't even know, had tried to help her.

She should have known that Tony wouldn't just go. She should have been more careful. She closed her eyes again.

'I think I'm going to be sick.' She tried to turn her head which resulted in an intense jarring pain that radiated from the back of her skull around her head, and it felt as though it moved all the way through her body.

'The ambulance is on the way. What's your name? I'm Jordan, from number three, downstairs. You remember?' His voice was smooth and calm.

Cassie clutched his hand. 'I don't feel very well.'

'I know. It's okay. Help will be here soon. It's okay.'

'I'm Cassie,' she said. 'I live in number fifteen. I know you, don't I?'

'We've seen each other a couple of times, but I don't think we've been introduced,' he looked up for a moment. 'They said the ambulance is just around the corner.'

Cassie closed her eyes and tried to swallow. Her mouth felt odd. She was very thirsty. Then she heard the sirens.

'Here they come,' Jordan said, still stroking her hand.

The two paramedics stopped in front of the apartment block and went straight to work. Cassie didn't really feel like talking to them and she allowed Jordan to answer for her. It seemed very hard to concentrate.

'We're going to take you to hospital. You've had a nasty bump on the head. It's hard to tell if you need stitches. Head wounds bleed a lot.'

'I'm bleeding?' Cassie opened her eyes to look at the paramedic, but the bright light from the ambulance made her close her eyes again.

'It's okay. But we'd like to take you to hospital and the doctors can do a scan of your head and patch you up.'

'Can he come?' She pointed to Jordan.

'Uh, sure. Do you want to ride with us mate?' The paramedic asked Jordan, who was still holding Cassie's hand.

'I, uh... I don't really know Cassie. I just sort of came across the scene. Shouldn't we call her mum or something.'

'My mum's dead!' Cassie gripped Jordan's hand.

'Okay. It's okay. I'll come in the ambulance.' He squeezed her hand and she relaxed a little.

Jordan stayed with her in the ambulance and in the hospital as they checked her out. He held her hand the entire time.

'Who can we call for you?' he asked her as the nurse left, drawing the curtain around their section of the emergency department. She could hear the bustle of the other patients, murmurs and beeps.

'Cassie? Is there someone who can come and sit with you?'

She tried to think but it was very hard. 'My aunt. Tessa. She would come. My sister... she can't drive.'

'Okay. That's great. Can you find your aunt's number for me?' Jordan looked tired.

'Maybe. I... my brain is fuzzy.'

'I know. Here's your phone.'

She found Tessa's phone number.

'Thanks.' Jordan called Tessa number and explained the situation.

'She's on her way,' he said.

'What time is it?' She felt she had imposed on him far too much already.

'Just after eleven. Not too late.' His thumb rubbed over the back of her hand.

Jordan didn't come with her to get her CT scan. It felt strange not to have his warm hand in hers. By the time she came back to the emergency department Tessa was waiting for her.

'I'm so sorry. Jordan's been telling me what happened. I didn't realise Tony was such a piece of shit.' Tessa gripped her shoulder.

'It's okay,' Cassie mumbled. Tears bubbled up and slid over her cheek. 'I got stitches.'

'I can see that. Have you made a report?' Tessa asked.

'A report?'

'To the police. Tony won't get away with this.'

'He didn't mean to. I wasn't talking to him and I guess he just got angry. I'll sort it out.'

'Being angry about a break-up is one thing, but this is two months later, and he's just split your head open.'

Cassie turned her head away and closed her eyes. Tessa sighed loudly and tuned to Jordan.

'You should go home now. I can't thank you enough for looking after my girl. If it were up to her, I'm sure she would have tried to shrug it off without even going to the doctor,' Tessa said.

'Yeah, she tried to tell me she was fine, but the bleeding head wound said otherwise. Anyone would have done the same.'

'Not everyone. Thank you. Now get off home. Do you need money for a taxi?'

'No. I'll check in on her in few days. I live downstairs.'

'You're a good man, Jordan.'

Cassie listened and pretended she was asleep. How many people had been dragged into this shit between her and Tony?

They kept her in hospital until just after ten the next morning. Her aunt slept in the chair next to Cassie's trolley.

'I'm going to come home with you today. No arguments. I'll stay with you tonight and then the doctor said you should be okay after that.' Tessa was firm.

'I wish Mum was here.'

'I know. But she's not, so I'll have to do.' Tessa smiled, but she looked sad.

Her aunt stayed all day and through the next night. She slept on the couch and left Cassie alone to doze in her bedroom. Tessa came in occasionally to bring her food, or a glass of water. She was very quiet and subdued.

The next morning Cassie came out into the lounge room as Tessa was folding up the blankets that she'd used to make up the couch.

'I'm glad you're up. You look awful,' Tessa said.

'I feel pretty ordinary.' Cassie stood in the lounge room; she couldn't quite remember what she'd gotten up to do.

'I'm going to head off to work today. They said you'd be alright after twenty-four hours. If you need anything, you call me at work. Do you promise?'

'I promise,' Cassie said.

Tessa was standing there with her arms full of blankets and a frown on her face. 'I've been trying to decide whether to say anything ever since I turned up to the hospital. I thought you were too sick but...'

Cassie swallowed; she knew what was coming. 'Don't,' she said.

'I know you don't want to hear it. You need to do something about Tony. Even before you broke up, I knew he was bad news, but there's no way to tell someone who's in love that their boyfriend is an abuser. Now you've ended it, and it was such a brave thing to do, but you need to protect yourself.'

'I know what I'm doing.' Cassie's head felt heavy and it throbbed where the cut was.

'I don't think you do. You've tried being civil. You need to make a police report and you need to get a restraining order. He knows where you live now. He's not going to stop turning up at your house or trying to get you back. He could have killed you.'

Cassie rubbed her hands over her face. The idea of dealing with Tony seemed so hard. Tessa took a couple of steps towards her and gave her a hug.

'I know it feels impossible. I'll help you whatever you need, and you don't have to do it now, but please, think about it?' She stroked Cassie's hair out of her eyes.

'I'll think about it.'

'Now get some rest. There's some food in the fridge, and the soup we had last night. You just have to bung it in the microwave.'

'Okay.'

'And you call me if you need anything?'

'I will.' Cassie's arms dangled at her sides, her aunt released her from the hug, and she swayed without the Tessa holding her up.

Tessa bustled around for another five minutes before she left. Cassie had made herself a nest on the couch with the blankets that Tessa had used. She switched on the TV and watched whatever dreadful morning show was on. Their voices made her feel less alone.

At about lunch time, Cassie's stomach rumbled, and she put a container of soup into the microwave. Her aunt had divided the leftover soup into three meal-sized containers.

As she stood by the microwave waiting for the bing, she remembered that she hadn't checked her phone in some time. She walked slowly towards her bedroom; it was probably in the plastic bag of belongings they'd brought home from the emergency department.

The battery was low and there were several messages. She plugged it in and tried to concentrate on the tiny screen.

Thanks for lunch. Do you fancy doing it again sometime? That one was from Jason. She would reply to that later.

Rachel's called in sick, can you cover 9:00-16:30? From Simone. It was from yesterday morning, early, before she'd even been released from hospital.

Then later; **Look, I get it if you're pissed but I'm trying to help. I won't bother next time if you're not even going to reply. We've found someone else.**

Even in her fatigue Cassie was angry.

I was in hospital. Long story, but I hit my head. I'm still good for those shifts from Monday. Cassie wanted to vent at Simone. It was another blow to the relationship she'd thought was solid.

I'm going to make it to those shifts, I'm not going to be the one who closes the door.

Cassie watched trashy TV all day. She was miserable and sore, but most of all ashamed. Tessa was right; Tony had demonstrated an escalating pattern of behaviour. His drinking was obviously a real problem and the fact he'd shown up at her work and then her home showed he didn't care about her boundaries.

Maybe he'd tried her at work that night and when she wasn't there had come to her house.

Tony showed up at my place the other day. That's how I hit my head. He didn't show up there did he? she texted Simone.

Yeah. Showed up at the end of dinner service, again, shouting. Can't you do something about him? He wouldn't leave. I nearly called the police.

Shit, I'm sorry… Cassie started to type, but she deleted it. She sat thinking about how to reply when another message came through.

What do you mean that's how you hit your head?

Cassie decided to call Simone.

'Hey.' Simone answered after only one ring.

'Hey.'

'What the fuck happened?'

'Tony was outside my house when I came home from a run and, well, he sort of knocked me over and I hit my head on the footpath.'

'Are you serious? What a fucking psycho. Seriously, babe, you need to do something about him.' Simone was breathless.

'My aunt said I should get a restraining order.'

'And charge the fucker with assault.'

'I know,' Cassie said. Simone was clearly on her side, and the weirdness between them seemed to be gone. On the other hand, the idea of going to the police seemed about as likely as climbing a mountain.

'You still there?' Simone's voice broke in.

'Yes, sorry. I keep vaguing out.'

'You know you don't have to come in, it's only lunch cover and we'll be okay without you, Monday's aren't super busy.'

'No, I need to get out of the house. And I need the money.'

'Okay. I have to go. We'll see you then.' Simone hung up.

It hadn't sounded like Simone was at work, but she certainly didn't seem keen to have a chat. Cassie sighed, maybe things would seem better in the morning.

She got up and went to shower. Since she'd come home from the hospital, she hadn't dared to try it. She must reek, after her run, her fall, and then two days of not washing. She put her hand up to feel the lumps where the stitches were, her hair was lank and greasy, but she decided it would have to wait till tomorrow.

The hot water felt delicious on her skin. She stood under the stream for a long time enjoying it. She reached up for the body wash and her vision swirled. She put her hands on the walls of the cubicle to steady herself.

Moving more carefully, Cassie soaped herself up and rinsed off within a minute or so. The hot water made her dizzy. She went to bed and fell asleep.

When she woke up on Monday morning, Cassie was wet with sweat, panting and her head pulsed. She took a few deep breaths, she'd been dreaming. All she could remember was being chased by a giant-sized Tony, twice his normal size.

She sat up and saw that she'd bled onto the pillow. It was still before seven. Cassie went into the bathroom and used a hand mirror to examine the back of her head in the big bathroom mirror; dried blood made clumps in her hair.

Wetting a face cloth, she gently dabbed at the wound until the scabby flakes of dried blood were all cleaned off. She brushed her hair carefully, not getting close to the cut, and tied it loosely. Using the small mirror again, she checked that you couldn't see the cut through her hair.

That's the last thing a lunch diner wants to see.

She arrived at the Fat Chef just in time to start her shift at eleven. Simone wasn't there, but Emma was out the back. She waved as she saw Cassie come in but didn't stop what she was doing.

'Who's managing the floor?' Cassie asked her, coming through into the kitchen.

'I'm in charge until Simone gets in later.'

'Okay.' Cassie looked down, she still felt very confused. Emma had never been her manager, in the year she'd been working there the chef had always been her equal.

'You just need to be out on the floor, Simone's given you the far side to keep an eye on, alright?'

'Sounds fine.' Cassie rocked on the balls of her feet.

'Listen, hun, could you take this out to Rachel? She's out there already.' Emma passed her a plate of poached eggs and avocado on toast.

'Right. Sure.' Cassie took the plate, hesitating.

'We'll catch up later. I'm a bit busy right now and that plate isn't getting any hotter.'

Cassie felt dismissed. She turned on her heel and walked quickly back out of the kitchen. She spotted Rachel immediately, the only staff member she didn't know. Still blinking to keep her tears in check, Cassie approached the new woman.

'Emma said these were for you.'

'Thanks,' she said taking the plate. Cassie fiddled with her apron as she watched Rachel taking the meal to a customer.

'You must be Cassie. It's so nice to meet you. I'm sorry to hear about your, uh, situation.'

'Thanks.' Cassie scolded herself for being surprised that Simone would have had to explain why she was off work. It should have only been for a few weeks, Simone could have got a backpacker to cover the shifts, there were always people looking for short term work.

They didn't speak much over the course of the shift. Cassie struggled to remember the details of her role; her code for the cash register, the prices of the specials, which options were gluten free.

The lunch hour was packed, and Cassie's head had started to throb. By the time it got to the end of her shift, Cassie was exhausted and felt as though she might throw up. She went through the kitchen to get her stuff and knock off.

'Come out the back for five minutes,' Emma said.

Cassie nodded and followed her out.

Emma handed her a bottle of water. 'Drink this. You look terrible.'

'Thanks.' Cassie took a couple of sips, and then pressed the cold bottle to her forehead.

'Are you alright? Like, really are you?'

'I don't know.' She looked up.

'Simone told you that Tony's been hanging around, right?'

'Yes. I'll deal with him. I promise.'

'Do you know what you're going to do?' Emma prompted, after several long moments had passed.

'My aunt says I need to get a restraining order. I dunno, it sounds a bit much.' Cassie took another sip of water.

'I think she's right,' Emma said.

'He showed up at my house. I was coming home from a run and he grabbed me. There was a scuffle and I ended up cracking my head on the footpath. My neighbour called the ambulance.'

'Holy shit! When was this? Babe, that's not okay.' Emma was gripping the tea towel so tightly her knuckles were white.

'I know.'

'When was this?'

'Thursday night.'

'Have you reported him?'

'No.' Cassie looked at the pock-marked concrete on the ground.

'It's just one thing after another for you at the moment. You'll get through this, but you need to take back control of your life, yeah?'

'Is that why Simone gave my job away? So I'd be back in control of my life?' Cassie hadn't meant to say it.

Emma took a deep breath in before she said anything. 'We had to have someone to cover your shifts. Simone never intended to give Rachel your job, but when you kept extending your time off, she had to offer her something so she'd stay.'

'All I see is that my mother dies and instead of sticking by me, my job, where I've worked for three years, just throw me over. I've got a dead mum, a stalker ex-boyfriend, family secrets coming out my ears, and now I'm broke and unemployed too. Gee, thanks.'

Cassie was glaring at Emma, who had gone red.

'And you never called me. Not once. I thought we were friends.' Her head was still painful.

'I'm sorry I didn't call. I meant to. I got caught up and then I didn't know what to say.'

They stood silent. Cassie heard the clatter of plates in the kitchen.

'I have to get back in there. If you stay here for a bit, I'll make you something to take home. You look like you could use a good meal.' Emma patted Cassie's shoulder before scurrying back into the kitchen.

The weight of everything that had happened felt overwhelming. At least Simone wasn't there to see her.

Emma made up two containers of food to take home. Cassie was grateful as she drove home. Her arms and brain were sluggish to respond.

I probably shouldn't be driving, she thought as she stepped out of the car at home. One container was vegetarian lasagne, one of Emma's specialities. The other was a Thai style chicken salad, Emma always thought it was comforting, although Cassie had never understood why.

I hope you are going okay today. Call if you need anything. The message was from Tessa.

Cassie ate her lasagne curled on the couch before switching on the TV and falling asleep.

She was woken a couple of hours later by the phone ringing. It was Tessa.

'Hello?'

'Oh good. I thought something might have happened when you didn't answer my text.'

'No. I did four hours at work and when I got home, I fell asleep.'

'Do you really think you should be working?

'Don't start. I don't need any more advice today.' Cassie was exhausted rather than angry.

'I'm not starting, but if you need to have some more time off, we can make sure you have enough to cover the bills, you know. You don't have to go to back to work.'

'I don't want to be stuck at home anymore. Wallowing. Waiting for Tony to show up.'

Tessa said nothing, but Cassie heard her draw breath as though she were going to.

'Do you think Dad knew about Kerry?' Cassie said, finally.

'I don't know. Have you spoken to him since the funeral?'

'No. I don't really want to, but I... when he left he said it was because of all the lies. I guess I never asked what he meant.'

'I—' Tessa started, but fell silent. 'The only way you'll ever know is to ask him.'

'Yeah.' Cassie said. Her eyes felt heavy again and she thought she should probably go and lie down in her bedroom.

'You promise you're alright then?'

'Yes. I'm just tired. I'll let you know if I need anything.'

'Okay, sweetie. I'll call you tomorrow.'

***

The next week went by in a blur of working and sleeping. Even with the reduced hours Cassie could barely do anything other than fall into bed when she got home. Cassie had hoped to talk to Simone to figure out what the issue was between them but every day she came in to find that she'd just finished or wouldn't start until after she left.

'I'm starting to think Simone isn't talking to me,' she muttered as she picked up her bag to go home after the Saturday lunch rush had died down.

'I'm sure it's nothing to worry about. With Rachel here now Simone's been doing the evening shifts,' Emma said, a little too quickly. She waited for more.

'I mean, it's natural for you two not to cross paths. Shift work is like that and you've only been doing short shifts,' Emma's cheeks flushed.

'She does the roster. I think she's avoiding me on purpose.'

'I'm sure you'll get different shifts next week. It'll sort itself out, you'll see.'

Cassie made a noise of agreement and plodded out. She had decided to drop in on Penny on the way home, just to see how she was going. They hadn't really spoken since the overdose.

When she pulled up to the house in Brunswick, she saw that all the curtains were closed and there were no lights on. In the middle of the afternoon on a Saturday it seemed a bit strange.

She knocked on the door and there was no sound. Penny didn't have a car, so that wouldn't help to know if anyone was home. Cassie knocked again, louder this time and tried to look through the gap in the curtains.

'Penny? Kev? Are you guys in there?' she called through the door.

She knocked a third time and thought she heard movement inside.

'What?' Her sister looked like she'd had a big night. Her hair, unruly curls at the best of times, was more like a halo of fuzz, and her eyes were rimmed in last night's makeup.

'I just finished work and wanted to see how you were.' Cassie stood on the front step of the brick veneer house waiting to be invited in.

'I'm fine. You've seen me, now go away.' Penny started to close the door, but Cassie put out her hand to stop it.

'Are you really alright? I mean, I haven't heard from you in a while and after out last conversation I was worried you were mad at me.'

'I am mad at you. You're always trying to tell me I'm not good enough and I need to clean up my act. You hate Kev and you think I'm a failure and I don't want to hear

it. So just fuck off back to your stupid perfect life.'
Penny pushed her back and closed the front door.

'What are you talking about? I don't hate Kev. I don't
think you're a failure and I certainly don't have a perfect
life.' Cassie was yelling at the closed door. She banged
her fist on the door a few times trying to get Penny to
come back out.

The yelling had caused her head to ache again.
Feeling alone, Cassie sat on the swing Penny and Kev
had on their front veranda and closed her eyes. She
wouldn't cry today.

Cassie had been sitting on the swing, rocking gently
back and forth, for about five minutes when she heard
the front door open. Penny padded out and sat down next
to her.

'Do you want a smoke?' she asked.

'Sure.' Cassie took the rolled cigarette.

'I'm sorry I slammed the door on you.'

'It's okay.'

They smoked in silence. Cassie opened her eyes
briefly to look at her sister. She seemed small in her
stained dressing gown.

'I miss Mum,' Penny said.

'Me too.' Cassie's cigarette had burned down to her
fingers, she dropped it onto the concrete. She'd only had
two drags. Beside her, Penny lit a new cigarette from the
ember of the last.

'I was in hospital last week.'

193

'What the fuck? Why didn't you tell me?' Penny turned to look at her sister, frowning.

'I dunno. I didn't want to burden you. Tessa came to pick me up.' Cassie poked the pile of ash with the toe of her shoe.

'No one tells me anything. What was wrong with you?'

'Tony.' Cassie swallowed; she didn't want to tell the story again. 'He pushed me, and I cracked my head open.'

Penny was silent, her eyes fixed on Cassie. Slowly, she laid out the whole night, and the horrible week she'd had at work, what she'd found out about their mum, and the fact that she wouldn't be able to pay her rent without money from her aunt.

Cassie wished she'd never started talking, she felt wrung out. Penny hadn't stopped smoking the entire time and the smell of her cigarettes was nauseating.

Cassie got up and paced up and down, the movement seemed to help.

'What're you gonna do now?' Penny asked. It was the first thing she'd said for nearly twenty minutes.

'I don't know.' Cassie turned to look at her sister. 'What would Mum say? I've let everyone down and now I don't know what I'm doing with my life.'

'Mum would probably say "If you don't like something, either change it or shut up."'

Cassie laughed at the imitation of their mother's tightly reigned voice.

'She probably would too, but where do I start?'

Penny had never really been someone who thought deeply about problems. She looked uncomfortable with the effort. 'Do you actually want to keep working in hospo?'

'Of course I do! It's what I've done ever since I left school—' Cassie broke off. She'd answered automatically. 'I mean, what else would I do? What am I even good at?'

'I'm not saying that you should find a new career, but y'know, have you ever really thought about what you want to do with your life? I mean, instead of just getting a job and sticking with it.'

Cassie went back to sit next to her sister. She leant her elbows on her knees and let her head dangle.

'Fuck,' Penny said quietly.

Cassie put her hand up and discovered that her hair had fallen out of its carefully arranged style and her injury was exposed.

'Yeah.'

'Does it hurt?'

'Not much. I have headaches sometimes; by the time it's the end of the day it's pounding pretty badly.' Cassie ran her fingers over the wound.

'Leave it alone.'

'Sorry.' She sighed loudly and dropped her hand back to her knee.

'Kev'll be home soon. I can get him to bring takeaway and we can watch TV. You don't have to go back to your apartment.'

'I'm not lonely.' Cassie lied.

'I know you're not, but y'know, I feel like we've been a bit distant, or something, since Mum.'

'Yeah. I'll stay for tea.'

The three of them had KFC. Kev picked up an obscene amount on his way home from work at the hardware warehouse. He hadn't even snuck any of the chips before he got home.

'Is that business with your Mum's will all sorted then?' He asked as he washed his hands in the kitchen sink.

'Mostly. There are a few loose ends I have to tie up.'

'Have you sent that stuff over to that woman? The American?' Penny said.

'I spoke to her and I have her address. I think I've been avoiding finalising it all.'

Penny looked at her and bit her lip.

***

Simone hadn't scheduled Cassie on for Sunday, and she was grateful not to have to get up for work in the morning. She'd fallen asleep on Penny's couch at about ten, and they had left her there. In the morning Kev had already left for work when she woke up.

My Mother's Secret

It felt very strange to wake up in her sister's house. Penny wouldn't be up till later; she'd never been an early riser.

She found her shoes and drank a glass of orange juice from the bottle in the fridge before she left. She thought of leaving a note but couldn't find anything to write on.

Driving home Cassie felt sticky from not having showered. When she came in the door she stripped off and had a very quick shower. She still wasn't game to wash her hair; the doctor had told her to try to keep the stitches dry for at least a week.

After sleeping on the couch Cassie expected to find herself tired and cranky, but instead she felt energised. Now she and Penny were back on the same team, she'd solidified her resolve to change her life.

The first thing was to settle the details of her mother's estate. The flat her mother had rented was still sitting partially emptied. There wasn't much left in the house, and Cassie thought she may as well take advantage of her current energy.

As she drove back out of her block of flats, Cassie saw Tony leaning against a tree on the far side of the road. If he was still there when she got home, she'd call the police.

I hope you slept okay. You can always call if you need to talk. Penny sent a message at two o'clock, as Cassie was packing away Eleanor's linen.

She worked slowly, not wanting to give herself a headache by overdoing it. There were seven boxes in the lounge and some smaller ones in the bedroom. Cassie figured if she folded down the back seats of her car, they'd all fit.

Thanks. I'm just putting the last of mum's stuff in my car. Do you wanna see it one more time before I go? Cassie sent the message to her sister and her aunt. It didn't feel like her mother's house anymore, just an empty shell.

The last box squeezed into the front passenger seat of Cassie's hatchback. She pulled the door closed on the empty house and knew that she wouldn't be back. She'd arrange to sell the remaining furniture to an estate seller, and have cleaners come through after that. Everything left of her mother was in those boxes.

Kerry would probably like to see the letters, Cassie thought, but she didn't want to let them go. Those letters where the only window she had into the woman Eleanor had been before she'd put up a wall around herself.

'There have been so many lies, Eleanor, I can't do this anymore.' Those were the words that her father had said when he left. Cassie wasn't supposed to hear, they were fighting in whispered voices, but it was a small house.

Cassie had moved out when the marriage broke down. Eleanor couldn't afford a three-bedroom house.

My Mother's Secret

'It's time for me to live on my own, Mum, I've been working for four years already,' Cassie had said when her mother insisted that she move with them.

'You'll always have somewhere to stay with me. I'll never love you any less, no matter what happens.' Eleanor said.

In the car, filled with her mother's things, Cassie thought maybe her mother felt abandoned. She'd had always been very reserved and those words, 'you'll always have somewhere to stay with me,' might have been her way of begging Cassie not to leave. It was enough to make her cry again, the road in front of her swimming as she rubbed the back of her hand across her eyes.

Cassie didn't know what else to do with the boxes, so she picked up a couple of them and started to climb the stairs to her small apartment. Putting the boxes on the floor next to the door so she could get out her keys, she saw that the door was ajar.

She gently pushed the door open. The apartment looked normal, but her breath was shallow and ragged; something was wrong.

Cassie picked up the boxes and manoeuvred her way inside, closing the door with her foot. She placed her load next to the TV and went to put her handbag in her bedroom.

Then she saw it; her bed was covered in tiny pieces of fabric. Her hands felt cold, her skin prickled as goosebumps of fear popped up all over her.

Her handbag fell from her hand as she rushed to the bed to pick up a scrap. It was a triangular shaped slice of her favourite formal dress, the shimmering wine-coloured cloth danced as she let it fall back to its companions.

Her wardrobe was standing open, and empty, her chest of drawers were all half out. Cassie felt a cold nausea; someone had been in her house. They had pulled out her clothes and cut them into tiny pieces.

She remembered the figure watching her apartment block as she left that morning and she knew what had happened.

She grabbed her bag off the floor and scrambled out of the apartment. She ran down the stairs and into her car, locking the doors. Cassie pulled out her mobile and dialled her aunt. Her breath was ragged.

'Hello?' Tessa answered.

'He's been in my house.'

'Who has?'

'Tony. Tony's been in my house.'

'Are you sure? What's happened?' Her aunt's voice was urgent.

'I—' Cassie burped, feeling as though she might vomit all over the interior of her car. She took a slow breath and started again.

'I came home from cleaning out Mum's place and the door wasn't shut properly. I thought I must have left it open coz I've been a bit vague since, well, since I hurt my head. And then I went into the bedroom and—'

'It's okay. Take your time. Where are you? Is he still there?' Tessa was calm.

'I'm in my car. I don't know where he is. He's cut up all my clothes. It must have taken hours. All my dresses, my jeans, all the drawers were open, but I didn't stay to look properly.' Cassie's hands were shaking.

'I think you should call the police. Now. Hang up and call them, I'm coming over and I'll help you with the police report. Then you're staying with me for a few days.'

'You don't have to do that,' Cassie said.

'I don't want to hear any of that nonsense. You do as I tell you, and I'll be there soon.'

'Alright.' Cassie didn't have the strength to resist her aunt. She didn't want to go back inside, the safe space she'd created for herself to live in was no longer safe.

She called the emergency number for the police from her car. The operator was very kind as she hiccoughed through the story again.

'We'll send someone out to you soon. It's probably better if you stay out of the apartment until they get there, alright?' the operator said.

'Don't worry, I'm not going in there on my own.'

Alone in her car, Cassie tried to calm herself. Her head had started to throb, but her painkillers were in her bathroom cabinet. She took long, slow breaths, and tried to think about waves lapping a shoreline.

The police were there within ten minutes, but it felt a lot longer than that. Cassie was terrified. The two officers who attended were quite young, both men. When they knocked on her window she squealed.

'I'm sorry about that. I'm a bit upset,' she said as she got out of the car.

'I understand. It's a very upsetting thing to come home and find that there's been someone in your house,' the older one said.

'I'm Senior Constable John Knight, and this is Constable Will Brent. We'll need you to take us up to your apartment so we can have a look around and then give us a statement about what happened. It shouldn't take too long. Are you ready?'

Cassie nodded. 'It's just up these stairs.'

She unlocked the door for the police officers and swung it open. 'You go in first, in case he's still in there,' she said.

'Alright, you wait with Constable Brent and I'll have a quick look around.' Knight went into the apartment.

Standing in the hallway with Brent felt awkward. Cassie wasn't sure if she should make conversation, but she didn't really feel like it.

'Have you lived here long?' Constable Brent said, after a long pause.

'No, only a couple of months. I had a breakup and I moved in here on my own. I'm pretty sure it's my ex who broke in, actually.'

'Okay. A rough break-up then?' he asked, as he pulled out a small pad of paper and wrote something down.

'You could say that. I thought it was okay, but it seems to have gone all wrong in the last—' she paused, 'over the last few weeks.'

'I see. And has anything changed in those few weeks that you think might have, uh, precipitated that change?' he said.

'I don't know. I mean, my mother passed away and my ex was pretty unhappy that I hadn't told him.'

Senior Constable Knight reappeared in the doorway. 'Seems to be all clear.'

They all went in to record her statement. Cassie's little apartment didn't have a dining room table, she only had one couch and no additional chairs.

'Have a seat,' Knight indicated to the couch. When Cassie sat down Knight sat at the other end of the couch with his notebook open. Brent remained standing by the fridge. He didn't seem curious to look around the house, or into the bedroom.

It was difficult for Cassie to be completely honest; she didn't want to get Tony into trouble. Just as Knight became frustrated with her and turned to his partner to ask something, there was a loud knock on the door.

'That'll be my aunt, I asked her to come,' Cassie said, as she got up to answer it.

Tessa looked furious, her face was tinged pink and her lips were pressed together in a thin line.

'Has she told you about the assault last week?' she asked, she didn't even wait for the two officers to introduce themselves.

'We haven't heard anything about an assault,' Knight said calmly. 'Can I have your name please ma'am?'

'Yes, I'm Tessa Beechworth, Cassandra's maternal aunt. I was called to the hospital after her psycho ex-boyfriend threw her onto the footpath and split her head open last Thursday night.'

'I see. And was a report made at the time?' Knight addressed the question to both women.

'No, the stupid girl refuses to make a report. And now see where it's gotten us!'

'There's no need for name calling, Ms Beechworth.'

Tessa harrumphed. She turned sharply and went into the bedroom.

'Holy shit. I thought you must have been exaggerating when you said he'd cut up all of your clothes,' she said. 'Will you be getting that restraining order now? You need to do something before he kills you.' Tessa stomped back into the living room, which now felt quite crowded.

'It's certainly worth looking into that option, especially if you feel he's an ongoing threat,' Knight replied.

Cassie was silent as she thought about the implications of what had happened. She didn't feel secure in her home, Tony had attacked her and then watched her, waiting until she left to break into her house and destroy her possessions.

'He's not a bad guy, deep down. I don't know what to do.' Cassie rubbed her hand over her face.

'No, he's not a bad guy, he's just a fucking drunk who breaks your head and then breaks into your house. I mean what was he trying to achieve?' Tessa addressed the question to the police officers.

The younger officer answered. 'Why a woman would want you back when you stalk her is beyond me. I mean if you'd just broken up with him and he'd thrown all your stuff out onto the grass in anger, y'know, that seems understandable to me, sort of, but this....'

'And given that he has assaulted you already, this situation isn't likely to resolve itself. It's up to you, of course, but I would recommend making your report and getting an interim order put in place. Perhaps that will be the end of it,' said Knight.

It took some time for the two officers to take Cassie through the formalities. As they left, they asked again if she wanted to come with them to the station and make any further reports.

'Not today, I'm sorry. I will think about it. I promise.' Cassie closed the front door, which now stuck where Tony had broken in.

Tessa was leaning on the kitchen bench, her face pinched.

'I know what you're going to say,' Cassie said.

'Do you?'

'You're going to tell me that I need to stand up for myself and make sure Tony can't hurt me anymore. His drinking is out of control, and if I'm not careful, next time he breaks in I'll be home, and he'll kill me.'

'Right. So, what are you going to do about it?'

'For today, can I just stay at your place and try to get some sleep? I'll go to work tomorrow, it's only a couple of hours, and then I'll go back to see the cops and work out what's involved.'

'I suppose that will have to do.' Tessa pushed away from the bench and hugged her. 'I worry about you. It's been a rough time lately. Let us look after you.' She stroked Cassie's hair.

Chapter 14

Jason's daily routine had had to be completely rewritten with Knox staying there. They had to be up, make breakfast and pack a lunch, and Knox dropped at school all before half-past eight—tough but doable. Picking him up in the afternoons posed a bigger problem. School finished at quarter past three, and Knox's school was in Brighton, forty minutes' drive—in good traffic—from Jason's apartment in Hawthorn.

'I've got my younger brother staying with me at the moment, there's some stuff going on at home, anyway he can't stay there. I need to leave work early a few days each week to collect him from school,' Jason said to Mr Pierce.

'You expect me to be happy with you off gallivanting after some kid? What if we need something done urgently?' Pierce's face was red.

'There are three other juniors here who are perfectly capable.'

'Would you trust them with correspondence? I don't know how to handle any of them, that's your job. And what does "a few days each week" mean?'

'I have someone to pick Knox up on Monday, Tuesday and Wednesday, but I need to pick him up on Thursday and Friday,' Jason replied.

'The two busiest days! What about all that stuff that needs doing on a Friday night? You can't leave us in the lurch.'

'I've never asked you for flexibility before. I always take leave when you do, so I don't disrupt the business, I've only had one pay rise and taken on looking after the three juniors without complaint. I don't think it's too much to ask.'

Jason bit the inside of his cheek to stop himself from saying any more. He knew he'd crossed the line. Pierce was liable to let go of a long angry tirade at the smallest thing.

'You're lucky I don't fire you right now, Jason.' Pierce's face had turned a darker shade of red. 'But as you say, you have been here for some time and you've shown you're a good worker. Usually.'

Jason kept quiet, in case Pierce said anything else. His breathing had started to slow down, and his flush receded away a little.

'I will agree to a trial of this new arrangement for four weeks. If there are any problems in that time, if we have any screw ups because you're not here, then I'll be rescinding my agreement. And of course, we'll have to adjust your salary for reduced hours.'

'Of course.' Jason was struggling to pay for all the new expenses of having a child staying with him as it was. He was reluctant to ask his father for money, but with reduced hours Jason would have to.

Jason loved having Knox stay with him, it brought a sense of joy into the house. Lucas had started to bond with him and had convinced him to learn drums. When Jason got home from work in the evenings, they would all make dinner together and then he would help his brother with his homework.

Knox didn't seem to mind sleeping in the lounge room; it was still an adventure. But Jason and Lucas couldn't watch anything too graphic and after nine, Knox's bedtime, they had to stick to their bedrooms.

'Mate, having your brother stay here is all good for the moment, but like, he can't sleep in the loungeroom forever, y'know?' Lucas said when Jason told him about the conversation with his boss earlier that day.

'I know. It's not permanent. He has parents and he's their responsibility. I'm gonna have to ask Dad for some money though.'

'How is your dad so rich and yet such a tight arse?'

'That's why he's so rich. I don't really know how he deals with the amount of money Becca spends, but it's not for me to judge.'

# Fleur Blüm

'Yeah, you might have a point. I'd chip in but it seems weird. Better your dad gives you some money.'

Jason had barely heard from his father in the two weeks Knox had been staying with them. Becca had called Knox a couple of times, but apart from a couple texts Jason had sent to update her, he hadn't spoken to her either.

'Dad?' Jason said into the phone late that evening. He'd gone out onto the balcony so he could keep an eye on Knox without him hearing.

'What is it? I'm pretty busy here.' David didn't even say hello.

'I wanted to talk to you about your son. The one who ran away and is staying with me? You remember?' Jason couldn't help his sarcastic tone.

'What about him? Is he complaining or something?'

'No, he's doing great.' Jason hesitated. 'It's just, well, there's two things.'

'Spit it out then.'

'Firstly, you need to give me some money. I can't afford to have him here otherwise.' Jason hadn't asked his father for money since he was a teenager.

'Is it really that expensive? Doesn't your job pay you well enough?'

'Come on, Dad. He's not my son. I didn't ask to have him here. I'm doing you a favour. I need at least a couple of hundred a week.'

210

'Fine. I had hoped—' he broke off. 'What was the other thing?'

'Well, what are you doing about making it up to him? When are you going to have him back? He can't sleep in my loungeroom indefinitely. He needs his parents. He needs his own space. I need my lounge room back.'

Jason sighed, he didn't want to admit having Knox stay with him was a strain, but not being able to chill out in his own home had started to be a burden. He was sure Lucas felt the same, although he would never say so.

Jason listened to his father's breathing.

'I don't know when we'll be able to take him back.' David's voice was quiet.

'What do you mean? What the fuck is going on Dad?' Jason said.

'Don't swear at me, you ungrateful shit. I've got enough stuff going on without this as well.' His father panted on the end of the phone. 'Listen, I'm not going to say any more. Is there anything else you want?'

'No. All I want from you, Dad, is your money and your contempt.'

'Fine. I'll transfer some money tonight.'

'Good.' Jason hung up. He wasn't sure how the conversation had gone so off the rails so quickly. David had left when Jason was about Knox's age, and the memories made it harder for Jason to keep his emotions under control.

More than anything else, Jason remembered the way his parents had spoken about each other; 'your father is an asshole,' 'your mother is a money-grabbing bitch'.

Jason had always wanted to live with his father, in his big house with all the latest gadgets. In the beginning he had gone to his dad's place every weekend, they had played video games and eaten pizza and Jason had anything he wanted. Over time it dropped to once a fortnight, then once a month, and then he saw Dad only on holidays.

David had met Becca less than a year after things went bad with Renee. It affected Jason deeply when his mother wanted nothing to do with his father, but neither of his parents would speak to him about it. His mother didn't want to dwell on unpleasantness, so she said, and his father simply refused to speak about it.

His father's second wedding was an enormous affair, at which Jason was a groomsman, and the pregnancy announcement followed within a month. When Knox was born, Jason had value to his father again—as a babysitter.

Over the years, he'd tried to build a relationship with his father, but David wouldn't be drawn. He worked long hours, and when he got home, he went to his study. Sundays were with the boys. Even Becca only ever saw him on Saturdays.

'It's like I'm married to a ghost,' she'd once told Jason when he'd come to pick up Knox.

'I, uh... he barely speaks to me either,' he'd replied. He'd watched as Becca became thinner and thinner, as she spent more money on her appearance to keep David's interest.

Now standing on the balcony with his phone gripped in his hand, and his jaw clenched, Jason tried to remember his father was human before he went back inside.

'At least I've got the money situation sorted out,' he said quietly to himself. He sat down on the couch next to Knox, who was watching a movie. Jason wasn't sure but he thought it was one of the *Fast and Furious* movies. They weren't his sort of films, but Lucas had all of them.

'Why don't you have a girlfriend?' Knox asked, as the cars were screaming across the screen.

'I dunno.'

'I've been here for like, weeks, and you haven't had a single date. It's not good for you.' His small face was serious.

'Are you worried about something, buddy?'

'It's just that most grown-ups have a girlfriend, or a boyfriend.' He was pulling at the hem of his shorts.

'Do you want to know a secret?' Jason leaned over.

'Yeah!'

'I did have lunch with a girl a while ago, she was very nice, but... she's a bit sad, because her mum died, and she might not want to have a boyfriend right now.'

'Have you asked her?'

'Asked her what?'

'If she wants you to be her boyfriend?'

It hadn't occurred to him that he could ask Cassie how she felt. He was so caught up in work and Knox and that he had barely contacted her since their lunch. 'No. I haven't. You reckon I should ask her then?'

'Mum says the only way to know what anyone else is thinking is to ask them. I used to think she was mad all the time, but when I asked her, she said she wasn't mad, but sometimes she was a bit sad.' He looked up to Jason's face briefly, before going back to examining his shorts. 'She also said sometimes we have to tell people how we're feeling. Otherwise they might not know. Right?'

'Exactly right. People won't know you like them if you don't say so.'

Jason was quiet after that; Knox went back to watching the movie. It was getting late, already well after nine. He wondered if it was too late to ask Cassie out again.

Hey. It's been a while, sorry. I've had some hectic stuff going on. You never said if you wanted to do lunch again. Jason texted Cassie and hoped she would still be interested. Then he realised, her mother's probate wasn't resolved. If she said no that would make his work with her uncomfortable.

You're such an idiot, of course she doesn't want to hang out with you. It's been two weeks and she hasn't talked to you either. Now you're hassling a grieving woman, well done.

He made sure Knox had cleaned his teeth and had a shower before tucking him into the sofa bed. Every day he did this and felt a wave of guilt that Knox didn't have a real bed, or a real bedroom.

I didn't realise it had been so long! I've been busy too. Lunch is hard for me with work at the moment, but maybe a drink after work? Cassie texted back just after eleven.

Jason had already gone to bed and was lying in the dark trying to drift off. He almost didn't check the message. His heart beat a little faster and he decided to leave his reply till the morning.

***

They arranged to meet for drinks on Tuesday, one of the nights Lucas could pick up Knox. The money David had promised had come through, so Jason had given Lucas some money to take Knox to the movies.

'I know you're taking on a lot of looking after him. You just let me know if you need a break or whatever,' Jason said, handing over some cash.

'You know I love this kid, and I love you. It's a temporary situation.' This is as close as Lucas would ever get to saying that he couldn't live like this permanently.

'Yeah, I'm working on it.'

The day at work was dreary; Pierce had taken to barking orders at him and the other staff.

'I think he's mad that I went part-time. I'm sorry, you guys.' Jason had waited until Pierce was back in his office before commenting.

The three other staff were silent. Jason was the buffer between them and the partners; he took the tasks and delegated them, he would give them advice or feedback when they did something that wouldn't be good enough for the partners.

'As long as he doesn't start going around you straight to us,' said Daniel.

Jason nodded and went back to the letter he was typing. He had arranged to meet Cassie at a bar in Federation Square at half-past five, hoping he'd be able to slip out of the office ten minutes early to get to her on time. As the end of the day approached Pierce was still in his office, and Jason realised he wouldn't be able to leave until he did.

I'm stuck doing something at work. Sorry. I might be a bit late. I'll keep you posted. Jason hated making people wait. A clot of guilt crept into his stomach at sat there making him feel slightly sick.

No worries. I'll do some shopping or something. Let me know when you're on the way and come I'll meet you.

Pierce left the office at ten to six. By this stage Jason has started to sweat. He let Cassie know he was on the way and went to splash some water over his face.

'It's alright. She won't mind,' he said to his reflection. He looked tired.

Jason arrived at the bar and found a table. There weren't many people out on a Tuesday night. He was sitting on a covered balcony facing the river, watching joggers running along beside it.

'Hey.' Cassie's voice came from behind him, he turned to face her and smiled.

'Hey.'

She sat down in the chair opposite him.

'Did you get any shopping done?' he asked, noticing she didn't seem to be carrying any bags.

'No, I don't really have any money for frivolous spending. With Mum and everything I haven't worked as much as I would normally.'

Jason looked at her face, she seemed thinner than last time they met, and her face was pale.

'Have you been alright?' He resisted the urge to reach out and grab her hand.

'I've been okay I suppose. As good as can be expected.' She shifted in her seat.

'Righto.' He wanted to know more, to know why she looked sick, but he didn't want to push it.

'Should I get us some drinks? What are you having?' he asked.

'White wine, I think.' She gave a small nod.

'I'll be right back.'

As he turned to go back to the table with the wine, he took a deep breath and decided that he would start the conversation again with a lighter tone.

'Here we are,' he said, placing the glasses down on the table.

Cassie had been staring out over the river, but she turned back as he spoke. 'Thanks.'

'Sorry, again, for being late.'

'It's okay.'

The silence felt awful, Jason's mind scrambled to fill it with something easy.

'My little brother has been staying with me. He's ten,' he said without meaning to.

'That's nice. For the school holidays or?'

'The holidays aren't for a few weeks—' he broke off.

'But?' She was looking into his face intently.

'His parents, well, they're having some problems. He's sleeping on my couch. I feel quite guilty about it actually, but what can I do? He says he won't go home.'

'You're a single parent now?' She smiled, it was good to see her smiling. It lifted some of the darkness from her eyes.

'Yeah I guess.'

'Tell me about him.'

Jason told her about Knox, about Lucas and David and Becca. He hadn't intended to, but he told her everything. He just kept talking. She listened and nodded; she didn't say much.

'I honestly don't know what to do. He can't stay with me forever, but how can I kick him out?'

'Yeah. It's tough.' She looked out over the river again and sighed.

'I've been staying with my aunt,' she said, without looking back.

'Sounds nice.' He let the silence stretch out.

'She… my ex… it's complicated. I don't want to burden you.'

'Hey, I just dumped my whole family history on you, and you listened. You're welcome to do the same but, only if you want to.'

This time he did reach out to touch her hand. She snapped her head back to face him and pulled her hand away. She folded her hands in her lap and went back to looking out over the river.

'I'm sorry. Maybe I should go.'

'You don't have to go. But, uh, you don't have to stay either.' Jason didn't know what to do. He wanted to get to know her, he wanted to know why she was thin and pale and jumpy, but it had to be on her terms. He couldn't force her to confide in him, they barely knew each other.

'The short version is that my ex is stalking me, and I can't stay at my apartment anymore,' she said quietly.

'I'm sorry, that sounds awful.' Jason barely breathed. He didn't want to miss anything else she might say.

'It is. I nearly didn't come out tonight. I don't feel like very good company.' She sipped her drink. 'And I don't really think I can date right now.'

Jason let out a disappointed sound. 'That's totally understandable.' He felt like he'd been punched in the guts. This was the first date he'd been on for a long time, apart from their lunch. He picked up his wine glass and saw that his hand was trembling. He put it back down without drinking. Cassie was still looking at the river.

He looked at his watch, it was nearly seven. In the silence he heard his belly grumble and he remembered how long it had been since he'd eaten lunch.

'I don't know if you'd be interested in ordering some food?' he asked.

'Another time. Thanks for inviting me out.' She collected up her bag and stood up. He stood up too.

'Should we hug?' he asked.

'I don't think so. I'm not... I'll see you around.' She turned and walked away.

Jason sat back down, his glass only had the dregs of his wine left but Cassie had only drunk half of hers.

That's blown it then, she's not going to be interested in seeing me again. Jason drained the last of his glass. He turned to look over his shoulder in case he could still see her, but she was gone.

My Mother's Secret

He bought McDonald's from Elizabeth Street on his way home. It was a seedy place, there were always homeless people camping down outside. It was open twenty-four hours a day, seven days a week. Every day there would be a new drama, he was sure.

He was home by half-past eight, Lucas and Knox were still out. He loosened his tie and sat down heavily on the couch. Something sharp dug into his side, it was a game cover that Knox must have left around when he went to school.

Jason looked around his lounge room, Knox had so little here. He couldn't afford to ask Lucas to move out so that Knox could have his room, he couldn't share his own bedroom, that wouldn't be any better than the couch and it would mean Jason had no space of his own.

It seemed like a basic need, to have a place of your own. He thought about it sometimes, about wanting to have somewhere to escape to. When Dad had left them, he and Tamara had to share a room until he moved out. David paid child support, but his mother still couldn't afford to rent a three-bedroom place.

Back then Jason had been heartbroken; the girl he thought he was going to grow old with had chosen to abort the pregnancy and break off all contact. For two weeks afterwards he couldn't face going to school and his mother had let him mope around the house.

But Tam was there, his ten-year-old sister, who shared his bedroom. He lay in bed at night listening to her breathing and only when he was sure no-one would hear him, he cried. The trembling sobs were silent except for his erratic breathing but even so he was terrified someone would hear him.

Jason brought his mind back to the present. His cheeks were wet. He felt sorry for his brother caught between warring parents, and for himself; an instant single parent. After being shut down by Cassie he felt alone.

But why had she walked out? Surely it wasn't her mother, that was weeks ago, she would be starting to come out of that now. Her eyes were ringed in purple, as though she wasn't sleeping, and her fingers fluttered around the table; she couldn't settle.

Just as he was descending into self-pity, Knox and Lucas came home, both beaming. He rubbed his hands over his face and smiled back at them.

'What did you see? Was it good?' he asked.

'We saw the Star Wars one. It was so great, honest, you should have been there!' Knox bounced over to him and sat next to him on the couch. Lucas smiled, and said nothing.

Knox was so excited that he told Jason the entire plot of the film, as well as everything they'd had for dinner and everything that had happened that day at school in one long stream.

'Sounds like you've had a pretty awesome day all round then.'

'Yeah, it was the best.' Knox swung his legs, his small feet kicking the couch.

'Do you have homework?'

'Not really.'

'That doesn't sound like the truth to me.' Jason looked at the side of Knox's head, who seemed to be avoiding his gaze.

'I have a little bit of maths homework.'

Jason looked at his watch. 'Maybe we'll do it in the morning, it's pretty late. Time for teeth and bed.'

Knox looked at him and grinned, before jumping off the couch and sprinting into the bathroom. Jason remained on the couch, listening to the brushing and water sounds coming from the open bathroom door.

'Help me make up your bed, mate,' he said as Knox returned smelling of mint.

Together they moved the coffee table and pulled off the extra cushions to convert the couch into a bed. They left the sheets on the bed each day, but the blankets and pillows were pulled off and shoved into a corner.

Knox climbed into the bed and lay flat on his back, starring at the ceiling and grinning.

'Good night, mate.'

'Goodnight,' Knox replied. Jason turned off the light in the loungeroom and went into his bedroom.

***

Jason found things always seemed better in the morning. He rolled over to turn off his alarm and checked for any word from Cassie. There was nothing.

Thanks for having a drink with me last night, I hope we can still catch up sometimes. I understand you can't date right now, thank you for letting me know, he texted her.

He'd lain awake in bed for what felt like hours coming up with the right words to send to her.

As he got Knox ready for school, and headed off to work, he was more aware of the presence of his phone than ever before. He arrived at work and there was still no reply.

He compulsively checked if she'd said anything back, but she stayed silent until nearly five. He'd been in a meeting with Pierce and one of clients for an hour and didn't realise she'd sent anything until he'd packed up to go home at quarter to six. The other staff had gone home for the night and locked the front door of the office suite.

'Now you say hello to that wife and lovely daughter of yours, won't you?' Pierce said as he slapped his friend on the shoulder.

'Of course!'

It seemed inappropriate for Pierce to refer to his friend's daughter as lovely.

I've gotta get a new job. When he locked the door behind him, Pierce was already at the lifts. Jason would have held the lift for him in his place, but Pierce let the doors close on his employee.

I've got some stuff going on right now. Not just Mum. I'll let you know when I'm ready to catch up, Cassie sent.

Jason read the words over and over. It seemed like she was telling him to leave it. He stared at the illuminated face of the phone until it turned itself off, then realised he was still standing in the corridor.

He used his phone to sign up to a bunch of job websites as he walked to the tram; putting in the titles, salary range and other details for the job he wanted to have. He was confident he could get something in the city, but he would also consider a firm that was closer to home.

He thought about the possibility of walking to work or being closer to where Knox's school was. He missed his stop while reading through the job ads and had to walk back from the stop after.

'I've decided to get a new job,' he said as he walked in. Knox was sitting at the kitchen table.

'You've said that before,' Lucas said.

'I mean it, though. I'm sick of it.'

Lucas nodded, but didn't say anything.

'I know, I know, I say this every few months, but I actually worried they might refuse my request to change my hours to pick up Knox. It would be cool if I could get a job with a firm over the side of town where the school is, that way I wouldn't have to drop him off so early.'

Lucas frowned slightly and took a sip of the beer he was holding.

'What?' Jason asked.

'Nothing.'

'What?'

Lucas sighed. 'He's not your kid, remember? Don't go getting another job closer to his school when Knox will be out of here in a few weeks.'

'Keep your voice down,' Jason said. Knox didn't seem to have heard them; he didn't look up from the page of sums that he was working on. Jason turned up the volume on the music Lucas had put on through the TV and beckoned him out onto the balcony.

'Sorry, man,' Lucas said, as Jason slid the door shut behind them.

'I know it's supposed to be temporary, of course I do, but I know my dad and he doesn't want kids around. He likes to tell the other money men he has them, but he doesn't want to spend time with us. I don't really know what Becca's like, but she hasn't even been to visit.'

Lucas took a sip and looked at Jason.

'I guess I'm just trying to be realistic. It could take them months to sort their shit out, and if they separate and divorce it will take forever. I like having Knox around, and I want him to feel like he belongs here.'

'It's important for a kid to feel wanted,' Lucas said slowly. 'I know you didn't always feel wanted. It's good you don't want the same shit to happen to your brother.'

'But?' Jason asked.

'But nothing. It's a good thing you're doing here.'

They turned to look out over the rooftops and Jason remembered why he'd always liked Lucas.

Chapter 15

Cassie moved away from the bar conscious not to run. When he asked her how she had been lately, and she told him about living with Tessa, her urge to leave had been overwhelming.

She stood on the platform at Flinders Street Station, waiting for the train. Tessa and Ian lived in Fairfield.

Tessa's words repeated in her head. Cassie was afraid if she went to the police, Tony would lash out at her again. What if the restraining order didn't stop him? He might find out where she was staying and harass her.

On the train ride her mind was focussed on the reasons she deserved to have Tony making her life miserable.

'How did your date go?' Tessa asked when she walked in.

'It wasn't a date,' Cassie replied.

'I thought you said that it was. Never mind.'

Cassie had said it was a date, she'd even allowed herself to feel excited about it. She'd come home from a short lunch shift at work and dolled herself up. Tessa had seen her preening.

The two women sat together on the couch.

'I made some pasta. If you haven't eaten, you're welcome to it,' Tessa said.

'Thanks.' Cassie's body felt heavy and although she was hungry, she didn't want to eat.

'I'll put some in the microwave for you.' Tessa patted her knee. She made little humming noises as she padded softly around the kitchen in her bare feet. Cassie closed her eyes and laid her head on the back of the couch, there was a slight twinge on the left-hand side where the cut was still healing.

'I got really freaked out and told him that I couldn't date anyone right now.'

There was a small pause. 'What did he say to that?'

'He seemed a bit shocked. He touched my hand and I pulled away like a weirdo and then I couldn't have dinner like everything was normal.'

The microwave pinged and Tessa came over with the bowl of carbonara.

'I'm very proud of you for going. It will be hard to get to know someone given, well,' she handed the bowl to Cassie. 'Try not to be so hard on yourself.'

'Thanks.'

Tessa switched the TV on, and they watched a reality cooking show.

'Tony's not going to stop, is he?' Cassie said when the episode finished.

'No honey. He's not a nice man. You should protect yourself.'

'What if he comes after me again?'

'One of us is home most evenings. You won't be alone. And if he comes near you again, we'll call the police.'

Cassie started to cry. 'I wish Mum was here.'

'I know. I miss her too.'

She rested her head on Tessa's shoulder while she stroked her hair.

'I have to get to bed. You can stay up out here if you like, but I think you should go to sleep too, it's late,' Tessa said.

***

In the morning she woke up to the sound of her text message alert. She realised she'd fallen asleep almost immediately after lying down. The message was from Jason.

Hey, hope you got home alright. I'd love to hang out again sometime.

It brought all of her self-doubt and self-criticism flooding back into her brain. She couldn't face replying to him now.

She woke up again to the sound of her alarm. She set an alarm for nine thirty so she'd make it to work on time, but both Tessa and Ian had left by then. In the empty house, she wished she could go home. She'd been so frightened to come home and find that Tony had broken in she hadn't even gone back for basic items from the apartment. She had the clothes she was wearing and her handbag. Tessa had organised for a locksmith to repair the damage to the front door.

'At least this way you won't come home and find someone else has stolen your things. I know you don't feel like you want them now, but in a few days, you might change your mind.'

Cassie had been too angry to say thank you. Now she stood in her aunt's kitchen, drinking her aunt's coffee from her aunt's cups.

'I'm going to the cops today after work,' she said aloud to herself. *Maybe I'll even look for a new job, since I've been pushed out of my old one.*

Simone had rostered herself on in the afternoon and Rachel was in charge, she was quite competent, which made it harder for Cassie to hate her.

Simone walked into the restaurant just before Cassie's shift was supposed to finish after the lunch rush.

'Hi,' Simone said.

'Hi,' Cassie replied. She was counting money to take to the bank and didn't look up. Once she'd finished

Cassie went into the office out the back to talk to Simone.

'Hey, can I talk to you?' she asked.

'It's not really a good time. Can it wait?' Simone's cheeks were pink, and she looked sweaty.

'Is there anything wrong?'

'Nothing's wrong. Why would anything be wrong?' Simone was talking very quickly.

'No reason. You seem upset, that's all.'

Simone moved some papers around on the tiny desk in the cupboard that was the office.

'I need to ask you to be a reference for me.' Cassie hesitated. 'I need to get another job.'

Simone opened her mouth to reply but Cassie held up her hand.

'I get that it's awkward for you, Rachel is a good manager. You don't want to fire me, but you clearly don't want to work with me. So, help me get another job.'

Simone looked at the desk. 'Of course, I'll be a referee for you. I'm sure Emma will too, if you ask her.'

'Thanks.' Cassie gripped the tea towel she held and walked out. She was angry. It was one thing to suspect that your boss was trying to force you out, but Simone hadn't even tried to deny it. Cassie clenched her teeth and started to sweep the floor.

There were still one or two customers hanging around from lunch, one had his laptop open on the table and, from the look on his face and the suit he was wearing, was doing something very important. The other was a middle-aged woman with a Jodi Piccoult book, her back resting against the window and the early afternoon sun picked up the silver in her hair.

It was too far to walk from the restaurant to Tessa's place. It would have taken more than an hour, so Cassie got onto the tram packed with excited school children.

'Do you mind if I sit there?' she said to a teenaged boy who was sitting in the priority seat.

He looked at her and leapt out of the seat without saying a word. Once she was sitting down, her thoughts went back to Jason's text. She liked him, but it didn't seem fair to do anything until she had her shit together. *If he's moved on by then, well, maybe it wasn't meant to be.*

Back at Tessa's place, she logged onto the computer and started looking for jobs. It seemed like there were plenty of hospitality jobs going, wait staff, bar staff, supervisors and managers. Cassie clicked on the ads to read them over and each one she read sounded exactly like the job she already had. If Simone stopped acting like an idiot and gave her her old job back, she wouldn't have to wade through these.

Tessa arrived home from work after five. 'Hey, you applying for jobs?'

'Yeah. Work don't want me there anymore. I asked Simone to be a referee today.'

'Well done. That would have been hard.'

'Yeah.' Cassie sighed and closed down the job ads.

'And how did it go with the police?'

'I was so angry with Simone I didn't go. There are so many things I have to get sorted.' Cassie sighed.

'I know, one step at a time. But don't leave it too long to deal with Tony.'

Tessa went to the kitchen to work on dinner and Cassie remembered she still hadn't replied to Jason's message. She really liked him, and he was sweet and totally hot, but she'd jumped when he touched her hand.

Got home alright. Sorry about that, I'll let you know when I'm free. She hoped the message would buy her some time to sort herself out.

Ian arrived home a little while later, and Cassie watched as he and Tessa greeted one another with a kiss. She envied the way they were so comfortable with each other. Cassie felt a deep longing for what her aunt had.

Dinner was burritos. Tessa was trying new recipes and Ian, who was an accomplished cook, encouraged her.

'How was work then?' Ian asked.

'Cassie's looking for a new job,' her aunt replied.

'Is that right? I thought you liked it there,' he said.

'I do like it there, but Simone has a problem with me.' Cassie broke off. 'It's probably because of Tony. I think he's popped in a couple of times looking for me.'

'That's a possibility. Sounds like they're dicking you around in any case.' Ian punctuated his comment with a firm nod of the head.

Cassie chewed her mouthful. 'Maybe I'll do something else, get out of hospitality, but I don't know what I would do.'

'What are you passionate about?' Ian asked.

'When she was a little girl, all she wanted to do was help people. You were going to be a social worker, I remember. What happened to that?' Tessa said. She knew the story, perhaps she was asking on Ian's behalf.

'I did two of three years of the degree. The first placement I ever did I had a really bad time, I was left alone with this group of kids and I couldn't keep them on track. I kind of gave up,' Cassie said.

'You didn't finish the degree?' Ian asked.

'No. I dropped out and started working full time at a café. That business folded a couple of years later and I got my job at the Fat Chef.' She shrugged.

'If you went back to school would they give you credit for the subjects you've already done?' he asked.

'I'm sure they would. You would have to decide if that's what you want to do though. It will be very different but it's what you always wanted to do.' Her aunt's brown eyes looked sad.

Cassie sat quietly and Tessa and Ian soon moved on to other topics

***

Over the next few days, Cassie looked at jobs in hospitality and became increasingly discouraged. On a whim she started looking for social work jobs; there were hundreds. She'd prefer to work with young people, maybe helping them get on track with school, or maybe refugees, there were plenty of people in the world who needed help.

The pay wasn't great, but she could make it work. If she gave up her one-bedroom apartment and got a flatmate it might even be fun. The longing inside her sprang up again, she wished the person she came home to was more than a flatmate.

One thing at a time. She'd started her degree at La Trobe, a university in the north of Melbourne but had never finished. She wasn't sure if she could handle going back to study; living out of home, struggling to earn money to cover rent and bills and have enough time for assignments and readings. She hadn't been eligible for welfare payments back then and she couldn't ask her mother for money.

'I don't know how I'd support myself if I went back to study,' she said to Tessa on Saturday afternoon. She hadn't got a weekend shift; the weekend penalty pay would have been a nice bonus with so few shifts.

'Well, I would have thought you'd get Centrelink this time, but even if you didn't, maybe I could help you out. I mean, I've been working a long time and I never had my own kids.'

'I couldn't take your money.'

'It could be *The Tessa Beechworth Scholarship fund*.' She laughed, and Cassie smiled.

'I called La Trobe and they said that they would be able to count my prior learning. I'd need to do my placements over again, but I could graduate and be a social worker in about a year.' Cassie's felt silly even hoping for the future like that.

'Look at you! Your mother would be so proud.'

Cassie's smile faltered.

'I'm sorry, hun. Did you end up sorting out that woman, Kerry was it?'

'Yeah, I sent the stuff over to her a while ago.'

It had been several weeks since Cassie had thought about her mother's secret lover. She remembered the words her father had said as he left.

'I don't know who you are anymore, Eleanor. How could you keep this secret from me all this time? How many more lies are there?'

'Everything I've ever told you is true,' Eleanor had replied, her voice flat and quiet.

'In that case, what other fucking secrets are you keeping from me? I can't deal with this. I could live with cold and distant but this, this is something else.'

'I never lied to you.'

'But you didn't tell me the whole truth either. You have your faults, but I thought we were a team.'

And then he'd walked out the door. Cassie had always blamed him for the breakup; she thought he was being unreasonable. He was a passionate, hot-tempered man; so much the opposite of her mother.

Cassie and her father had never been close and when he left, she stayed with her mother. She let him drift away. He'd kept contacting her for a few years, but she wasn't interested and eventually he stopped.

He came to the funeral, but Cassie had wondered why he would want to go to his ex-wife's funeral. Now Cassie knew her mother's secret, she could see why her father would have been so upset. Never telling your husband about something so important would have hurt him. Cassie still struggled to forgive her mother for keeping it secret. On an intellectual level, she knew Eleanor had her reasons, perhaps she wanted to forget about it.

Cassie called her father. 'Hi Dad.'

'Cassie? Goodness, this is a surprise. How are you?'

'I'm alright, I guess.'

'That's good to hear.'

There was a silence, the last call she'd made to her father was to tell him Eleanor had died.

'Was there something you wanted to talk about?' he asked, his voice was calm.

'I don't know.'

'Well, that's alright. It's very nice to hear from you anyway.'

Cassie took a deep breath before she went on. 'I want to ask you about mum.'

'What did you want to know?'

'I found some stuff in her house, when I was cleaning it out, and—' she trailed off.

'You wanted to ask me about it.'

'Yes.'

'I would love to chat with you about your mother, and to hear how you're going. But it might be better to do it in person. Do you think that would be alright?'

'I guess so.'

'I have to rush off to meet with a client now. Let's have dinner tomorrow night?'

'Yeah, okay.'

Cassie had never been to her father's new house. After he'd left the family the few times she'd seen him had always in a coffee shop or restaurant. Had she been too hard on him? He might not be the arrogant, impulsive man she'd decided he was when he left.

'It's good you're reconnecting with your father,' Tessa said. 'He's a good man, and I think he took the marriage breakdown quite hard. He said neither of you would speak to him, so I've kept him up to date with how you were doing.'

She was surprised to hear Tessa had been in touch with Ben. She had thought they hadn't got on, but perhaps she was more forgiving than Cassie.

***

Dad had bought himself a two-bedroom apartment in the city. He worked in business development for a consulting company, which had always seemed to Cassie to be a job that didn't really exist selling something she didn't understand. He did well for himself, although he'd never remarried.

'Cassie! My darling!' he said as he opened the door. Ben seemed to have aged since she last saw him, his hair was mostly grey now, short as always, and his belly stuck out over the top of his pants.

'Hi Dad.'

He leaned in to hug her with his hands out wide, Cassie accepted the hug, despite the feeling she no longer knew the man giving it. She pulled away quickly and moved past him into the apartment.

'I've got cheese and biscuits and wine to start, and then I thought we could order some gourmet pizza.'

'That sounds nice.' Cassie was hovering in the middle of the room.

Ben indicated the coffee table, where the cheese platter sat next to red wine already opened to breathe. She sat on the ottoman beside the table. She wasn't ready to sit next to him on the couch.

'Help yourself. I've got a bitey cheddar, a lovely soft blue, and some of the orange Leicester. That one is quince paste; I love it with cheese, especially the blue.' He pointed to each on the platter before pouring them each a glass of wine, using both hands to hold the bottle, that only shook a little.

'How have you been?' he asked.

'I don't really want to do small talk today... Dad.' In her mind she'd been calling him Ben since he left. 'I was hoping you could tell me about why you and Mum broke up. She, well, she never really said anything about it, and uh, I'd like to hear your side.'

Ben took a sip of wine and loaded up a biscuit before he looked at her. He popped the morsel into his mouth.

'I thought maybe you hated me for leaving. I know that it was very hard on Eleanor.'

Cassie waited for him to go on. She held her glass in her hand, but she had not had any of the cheese or the wine. Her stomach gurgled and churned; she thought she might be sick but pushed the thought away.

'You found the letters then, if you went through her things.' Ben looked across the table at his daughter, she nodded.

'You know about Kerry and the damage that did.' His eyes were dull, he looked far away.

'We met when your mother was twenty-one, I was thirty, so not quite so young. We worked in the same company. I don't know if maybe we'd met later, we might not have stayed together so long.' He sighed and reached for another piece of the cheddar.

'Your mother was a cold woman. She was distant and silent, and I thought that was just how she was. I could

241

never be sure if she was angry or just quiet. Sometimes I wouldn't know for days or even weeks if I'd done something to upset her. It was very difficult.'

Cassie wanted to reach out to him. She knew what her mother was like, she was sparse in her words and her praise.

'One day I was trying to be helpful around the house, I was putting the laundry away and I saw that your mother had a bunch of letters in with her stockings and pantihose. They looked like old letters, bound with ribbon.'

Cassie knew them well; she had known they were love letters the moment she saw them.

'I don't know why I did it, I shouldn't have read them. But you were all out. No one would have known, so I opened one. Once I had started, I had to read them all. I put together h bits and pieces from Kerry's letters and I couldn't believe this was the same woman I had married.'

'I know what you mean,' Cassie said.

'I was still reading the letters when your mother came home. Her face was pale and full of cold fury. She snatched the letters away from me and hid them somewhere else. She barely spoke to me for almost a month.

'I tried to find them a couple of times, but I never could. I tried to talk to her, to ask her why she'd never told me. I mean it was only a year or so before we'd met, surely something that big, you would have told your husband.'

'She never even hinted?'

'Not so much as a whisper. I didn't like to pry, given how she was, but I'd always thought I was her first.'

Cassie shifted forward on the ottoman and cut a portion of cheese her hunger had returned with a burgeoning affection for her father. *It must have been hard to be married to someone so closed.*

'After she started talking to me again, at least as much as she ever did, I tried to ask her about the letters. Bit by bit she told what had happened. I expected her to be sad or something, but she was stony and cold like she always was. It was like she was telling she'd made a cake. She was still heartbroken after all that time.' Ben drained the last of his wine and refilled it. His hazel eyes were wet.

'I knew then your mother had never loved me. Our whole lives, everything we'd built, had been built on a lie. Not to be too personal, but we never had a particularly active sex life. I accepted that. I was never with anyone else, I just kept myself going, so to speak.

'But once I knew about Kerry, I couldn't tell if she was even attracted to me. If she married me because I was the least objectionable male suitor. I started to wonder if her classes were really classes, or if she'd been keeping a lover on the side.' He looked down. 'I didn't trust her anymore.'

Cassie had never thought about how much it must have hurt her father to have to leave a marriage after over twenty years. She had only thought about what it was like for Eleanor, suddenly without her husband, having to be a single mother to two troubled daughters. Ben had made some effort to be part of their lives, but Cassie had pushed him away, and Penny always followed what her sister did.

'I'm sorry, Dad' she said quietly.

'I'm sorry too. I should have told you, but I, I felt very guilty. And I still loved Eleanor very much. Seeing you girls reminded me what I'd lost. Something I probably never had in the first place.'

Ben's hands hung limply over his knees. He'd finished the second glass of wine and was staring down at the carpet. He looked exhausted. Cassie stood up and moved to the couch and patted his shoulder awkwardly. He seemed so small as he turned his face towards her. The irrational, selfish man she had built up in her mind was not the man in front of her.

He wiped his face with his sleeve and stood up. He walked out of the loungeroom and into the bathroom.

She thought about all the short flings he'd had since he left Eleanor. When her aunt or her mother had told her about them, she'd hated him. She assumed that he was using these women and throwing them away. But seeing the hurt in his eyes when he spoke of her mother, she wondered if he was afraid to open himself up to the hurt he'd felt with her.

Cassie wasn't sure if she could handle this version of her father. Through her childhood he had been largely absent, always working.

'Do you want me to get the pizza menu?' he said, when he eventually came out of the bathroom.

'I don't think I'm ready to eat just yet.' Cassie couldn't bring her mind away from her father's sadness. 'Did you try to make it work?'

He lifted his head, his eyes were red. 'I tried a few things. After I left, I tried to stay in touch, to see if there were any feelings on her side. She never once said she missed me. I hoped for a while she would say sorry, tell me she loved me and ask me to come back, but she never did.' He rubbed his palm across his cheek, the stubble of his beard under his fingers crackled like static. 'I think it was a relief to her when I left.'

'I waited nearly two years for her to come around. I sent her messages and letters. She didn't love me. She tolerated me.'

'I always hoped she would tell us she loved us,' Cassie said. 'I know she cared, she would check in and make me dinners, but I think she probably said she loved me twice in my whole life.'

Ben looked at her. 'I'm sorry. I never realised how cold she was until I read those letters.'

'How did you meet?' Cassie asked, she had heard the story before, but today she felt as though it might be different in the retelling.

'She was young; she'd just finished uni. I remember I wasn't invited to her birthday party because I didn't know her very well.'

Cassie refilled his glass as he talked, as well as her own, and sipped it.

'I worked in the office where she got her first job. I wanted to go out for a beer after work one night, I was celebrating because my boss had given me a huge bonus for sealing a deal.'

Ben looked at the cheese, his hand moved towards it, but he changed his mind.

'She was so pretty, and sort of quiet in an intriguing way. I said she should join us, my shout.'

Cassie thought of the photos of her mother when she was young she'd had a slim build with wild dark curly hair, Penny had inherited that hair, although she dyed it blonde.

'We all went to a little bar, down under street level. It was a sports bar, I think. I bought the drinks. In the end it was just me and her. I didn't think I should leave a lady to find her way home alone. I took a cab to her parents' place and dropped her off. I snogged her in the back of the taxi.'

Ben reached out for his wine and swallowed a third of it. 'And that was it, basically, we dated for years. When she, uh, got pregnant, I proposed and that was that.'

'Did she ever tell you she loved you?' Cassie asked.

'A few times. When she said yes, she said she loved me. When you were born, and when Penny was born. Those moments where maybe she felt like she had to say it.'

It seemed sad to Cassie her father, a man who had always loved her mother, had only heard it from her a handful of times.

'Did you ever ask if she loved you?'

'Sometimes when we'd fight, or if I needed comfort, I'd say, "do you love me, darling?" and she would say "what do you think?" It's not quite the same, but when it's all you get from someone, you tell yourself a story it's enough.' Ben stood up and paced over to his fridge. He opened the door and stood looking into it for a long time before he spoke.

'More wine?'

'I'm okay I think,' Cassie replied. He walked back to the couch, the flush in his cheeks fading.

'Should we get that pizza then?' she asked. He glanced at her and smiled.

They ordered a pizza each even though they knew it would be too much to eat. They talked about unimportant things. Cassie's belly was full, they'd finished the first bottle of wine and were halfway through the second.

'You really had no idea? She never said anything to you about Kerry? Tessa never said? Her parents?'

'I knew Eleanor's relationship with her parents was tough. They were not really warm people, and I thought that was probably why she was so reserved. Perhaps they had never really forgiven each other. When we told them we were getting married they were more relieved than anything else.' He stared at his half-eaten pizza and poked an olive around his plate before popping it into his mouth.

'Perhaps there were signs, things I never really understood but now I know I guess you could say it was obvious. I don't think she ever had an affair, that wasn't in her nature. I wish I'd realised sooner.'

'Would you have married her if she told you when you proposed?' Cassie asked, a sudden fear came through her chest that if her mother had been honest, she wouldn't exist at all.

'I don't know. I loved your mother. I suppose I still do. I think I would have been upset, I would have needed time to process that she would never love me the way she loved Kerry, but perhaps we could have been happy anyway.'

Cassie looked at the time, it was nearly midnight. 'I should go home.'

'Did you drive over? You'll be over the limit if you drive back now. Let me get you a taxi.'

Cassie smiled, her father, the man she had thought was weak and thoughtless. He was doing his best.

'I love you, Dad,' she said. It might have been all the wine, but perhaps for the first time she felt love for this man. All her life she had an idea of father; she had loved him because it's what you're supposed to do. She felt as though now she was starting to know him as a human being it felt more real than it had.

'I love you too, my gorgeous baby all grown up. I'm so proud of you. Thank you for coming to see me. I missed you.' He gripped her hand.

'It's okay.' She took the serviette and gently dabbed away his tears. They had barely seen each other since he left Eleanor and, in that time, he'd become an old man.

'You're not allowed to die alright?' she said.

'I promise I won't die.' He smiled.

***

She crept into Tessa's house when the taxi dropped her off, the lights were all out. The couch was made up for her. Cassie slipped into the covers, the tight sheets and blankets made her feel safe; cocooned in the care of her mother's sister.

It must have been nearly an hour before she finally drifted off. Her mind was filled with who her parents were. Her mother, who she had thought had suffered with an arrogant and jealous husband, was really a cold and distant woman who had starved them all of love. And her father, a man who felt his emotions deeply, who loved his wife, flaws and all, and never stopped loving her.

* * *

In the morning, Tessa and Ian woke her as they shuffled around in the kitchen.

'I'm sorry love, we didn't mean to wake you,' Ian said, toast in hand.

'It's alright.' Cassie sat up, squinting her eyes in the daylight.

'Do you want a bit? It's lovely sourdough from down the road.' He waved the toast in her direction.

'If you don't mind,' she said. Lining her stomach with something should help with the sick knot she felt there.

'I'm going to go back to my apartment tonight,' Cassie announced as she scraped vegemite onto her second piece of toast.

'Okay then. You know you're always welcome back here if you get frightened in the middle of the night or you fancy some company.' Tessa's mouth was tight.

'Thank you. But I can't live my life in fear, can I? I have to tell Tony it's over and he can't terrorise me anymore. If that doesn't work, I'll get an intervention order. I just don't think it's fair to do it without giving him a chance.'

I have to believe he has the ability to be better. What happened between us isn't entirely his fault and I loved him once.

Tessa and Ian exchanged glances. 'Whatever you think is best, you know we'll support you,' Tessa said. They didn't agree with her, but she was glad they didn't say so out loud.

Back at her own apartment Cassie wrinkled her nose as the rotten smell hit her. The bananas were black and mouldy and the not quite empty milk bottle in the recycling bin had gone sour.

She threw them out and started on the mess in the bedroom. She'd just walked out and left it when it had happened. She'd borrowed a few items from her aunt and bought some new underwear.

When she entered the bedroom, she wanted to turn around and go back to Tessa's. All her clothes were destroyed. The green satin dress she'd worn to her high school formal and sometimes pulled out for weddings and other fancy parties was in pieces. The black pants and jacket she'd worn to her mother's funeral were destroyed. The jeans she'd worn for years and repaired more times than she could remember because they were exactly the right size and shape were gone.

She took a breath and grabbed a black plastic bin bag from the kitchen. There was still a smell in the house, but she hoped that it would pass once she aired it out. She opened the bedroom window as well as the lounge and kitchen windows. She considered propping the front door open too but decided against it.

She cleared the floor first, there wasn't much there, she suspected it was only what had slid off the bed. Each time she grabbed a handful of fabric and shoved it into the bag the smell was stronger. The last few handfuls of fabric were left in the middle of the bed and as she grabbed them, she realised that the fabric was stiff. She moved the fabric closer to her face and saw that there were white crusted marks on some of them. A lump of bile rose in her throat as she realised that Tony had cut up her clothes and then fucked her bed as though it were her.

She shuddered; he had been turned on by the idea of destroying her possessions. The bedclothes were also stained with white. When she had collected all the fragments of fabric, she stripped the sheets and put them into another rubbish bag, and then the doona followed. The smell wasn't just cum, he'd probably pissed on it too.

Surely there can't be any more surprises left. She took the bag and doona down to the bins at the back of the apartment block.

I'm going to have to buy a new doona and sheet set as well as new clothes, she texted her aunt.

Oh no, what did he do?

Cassie told her the short version of what she'd found.

Disgusting. You need to get that restraining order, he's not going to leave you alone.

Cassie didn't want to admit Tessa was right. She decided to clean her entire apartment; Tony had soiled it with his presence and what he did. She needed to remove any trace of him; emptying the fridge, scrubbing the bathroom and toilet, vacuuming the floors, wiping down the benches and cupboards. About halfway through she had decided it was much too quiet and had put on one of her mother's CDs to keep her company. Once she was done and she couldn't think of anything else that needed washing or wiping she stood in the middle of her living area, sweaty and exhausted, but feeling more in control.

She showered, dried off with a fresh towel and sat on the couch looking at her phone.

'Hello? Cassie?' Tony answered after letting the phone ring for so long Cassie was sure she would get the voicemail service.

'Yeah…'

'How are you?'

'You need to stop trying to contact me. I don't want to see you, I don't want to talk to you, I don't want you to show up at my work or my house. I know you broke in and cut up all my stuff. It's not going to make me want to get back together with you.'

'I just wanted to see you. You know how much I miss you, how much you mean to me. I only do those things because you make me crazy.'

'No, you do those things because you're an arsehole. I don't want you in my life. Leave. Me. Alone.'

'You sound angry babe; I don't know what you're angry about. I'm the one left out here in the cold. What did you expect to happen?'

Cassie closed her eyes and counted to five before she answered. 'You need to stop trying to contact me. I'm never going to take you back. If you don't leave me alone, I'm going to the police.'

He laughed, a cold sound down the phone line that sent a chill through Cassie.

'You're going to the police? And exactly what are they gonna do? You filthy slut, you belong to me, don't you understand that? The police are gonna laugh at you for being the pathetic cock-teasing whore you are and then you'll come back to me. No one else wants you Cassie.'

Cassie felt the heat rising in her cheeks. He'd done it before, but somehow it felt like it was the first time. She saw his words for what they were; empty and manipulative. She wasn't having it; she'd seen what he was really like. She wouldn't make excuses for his behaviour anymore.

'That might well be true, but I don't want you Tony. I don't want you in my life, and if you don't stop stalking me, I'll set the cops on you. I'm changing my phone number. Just move on.'

She hung up on him before he could say anything back. She hoped it would be enough to threaten him with the police. She didn't want to have to subject him to that.

He was clearly not coping with the breakup and she wanted to give him time to heal without bringing the authorities into their relationship. It certainly wasn't winning him any favours.

She had expected to be shaken by the phone call, but instead she was calm and determined; she knew what her options were.

She flicked on the TV and pulled out her laptop and spent the rest of the evening scrolling through job ads and watching trashy reality shows. None of the jobs were what she wanted and her decision to go back and finish her degree looked like her best option. She wanted to feel like her life had meaning. Cassie fell asleep on the couch with the TV on.

Chapter 16

Jason was on the phone to his father again.

'It's not fair to have him sleeping on my couch, Dad. He's been here for a long time already, more than a month, and I know I said take your time, but I need to know you're trying to fix this.' Jason was pacing on the balcony, Knox and Lucas were playing a car chase game inside.

'I don't know what the problem is, I'm paying for him. Can't you just look after him?'

'I am looking after him. He needs his parents. He needs his parents to love him and care about him and want to fucking see him. How do you think it feels to not even be missed?'

'If you're going to take that tone with me, I'm hanging up.'

Jason sighed. 'Are you sorting things out with Becca at least?'

'That's my affair, I'm doing what I can, and it will take as long as it takes.' His father's voice was businesslike. It sounded like a lie. Jason clenched his jaw, his father was doing what was best for himself and covering up any signs of weakness. If this was fatherhood, he wanted no part of it.

'Just remember that this isn't a permanent solution. You need to sort your shit out so Knox can go home.'

'I have to go.'

Jason knew there would be nothing more to be done. 'Bye.'

***

Hey. I'm sorry I've been such a mess lately. I have had a lot of stuff going on. I hope things are going well with you. Maybe we can catch up again soon. Cassie's message had come through while he was talking. It had been over two weeks since she had run off from their meeting in the city.

After the conversation with Dad, it was a nice surprise to hear from her again. His mouth was dry, as though he had suddenly forgotten how to speak at the thought maybe she was into him.

He wasn't sure what to say to her, so decided he'd leave it for a while. Lucas looked up at him when Jason walked back into the loungeroom, his smile fading as he took in his face. Jason tipped his head towards the kitchen.

'I'm gonna have a little break mate, you keep it going for me, will you?' Lucas said to Knox, extracting himself from the couch where they had been playing.

'Dad's being weird,' Jason said, in a low voice.

'Isn't he always weird?' Lucas and Jason had been best mates since high school.

'Yeah, but I feel like this is more than just that. It feels more like he's hiding something.'

'Like what?'

'I dunno. It's been too long for him and Becca to be just having some sort of tiff. Maybe they don't really want Knox back. Maybe they're happier now. Dad hasn't even seen him in all the time he's been here, Becca called a few times at the start, but she's only popped by twice. One of those was just to drop off some stuff that came from her parents.'

'I didn't even think about grandparents, I mean, does Knox see them?' Lucas asked.

Jason's grandparents were all dead, David was much older than Becca and had been the youngest in his family. Becca's parents were still around.

'I don't know them. People shouldn't have kids they don't want. Dad's got three. He only sees me coz I'm free babysitting for Knox.' Jason looked down and realised that he was gripping the benchtop. He ran his hands through his hair and it immediately fell back where it had been over his eyes.

'I guess they're going through their own stuff, y'know, David and Becca.'

'It's nice of you to give them the benefit of the doubt, but he's not my son. I can barely look after myself let alone a kid. And what do I do with him if he messes up? I'm supposed to be the fun older brother, the one who gets him into adventures we don't tell his parents about, not the one who makes sure he does his homework and eats his vegies.'

'You're doing a great job. You know that, right?' Lucas gripped Jason's shoulder.

'You think so?'

'Yeah. Nothing to worry about. I gotta get going though.'

Jason watched as Lucas swept his hair into a messy bun and checked his teeth in the bathroom mirror.

'Catch you later, mate,' he said over his shoulder on the way out.

Jason sat down on the white couch next to Knox. The apartment was small enough with just Lucas and Jason, but with Knox sleeping on the couch it was cramped.

'I reckon that's enough games now, buddy. You don't want your eyes to go square.'

'Mum and Dad never tell me to get off the games.'

'Well, they're not here and I think that's long enough. Have you read your book for school?'

Knox drove his car into a barrier and the game was over. He folded his arms across his small chest. 'I wanna go home,' he said.

Jason tried to put a hand on his shoulder to comfort him, but he pulled away.

'I know it's not the same as home. You've got all your stuff and you've got a massive backyard and a pool and you can run around and do whatever you want. It's hard not having a room here.'

Knox stared straight ahead, his bottom lip sticking out in a pout.

'Did Dad say when I can come home?'

'Uh, well.' Jason was unsure how much to tell him. Knox knew David and Becca were having problems.

'He didn't say. I think he and your mum need some more time to talk about things. It's hard to talk about grown up things when they're worried about you as well. This way they know I'm looking after you and they can focus on being nice to each other.'

Knox turned his head and look at his brother. The pout had been replaced with raised eyebrows.

'As if. They don't want me to come home. They hate having me there. Dad doesn't even barely see me and Mum's always on the phone.'

'I'm sure it feels like that but it's not true, mate. They love you and they want you to come home.'

They sat in silence for a while, Knox kicked his heels against the edge of the couch. Jason stared past his brother's head through the glass balcony doors and over the dark rooftops.

'Can I have a can of Coke?' Knox asked.

'No, it's nearly bedtime. You can have water or milk.'

'You're the worst. At my house I have cans of coke in the fridge in my bedroom. I don't even have to ask, I can just have what I want. I'm not a fucking baby.'

'What did you just say?' Jason knew he swore too much in front of Knox but it didn't mean he could let it slide.

'I'm not a fucking baby,' Knox repeated.

'That's not the sort of language I expect from you.'

'I hate you. You can't tell me what to do, you're not my dad.'

'No, I'm not your dad. But I am your brother, and I'm looking after you, so until you go back to your Mum and Dad's house, my rules apply and swearing is not allowed.'

'You do it.'

'When you're a grown-up, you can decide what words you're allowed to say.'

'That's not fair.'

'It might not seem fair, but if your teachers catch you swearing, they'll give you detention, so you better not get into the habit. I'm going to start a swear jar, and you have to put in a coin any time you swear. I'll do it too, but maybe you can help me coz sometimes I don't realise when I've said one. Can you help me with that?'

'I s'pose.' Knox's arms were still folded but he seemed to have accepted the deal.

'So, half an hour of reading and then bed. Do you want me to bring you some milk?'

'Yes, please.'

Jason was surprised that Knox had been so easily swayed, but he was a good kid.

***

When he went to bed Jason couldn't sleep. What if his father never wanted to take Knox back? As time passed, it seemed less and less likely David would do the right thing. He couldn't stay in that apartment if Knox lived with him permanently. He'd have to find somewhere else, somewhere cheaper and with a room where a kid going into adolescence had his own space.

He'd need to get a better job, but he was afraid to leave. Everything he'd ever known about working was from that job. He was used to the way things were done, and although he hated the partners, he knew their moods. In a new job, there would be a whole set of new rules he would have to learn.

What if he'd spent the last six years learning bad habits, learning the wrong stuff, and the people in the new office laughed at him? Or worse, he'd never get another job. He turned over and looked at the time on his phone, it was nearly two in the morning.

He sighed. He would be tired tomorrow. It was too late for a sleeping pill; it wouldn't have worn off by the morning and he'd be driving Knox to school like a zombie.

He could ask if Knox would change schools. If his father stopped paying the fees at the private school there was absolutely no way that Jason could afford them, even with a better job.

Then he remembered Cassie had texted him. He really liked her, she seemed sincere and caring and he was interested in her, but they both had so much going on in their lives.

Hey. I'm sorry I've been such a mess lately. I've had a lot of stuff going on. I hope things are going well with you. Maybe we can catch up again soon. He reread the text. Did she want to catch up as friends? Or as something more? Would he get his hopes up only to have her say she wasn't ready, or worse, she wasn't interested?

Hey! Good to hear from you. I'd like to catch up again, last time we didn't really get a chance to talk. Let me know when's good for you.

He sent the text. His mind calmed and it wasn't long before he drifted off to sleep.

Knox woke him up in the morning, 'Hey! We're going to be late for school.'

Jason looked at the time, he must have turned off his alarm without waking up. He had five minutes to get up and out the door and still make it to school and work on time.

'Oh shit! Why didn't you wake me up?' he said, eyes still blurred with sleep.

'Swear jar!' Knox grinned. Jason wondered if the swear jar had been a mistake.

'Okay, okay. I'm up. Have you made breakfast? Or lunch? We're going to be so late.'

'I had cornflakes already, and juice, and I made peanut butter sandwiches, but I can't find the cling film.' His chest was puffed up.

'Champion! You hardly even need my help in the mornings, do you?'

Jason swung his legs out of bed and hurried to dress. He wrapped the sandwich and packed it into the lunchbox with an apple, a banana and a muesli bar. The drive to school was quick, somehow the traffic was working with them, and Jason managed to get to the office with four minutes to spare.

He bought himself a coffee at the little kiosk in the foyer of his building to steel his nerves for the partners. They were unlikely to be in the office yet, but every time Jason was late it was one of the rare days that one of them would turn up at nine.

As soon as he walked in, he knew that Pierce was there, and that he was in a foul mood. Maybe his haemorrhoids were playing up again.

'Finally, you decide to join us then, Jason,' Pierce was standing in the waiting room, arms folded.

'It's one-minute past nine, I wouldn't call that late,' Jason replied, keeping his voice quiet.

'If you're not six minutes early, then you're late in my book.'

Jason took a breath and didn't say what he was thinking.

'I need you to put off all of your other work today and work on this.' He shoved a brown folder towards him. 'I need this will sorted out pronto, the client is just about ready to shuffle off this mortal coil, so just make sure you get it registered and all in order before he pops his clogs.'

'Okay, I'll get onto it now.' Jason took the folder. Pierce nodded and stomped back towards his office, slamming the door.

Jason put his coffee on the low table and dropped his bag on the floor next to it. He flipped through the file, still standing in the waiting area. The file seemed simple enough; the money was to be split evenly among the two listed children. Until he read the final comments, 'Absolutely none of the estate is to go to Bill Steddings, third son, who is also barred from attending any funeral or memorial.'

Jason read the sentence over again. What sort of father would bar his own son from his funeral and cut him out of the will? It would be contested for sure. His curiosity was now piqued, and Jason flicked through the rest of the file to see if any older versions of the will were in it. He found three different versions, one was thirty years old and didn't list a third son, but the most recent one was only six months old. The third son was getting his share of the estate in that one.

It didn't seem right to Jason that poor Bill Steddings miss out just as his father was dying. It reminded Jason of his own situation, two kids in one relationship, then a third child who was much younger in a second relationship. It seemed that Knox was the one being excluded from David's life, just as Bill was being excluded from William Steddings' will.

Jason realised that he was gripping the file very tightly. He tucked it under his arm, picked up the coffee cup and his bag and went to his desk.

The three other clerks had looked up when he walked in the door but given the mood Mr Pierce seemed to be in Jason wasn't surprised that they hadn't greeted him. He would have kept silent and hoped not to be noticed too, if he were in their position.

Sorting out the file meant Jason spent most of the day on the phone. More accurately he spent most of the day on hold. Listening to the hold music he was effectively alone with his thoughts. He kept coming back to his father's reluctance to have Knox back, and his apparent reluctance to give Jason the money he needed to feed and house his son. David had always been frugal but had also often used money as a replacement for affection. Now that Knox wasn't there, Jason would have expected to be receiving hundreds in guilt money to buy the child's love, but it wasn't forthcoming.

It was ridiculous to think David could be strapped for cash; he was a stockbroker, one of the best according to him. But what other explanation could there be? The arguments with Becca, from what he could gather, were about her spending habits. When he asked for money, he'd been shocked at how stingy his father had been. David must be hiding something big.

On Monday afternoons Lucas picked up Knox from school, and so it was almost six o'clock before Jason was able to leave the office. He wanted to call his father and ask him outright if he was having money trouble. He couldn't do it on the drive home, and nor on the balcony where Knox might hear him.

Jason parked his car outside his apartment, and he pulled out his mobile to call his father.

'Hello?' he answered.

'It's Jason.'

'I gathered. What do you want?'

'Uh,' Jason was struck by how rude it would be to just launch straight into his suspicions.

'I was just calling to see how you are…' he said.

'Why? I'm very busy. I don't have time for idle chat.'

'Oh, rightio.'

'Is that it then?' David asked.

'Uh, well, no. I was wondering-'

'Just say it, for fuck's sake, don't dither.'

'Are you broke, Dad?'

There was a silence that hung in the air, Jason heard his heart beating in his ears.

'What makes you ask that?' David said, he sounded out of breath, barely audible.

'A couple of things. Are you in some sort of trouble?'

'I've got it under control. Nothing for you to worry about.'

'Shit. You are broke? What the hell happened?'

'Look I said I had it under control, just leave it, will you?'

'Is that why you don't want Knox back? And why you and Becca are fighting?'

'Don't you say anything to either of them, you little shit. They don't know anything about my finances, and it's not any of their business,' David said.

'It is their business though. If you're in the shit they're affected by that. You can't keep everyone in the dark. Do you own the house? Are you going to lose the house?'

'I've got it under control. I gave you money for your stupid brother, I'm upholding my responsibilities, so is that it?'

'I can help if you'll let me.'

'I don't need your help.' He hung up.

Jason's hand, the one holding the phone, was shaking. He was so angry; adrenaline rushed through his blood.

Despite his assurances he had it under control, Jason was sure David was headed for a disaster.

He was sitting outside his apartment building and could see Knox and Lucas sitting on the balcony waiting for him. Lucas generally made dinner of some sort on nights when he looked after Knox, mostly pasta and sauce with some frozen vegies on the side.

Jason stomped up the stairs to the apartment, trying to shake off his anger. When he opened the front door, he had calmed down a little.

'How was work?' Lucas said as he walked into the lounge room.

'Alright. Had a weird case today, an old man trying to cut someone out of his will. It seemed a bit sad. And the partners were being total bastards. Barking orders and then disappearing into their offices.'

'Business as usual then?'

Jason sighed. 'Yeah, I suppose. Usually the other three will make me be the mediator for the partners but I spent most of today stuck on the phone, so they had to do it themselves.'

Knox was still out on the balcony, staring off at the city.

'Is he alright?' Jason said.

'He's been pretty quiet. Maybe you can talk to him.'

'Okay. Is there anything to eat?' Jason didn't want to have a tough conversation on an empty stomach.

'Yeah, I saved you some.' Lucas pointed to a bowl on the counter.

Jason ate his pasta at the kitchen table and watched Knox on the balcony. His shoulders were hunched, and he hardly moved.

'Hey, mate,' he said, stepping out onto the balcony and sliding the door closed behind him.

'Hi.' Knox didn't turn around.

'You okay?'

Knox shrugged.

'How was school?'

'Fine.'

Jason waited, a chill wind had picked up and was winding its way around the building.

'You look a bit cold. Should we go inside?'

'I'm not cold.' Knox shivered.

'What's up mate? You can talk to me.'

'Am I going to live with you forever now?'

'I'm not sure.'

'I don't really want to sleep on the couch anymore.' Knox was so quiet that Jason barely heard him over the wind.

'I know.' Jason put his arm around his brother's shoulder. The child's skin was icy to the touch. 'Come inside and we can talk about it.'

Knox turned and went back inside without a word. Jason was exhausted, he didn't know what to say.

'Would you like to swap for a while? I can sleep on the couch and you can sleep in my bed for a while?'

'I guess.' Knox was hugging himself. Jason got up and wrapped a blanket around his shoulders.

'If you have to live with me permanently, we'll make sure you have a room of your own. Somewhere you can put all your stuff and have time out when you're sick of me. It won't be as big or flash as the one you have with Dad and Becca, but it will be your room.'

Knox curled himself into a ball on the couch inside the blanket.

'I know camping on my couch is only fun for a little while. I'm sorry it's hard for you.'

Knox put his head on his knees and didn't look at Jason.

'Is there something else you want to tell me?'

'Mum and Dad don't care about me.' Knox's voice was muffled.

'That's not true. Why do you say that?'

'I haven't seen them for weeks. I haven't even spoken to Mum for ages.'

'Have you tried calling them?'

'No. They've forgotten about me.'

'Well. Maybe they think you've forgotten about them too. Let's give them a ring, how about that?' Jason reached into his pocket for his phone.

'What if they don't want to talk to me?'

'Let's just give them a ring and ask, eh?'

Jason dialled Becca's number. He knew David wouldn't answer another call so soon after the last one. He also suspected that Knox missed his mum more.

'Hi Becca.' Jason's voice sounded falsely high to his ears.

'Hi. What do you want?' she asked.

'Uh, well, Knox was hoping that he could talk to you?'

'Oh, uh, it's not a very good time.'

'It won't take long. He hasn't heard from you guys for a while.'

'Fine,' Becca said.

'Here, mate.' Jason passed the phone to his brother. 'You can use my room if you want.'

'Hi Mum.' Knox took the blanket and went into Jason's room, closing the door behind him.

Jason switched on the TV, there was nothing much on, but he couldn't go into his room for his laptop until Knox had finished.

Only about ten minutes went by before Knox came back out.

'You okay?' Jason asked.

Knox shrugged. 'Here's your phone. Mum had to go.'

'Well, she did say it would only be a quick chat. Do you feel a bit better?'

'No.'

'Why not?'

'She doesn't care about me. I asked her when I could come home, and she said she didn't know. She doesn't want me anymore.'

'She loves you, and I'm sure she misses you.' Jason felt as though he was lying to his brother.

Knox sat down next to Jason on the couch and drooped onto his shoulder. He thought about asking whether he had any homework, but decided it was best just to give the kid a night off.

'You wanna watch a movie?'

They put on a cartoon about cars, Knox's favourite at the moment, and the boy watched in sombre silence. Jason kept a hand on his shoulder, his head in Jason's lap.

Jason looked at his phone and saw Cassie had replied.

Yeah, I'd like to catch up. What did you have in mind?

He still had no idea whether she was interested in him as a friend or as more.

We could have dinner this week? I've got my brother staying with me, so it would have to be tomorrow or else he could come with us. He's a great kid, but I don't want to put you out, he wrote.

Dinner sounds good. Tomorrow is no good for me, but Wednesday would work. Your brother is welcome to come. How old is he again?

Jason turned to Knox. 'You wanna come have dinner with me and a friend of mine on Wednesday? Lucas will be out, and I can't leave you on your own.'

'Mum left me on my own all the time.'

'Well, would you like to come to dinner anyway?'

'Yeah, alright.' Knox seemed tired and sad.

He's 10, he's keen, Jason texted back.

He and Cassie chatted back and forth throughout the evening. Knox fell asleep halfway through the movie, but Jason didn't want to get up and wake him, so he stayed still until the end. Then he gently woke his brother, did a quick tooth brushing and face washing, and put him to bed in his own room.

Jason pulled out the sofa bed, set himself up with the laptop and applied for a couple of jobs before falling asleep.

Sleeping on the couch did not agree with his back, the fold-out bed sagged under his weight and he woke up in a hollow in the middle of the mattress. Knox seemed much perkier when he came out of Jason's room that morning. Jason felt guilty for letting him sleep on the couch for so long. The situation couldn't go on much longer.

Work that day was more of the same. Jason was tempted to look for a new job at work, but he knew he'd feel bad about it later; it felt like stealing. He had always had such high expectations of himself. David wanted his son to be a highflyer like himself, but his absence meant that Jason didn't get much in the way of practical help if he needed it. After Renee's abortion Jason's schoolwork was patchy for a year or so. Some subjects, like English, which he enjoyed, he managed to keep his grades up to the level he'd had before. But the subjects he didn't enjoy, like Chemistry, suffered significantly. He and his parents had been called into the principal's office to explain what had happened.

'We've all noticed that your marks are slipping Jason. You're distracted in class and mixing with some different friends. What's going on?' the principal had asked.

Jason stared at his shoes and refused to answer.

'There was a bit of trouble at home. It's all sorted out now. He needs to grow up and accept a few facts of life,' David had said.

'If there are troubles at home, we can always talk them through. We can be flexible in response to these sorts of situations. Even in VCE we can apply for special consideration. Jason, are you able to tell me a bit more about what's been going on?'

Jason flickered his eyes up from the carpet and was about to open his mouth to reply when David cut him off.

'We don't need to be airing our dirty laundry in front of everyone.' David uncrossed his legs and leaned forward in his chair. 'We know Jason needs to pull his finger out. There is absolutely no reason these issues should still be affecting his schoolwork. Thank you so much for bringing this to our attention, Mr Findlay.'

David stood up. Jason's mother, Lynn, who had been quiet for the whole meeting did the same.

'It's all in hand. Thank you for your time,' she said. She and David had been divorced a couple of years, but the friction between them was still palpable. Their divorce had been messy; each of them blamed the other.

Jason stayed in his chair, silently hoping Mr Findlay would ask him, just once more, what was going on. It would have felt good to tell someone, and the fact his parents didn't want the school to know added a sense of rebellion.

Mr Findlay stood with a sigh. The four of them walked out towards the reception area. Lynn and David walked stiffly, side by side looking straight ahead. Jason dawdled behind with Mr Findlay.

'It's okay to talk to someone about things that are going on. Now isn't the time, but sometime soon, make an appointment with the school counsellor. She won't have to tell your parents unless you're not safe.' Mr Findlay put his hand on Jason's shoulder briefly. 'Don't let this little obstacle ruin your chances for the future.'

'Okay,' Jason mumbled.

He went home with Mum, Tamara had stayed at a friend's house so both parents could come to the meeting.

The drive home was filled with uncomfortable silence. Jason turned the radio on in the car, but his mother wordlessly turned it off again. As they pulled into the drive, and his mother switched off the engine she turned to him.

'Your father doesn't want to talk about it. He's a bully but he's trying his best to do what he can for you. So am I. I hope you know we're on your side.'

Jason grunted.

'You can't throw away your future. I know you're still hurt from what happened with Renee. The age you're at is difficult at the best of times and you've had some tough things to deal with. I'm sorry fighting with your dad kept me so busy.' She put her hand on Jason's knee and absently stroked her thumb across the fabric of his jeans. He didn't move.

'I just want you to know you can talk to me. You don't have to deal with it all on your own. I know it's weird to talk to your mum, but I'm here when you're ready.'

'Okay.' Jason swung open the door and dragged himself to the house. He had a key, but he stood at the door waiting until his mother arrived to open it for him. He wanted her affection, he craved it, but whenever she showed it, he would flinch away. He had done exactly what his parents had feared – he'd gotten a girl pregnant because of his stupidity and now his mother was showing him kindness he didn't deserve. But he didn't want her to stop trying, either. He knew that Dad didn't really care. As long as Mum kept trying, he would be able to get up in the morning and go to school, even if he failed his classes, if she wanted him to go, he'd go. To make her proud again.

Thinking of his mother made him remember how long it had been since he'd called her. With all the business with Knox he hadn't spoken to her for weeks. He'd make Knox dinner, then call his mum, and then apply for jobs. Maybe he and Knox could go visit his mother. He wasn't her son, but she liked him anyway.

Where do you think we should go for dinner tomorrow? It will need to be kid friendly, and I'll have to leave by about 8:30. Thanks for being cool with it. I'm looking forward to it, he texted Cassie on his way home. He wanted to make sure that he kept their communication flowing. He thought of her often throughout the day, but he didn't want to overwhelm her too early.

I'm tempted to say McDonalds! Haha. Does your brother eat Vietnamese or Thai? I have a hankering, Cassie sent back not long after.

Good thinking. Knox is a pretty adventurous eater. He loves sushi, so I'm sure we'll be able to find him something.

They agreed to meet at a place in Brunswick Street, an area in Fitzroy known for its trendy restaurants.

It's my go to place. If you don't like it, we can't be friends, she replied.

The phrase 'we can't be friends' went around and around in Jason's head as he cooked burritos for their evening meal. He felt as though he was a helium balloon whose gas had slowly seeped out; drooping slowly, looking puckered and decrepit.

He hadn't wanted to admit it to himself, but now the option of a romantic relationship seemed to have been taken off the table, he knew it was what he'd wanted. He made an unnecessary amount of noise making the burritos, slamming the bowls down on the table.

'Dinner Knox.' His voice sounded sulky, even to him.

'What's wrong with you?' Knox said as he sat down and started piling his tortilla with filling.

'Don't put too much in or it'll burst. You can have more tortillas.'

Knox looked up, halfway through spooning beans onto the pile. 'Okay.'

'I'm okay, mate. It's not you, it's just stupid grown up things.'

Knox looked at him for a long moment before nodding.

Jason wasn't sure why he didn't want to say anything to Knox, but he told himself it was because it was too much to expect him to understand, not because Jason was afraid of how strongly he felt for Cassie.

***

The dinner with Cassie hung over him all day at work. He would find himself staring off into space imagining elaborate ways the evening could go wrong. Every time he caught himself out in these fantasies, he would remember the phrase 'we can't be friends.' She was beautiful and strong and interesting. He wanted her to want him the way he wanted her. If she wasn't interested in him, he couldn't stand being just her friend.

He left work at three to pick up Knox from school. If the partners happened to see him leaving on his early days, they'd scowl at him.

'This leaving work early nonsense has gone far enough,' Pierce said as he turned to the door to leave.

'What do you mean?' Jason asked, feeling the anger rising inside him.

'I'm sick of seeing you sneak off in the afternoons. You've coasted on our generosity long enough. From next week this trial period is over and you'll need to be in the office regular hours.' The veins in his neck were standing out and his face had turned a deep shade of pink.

'I can't do that. I have custody of my brother at the moment, as you know. I need to be able to pick him up from school two days a week. You don't pay me for the hours I'm not here. I'm getting through the same amount of work as I was before, even with the reduced hours.'

'If we wanted staff who had to run around after children, we would have hired women. But we hired men, who should be reliable and committed to their work. It seems to me that you're no longer putting the firm's interests first.'

Jason knew Pierce hated women, but this was one of the rare times he'd had actually said it aloud.

'I'm sorry you feel I'm no longer committed to the firm, Mr Pierce. I can't discuss changes to my hours at the moment. Knox is waiting for me. We can talk about it tomorrow, if you have some time.' Jason's fingers were gripping the doorknob so tightly his fingers hurt. He kept his voice civil, but it was all he could do not to resign on the spot.

'You're a useless, spineless little shit, Jason. I don't know why we keep you on.' Pierce turned away and slammed his office door.

'You keep me because I'm good at my job. And because I take your shit,' Jason muttered to himself.

He was still seething when he arrived at the school.

'Hey,' Knox came bouncing over to him as he stood at the school gate. His face changed as he registered Jason's mood.

'I'm not angry with you. I had a fight with my boss.'

'Is your boss nice?'

'No. He's a nasty old man.'

'Can't you tell him to be nicer?' Knox trotted alongside Jason as he took large angry strides to the car.

'I don't think it would help. I'll just get a new job and I won't have work with grumpy old men who are mean to me anymore.'

'Old men can be pretty mean. It's okay coz I think you're pretty cool.'

Jason smiled down at his brother. 'Thanks, buddy.'

When they got home, Jason was calm enough to think about the meeting with Cassie. He kept telling himself it wasn't a date, but the nerves in his belly felt like it was. He showered and shaved. Knox sat in front of the TV and played a car chase game.

'Are you ready, mate?' Jason said as he was running his hands through his wet hair trying to get it to behave.

'Yeah.'

Jason put his head around the doorframe. 'Fuck. Mate, you haven't even got shoes on and you need to change your shirt. What is that anyway?' He pointed to a huge white stain.

'Swear jar!' Knox replied, reluctantly getting up and pulling his shoes back onto his feet.

As they drove towards the restaurant Jason looked at the time; they were running late.

'Can you get my phone and text Cassie that we're late?' Jason said, his eyes scanning the barely moving traffic up Victoria St.

'Okay.' Knox reached over to where the phone was.

'What are you typing in?' Jason asked after about a minute of silence.

'Uh, so far I have "Hi Cassie. This is Knox. Jason says we'll be late."'

'Is that all? It seemed like you were typing a lot.'

'I had to change it. I wasn't sure what to write.'

'You can ask if you're not sure. You know it's okay to ask.'

'Yeah.' Knox turned to look out the window. Jason let the silence sit between them as the radio burbled in the background.

'Did you send it?' he asked after they had crawled a little further down the road.

'Oh, no.' Knox moved his fingers over the phone and dropped it back between them.

'Good man.'

They arrived fifteen minutes late. Cassie was already seated inside when they approached. She looked relaxed and was playing on her phone. She looked up as Knox pushed open the door ahead of Jason. She smiled and stood up.

Jason moved to hug her, but then hesitated. 'Would you like a hug?' he asked.

'Yes, I would.' She replied by embracing him, the hug lingered a little longer than he expected, and he inhaled the fruity scent of her hair.

'This must be Knox,' she said as they pulled apart. She put out her hand to his brother.

'Yeah, this is my brother. Knox, this is Cassie. Do you want to shake her hand?'

Knox murmured something and took Cassie's hand. 'He can be a bit shy.'

'That's alright. I used to be pretty shy. I'm sure he'll warm up.'

'Have a seat there, mate.' Jason pointed to a chair next to him as he took the seat opposite Cassie.

'I'm sorry we were late; traffic was worse than I expected.' Jason had been trying to fix his hair, but the traffic was an acceptable excuse.

'It can be pretty bad at this time of night.' Cassie smiled, and picked up her menu.

They each ordered a main and a couple of entrees to share. Knox wasn't sure what to eat but finally decided on a chicken and cashew stir fry.

The conversation as they ate was stilted. Knox was still being very quiet, and Jason was wary of keeping the topics child appropriate.

'And how's work?' Jason said as they were finishing their mains. He realised he hadn't even thought to ask earlier.

'I sort of lost my job. It was kind of mutual, I guess. I'm thinking of going back to study social work.'

'That sounds good. What will you do for money in the meantime? You were in hospitality, right?'

'Yeah, I was. I'll need to move, the rent on my place is too high to afford as a student, and there are some uh... bad memories there so I kind of want to leave anyway. I'll get an evening job in a bar probably, just enough to pay for rent and food—the basics.'

'Sounds like a pretty big change.'

'Mmmm,' she said.

She chewed her mouthful and looked off into the distance. Jason waited in case she was going to say more, but she took another mouthful instead.

'What's social work?' Knox said. It was the first time he'd spoken without being asked a direct question.

'Well, there people in the world who are having a rough time. Maybe they lost their job, or they can't get a job, or kids whose parents are struggling, and that means it's hard for them to find somewhere to live, that sort of thing. Social workers are there to help people get to a more stable place in life. It's a sort of professional helper I guess.'

Knox was silent again for a minute or so.

'Could a social worker help my mum and dad? They fight all the time and I can't live with them anymore.'

Jason was watching Knox and his heart broke for him. 'It's not your job to fix your mum and dad. You know that, right?'

'I know. But if they stopped fighting then I could go home.'

Jason shifted in his seat. He was embarrassed, he was sure Cassie would think he was a terrible carer. He could be the best big brother in the world, but he would never be Knox's dad.

'Sometimes a social worker can't make it better, sometimes it just takes time. I don't know anything about your mum and dad, but I'm sure they love you very much and they want to bring you home,' Cassie said.

Knox's closed his mouth, pressing his lips together to make an angry line. 'I want to go home now,' he said, barely opening his mouth.

'You don't even want any ice-cream?' Jason said, hoping to bribe Knox to stay.

'I want to go home,' the child repeated. He pushed away his partially-eaten dinner and folded his arms.

'I'm sorry. I seem to have said the wrong thing,' Cassie said, her eyes soft and sad.

Jason looked at his watch. 'I dunno. It's getting towards bedtime as well I think. We'd better go.'

He reached into his wallet and handed Cassie a couple of twenty-dollar notes.

'Can you take care of the bill?'

Knox was sitting with his arms crossed staring at the floor.

'Of course, but that's too much. I'll get you some change,' Cassie said, and she tried to hand one of the notes back.

'It's okay. Plus, you aren't working at the moment, it seems fair to me.'

'Alright, I'll get the next one.'

Jason and Cassie stood up, she held out her arms to hug him again and he held her close, breathing in that fruity shampoo. He wanted desperately to turn his head and kiss the smooth skin on her neck. He pulled away and saw that Knox was already at the door.

'I'm sorry about this,' he said, looking at his brother. 'He's got a lot going on.'

'It's fine, really. I hope he feels better.'

'Slow down, mate, I'm coming.' Jason jogged out into the street after Knox, who was already halfway to the car.

In the car Knox was silent. Jason waited for him to say something as he drove. When they arrived at the apartment and Knox reached for the door Jason decided it was time to ask.

'That was a bit rude, just rushing off like that. What happened back there?'

Knox clenched his teeth and stared straight ahead.

'I don't mind that you wanted to go home, I won't understand unless you tell me what's happening.'

'Your friend is an idiot,' he said quietly.

'That's not very nice. Why do you think Cassie's an idiot?' Jason was using everything he had to stay calm.

'She doesn't know anything.'

'About what?'

'She said that mum and dad love me and want me to come home. They don't love me. They've dumped me with you in your stupid flat with your stupid housemate and I'm sick of it.'

Jason took a deep breath. 'Do you want to go visit them?'

'No. They don't care.'

'They do care. They might be a bit crappy at showing it, but they do care.'

'Whatever.'

Jason wasn't sure what to say. 'Is there still ice-cream inside?'

'I dunno,' Knox said his arms still folded.

'Let's go inside and have a look. You can have some ice-cream and then sleep in the big bed.'

Knox grunted and opened the car door. Jason followed as he stomped all the way to the front door. There was chocolate ice-cream in the freezer, which Jason spooned out for each of them. They ate quietly and Knox took his bowl to the sink when he was finished. He went through his night-time routine before saying good night.

'Can I have a hug?' Jason asked.

'Yeah,' Knox said. He stood there and allowed Jason to hug him. It hurt to see how his brother was struggling, how he was stuck in limbo while his parents tore each other to pieces.

Jason lay awake on the foldout bed for a long time, thinking over his options. He'd have to move soon. It didn't look like anything was going to change.

Since he wasn't sleeping anyway, Jason pulled out his computer and started looking at rental advertisements.

Chapter 17

Being unemployed didn't suit Cassie. It left her with too much time to think about things. She was averaging an interview each day, however they were all wrong in some way.

The course she wanted to do didn't start until next year, late February, and she needed to find work that would give her a lot of hours for the couple of months between now and then and but could scale back when she needed to focus on her studies. It should have been fairly simple.

'Sounds like you're creating faults in them.' Tessa sipped her red wine. 'What are you afraid of?'

'Nothing,' Cassie said immediately. 'I don't know. Maybe I am wary of learning a whole new set of people's foibles only to find myself out of a job as soon as I take a day off.'

'I've told you before that your old job was clearly run by idiots. You'd been there for years, and when you struggle for a few weeks they fire you? It's weak. It's weak and you shouldn't stand for it. You should take them to Fair Work—'

'I've told you I don't want to do that,' Cassie said. She hoped Tessa would drop the subject. It came up almost as frequently as getting an intervention order against Tony.

'Alright, alright.' Tessa held up her hands in surrender.

'You never finished telling me about your date the other night.'

'I'm not sure it was a date.' Cassie sighed. Tessa put her fork and knife together on her plate and took a sip of wine.

'His little brother suddenly cracked it and wanted to go home. He couldn't get away from me fast enough.'

'What were you talking about?'

Cassie thought for a moment. 'I think we were talking about why he was living with Jason.' She was surprised that she hadn't thought of it before. 'I said that his parents would always love him and that the current situation didn't change that. Maybe he thinks it's his fault.'

'Kids always think discord between their parents is their fault. It takes a while to learn the world doesn't revolve around you.' Tessa laughed.

Cassie ran her hands over her face, she was so tired.

'If I wasn't allowed to stay with, or even hardly see, my parents, at that age. I'd think there must be something wrong with me,' Cassie was mostly talking to herself now. 'And there isn't any room at Jason's place. He's been sleeping on the couch.'

'It sounds like Jason is trying to make the best of a very difficult situation.'

Cassie started to clear away the dinner plates. She and Jason had exchanged a few brief text messages in the days since their dinner and Cassie got the feeling he was pissed off with her. He'd apologised several times, but he hadn't proposed another time. Cassie had suggested the dinner, so she didn't want to seem pushy by suggesting the next meeting too.

'You said you don't think it was a date. Did you want it to be a date?' Tessa was on the couch flicking through the TV channels.

'It doesn't seem fair to date someone when my life is in such a shambles. I really like Jason; I think he's really thoughtful, obviously he cares a lot about his family, and he's super-hot, but I just...'

'Have you been up front with Jason about your personal situation? He's got some pretty intense stuff going on in his life too, but I don't see him talking himself out of a relationship.'

'You might have a point.' Cassie left the dishes in the sink and wandered over to the couch.

Cassie heard the scratching of the keys in the front door and her whole body became tense.

'It's alright. Ian's probably had a few and can't find the keyhole.' Tessa laid a hand on Cassie's knee.

'I'm sorry. I'm a little bit jumpy still.' Cassie didn't like to show her fear to anyone. She didn't like to think of herself still being affected by Tony.

'I'd better head home,' Cassie said. She didn't really want to end up stuck with Ian when he'd been drinking. He always wanted to have long, rambling conversations.

Tessa stood up and opened the door for Ian. 'You're lucky I'm here to let you in, you lush!' she said, her smile was so wide it pushed out some of Cassie's fear.

'Gorgeous woman!' Ian stumbled in the door and embraced Tessa enthusiastically. She giggled like a teenager and batted away his wandering hands.

'And Cassie! Darling girl! How are you?'

'She's just going dear, you're not to bother her. You stink of whiskey.'

'Yes, boss.' Ian attempted a salute, but he was leaning to the left and it looked askew.

Tessa pushed him into the house, and he went; each step he took he looked in danger of falling flat on his face.

'Now, if you want to see this boy again, you'd better just ask him. Men often don't know when a woman is interested, and especially a man who has as much going on in his life as Jason. Don't worry about seeming pushy. He'll be falling for you in no time.'

'If you say so,' Cassie said. She wasn't convinced but given her history with men, perhaps she should start dating differently.

Coming home to the apartment filled Cassie with anxiety. She expected Tony to retaliate in some way to her threatening to go to the police, but so far, he hadn't done anything. There was something unsettling about not knowing what was going on in his mind. Cassie pushed open her front door and her apartment was there, just as she'd left it.

She really didn't have the money to keep paying the rent on this place, but she had taken her aunt's loan even though it felt strange accepting help.

She should start saving properly and have a real plan for her future so that next time something came and knocked everything out of balance she wouldn't be so unprepared.

She sat on the edge of her bed and checked her phone for a message from Jason: nothing. It was nearly midnight, but if she didn't send something now, she wouldn't.

I was thinking we could have a date, just the two of us, where neither of us has to run off early. I did it the first time, and you did it last time, so we're even. Maybe we could have a drink one night when you can leave

Knox with someone? Cassie put her phone down on the bedside table and went to shower.

She stepped out of the bathroom and climbed into bed. She knew she shouldn't, but she checked her phone just in case.

A drink one night sounds great. Let's get cocktails, my shout. How about Saturday? Jason had replied.

Saturday sounds perfect, she wrote back. Without a job where she was expected to work all hours, she could go out on a Saturday night for once.

Cassie was woken several times during the night by dreams about walking in and finding her apartment destroyed. She gave up on sleeping at six and got up.

With all her spring cleaning and the clothes Tony had destroyed, her bedroom looked bare. Without a steady income, she couldn't afford to buy herself new clothes either.

She'd splurged on an outfit for interviews, as well as one pair of jeans and two plain T-shirts. It was a frugal and depressing selection. She decided today she wouldn't apply for any jobs, and she'd go to charity shops in search of bargains. She set a limit of a hundred dollars and once she'd spent that she'd come home.

Having made a plan, her day looked brighter. She wanted something cute to wear out on Saturday night, but that could only happen is the shopping gods were smiling on her. If not, she was sure Jason would understand.

You fancy an Op-shop adventure today? I need to get new clothes, she texted her sister. Penny wouldn't be up yet, and the shops weren't open until nine or ten, so Cassie put her favourite DVD into the machine and watched a movie while she had breakfast. It felt very decadent.

Penny hadn't replied by eleven and by then, Cassie was sick of sitting around on her own. She put on the same pair of jeans and T-shirt that she'd worn for the last week and looked at herself in the mirror.

How had she come to this? No job, haunted by her crazy ex-boyfriend, and too shy to let Jason know that she really liked him.

Cassie got in her car and drove to Malvern; she fancied her chances would be better over that way where the donations were better quality and there were fewer people to pick through them.

There were two shops quite close to each other. The first one she walked into was playing classical music from a sound system behind the counter. It was jammed with items, mostly clothes at the front of the store but at the back there were a few pieces of furniture, a shelf full of books and another with assorted kitchen items.

There were no other customers, and two elderly ladies behind the counter. They must be volunteers; it didn't look busy enough to pay for two assistants.

One of the women was perched on a high stool knitting. It was shaped like a jumper for a baby, but in a drab khaki green. Cassie wondered whether the parents had requested army green or whether, perhaps more likely, the colour was left over from another project that she was trying to use up.

The other woman was fussing with the items in the display case. Neither of them seemed to notice Cassie walk in.

Cassie flicked her way through one and a half racks of women's clothes before they had addressed her.

'Are you alright, dear?' asked the woman knitting.

'Just having a look,' she replied.

'Anything in particular you're after? We can help you find something if you need it.'

'I should be okay, but I'll let you know.'

Cassie continued down the rows. There were plenty of pairs of jeans, and pants that might be suitable for a corporate job. She didn't need anything like that. What she needed were basics; staple items that she could wear in lots of combinations.

She got to the end of the women's clothes section and became overwhelmed by the task. Things were the wrong size, or the wrong style, and one skirt which she liked smelled of mothballs so strongly she put it back.

Cassie was staring at the wall of mismatched crockery and she felt her throat tighten. She didn't deserve this. She had tried to tell herself they were only clothes. But something about trying to repair the damage Tony had done made it seem real.

She rubbed her eyes; her hands were dusty, and she made herself sneeze.

'Bless you.' The other old lady had said it, her voice was wobbly as though she didn't get much use out of it. Cassie took a deep breath and wandered back towards the door.

The second shop was not as full and had only one person behind the counter.

'I'm just letting you know that all the clothes with yellow tags are half-price today,' he said as she came in the door. 'Are you alright? You look a bit, uh...'

'I'm alright, thanks,' Cassie said. Then she caught sight of herself in a mirror; her nose and cheeks were red, and her eyes were bloodshot.

'Oh! I was just in the Salvo's; it's a bit dusty in there.'

'We do our best to make sure the items are clean, but it's an occupational hazard I guess.' He smiled.

Cassie tried to concentrate on the task of sorting through the clothes. She flicked through skirts and dresses, all sorted by colours.

She picked up a couple of items to try on and she was starting to enjoy herself. The lurid pink parachute pants made her smile at how out of style they were.

'I'll take these two, and I'll leave those ones,' Cassie put two piles of clothes on the counter.

The assistant was a young man; his face heavily scarred by acne. He had a patchy beard, perhaps to try to cover some of the scarring.

'I really love these pants,' he said, holding up a pair of purple jeans. They were covered in paisley-style patterns.

'I would never have bought these a month ago,' she said quietly.

'But they're so fabulous! What changed?'

'It's a long story. I lost most of my clothes in a break in.'

'That's awful! Who would steal clothes? You can't sell them.' He shook his head.

Cassie didn't answer. It was hard enough to talk about it with her family. She was still waiting for them to say that she should have seen it coming or should have done something about it earlier.

'Thank you for your help,' she said as she turned to leave.

'Any time. Have a lovely day.'

Cassie knew that he probably said that to everyone, but even so she felt better.

It was nearly lunchtime, and she checked her phone as she wandered down the street towards the cafes. Penny had replied.

I'm always up for an adventure. Are you still shopping?

Yeah. I'm gonna get something to eat and then come over your side to see if the hipsters have left anything worth buying, Cassie replied.

Haha! Good one. I'll come find you when you get here.

Cassie thought that Penny was probably still in bed and would need time to get herself together.

She went into a quaint, small and mostly empty shop and ordered a latte and a toasted chicken and avocado sandwich. Cassie's mother had always made cheese toasties and canned tomato soup for them when they'd been sick. Cassie kept a can of soup in the house in case she needed it, but now every time she opened the kitchen cupboards and saw the can sitting there, she was reminded of her mother's death.

The traffic as she made her way back across the suburbs to Brunswick was busier than Cassie had expected. Punt Road was a complete nightmare as usual. No matter what time it was, it was chocked with cars.

There was an enormous charity shop on Sydney Road, not far from Penny's house Cassie was aiming for.

Alright, I'm at Savers. Come find me, she texted to Penny as she stepped out of the car.

It seemed to be a converted warehouse; blank, white and impersonal. Fluorescent lights hung on long chains from the high ceiling. In the lull between songs she could hear the tubes buzzing.

Cassie didn't quite know where to start, so she went to the 'Formal Wear' section, hoping to get something she could wear to a cocktail bar and impress Jason.

She was flipping through metallic crimes against fashion, leftovers from the eighties, when Penny spoke.

'Tell me you're going to get that!' Penny said.

Cassie was startled but refused to let Penny see it.

'It would be pretty funny, but I thought I might try not to scare the man off. Did you have any trouble finding me?'

'Nah. Took me a while to get out of bed, I was working last night.'

She knew she should be glad that Penny was working, that it was none of her business, and sex work was still work, but it was hard when the profits and contacts were fuelling Penny's ice habit.

'Right.' Cassie turned back to shuffling through the rack of hideous clothes.

Penny stood for a moment, her hands dangling by her sides. She sighed. 'You're going on a date? Is it the dude from the lawyer's office? He's cute.'

'Yeah, he invited me and then I realised I literally had nothing to wear.'

'You should do something about Tony. He should be paying you to replace all that stuff. You're not even working right now, and that's his fault too.' Penny grabbed a hanger.

'I know I should, but I just can't right now.' Cassie looked her sister in the eye and took a deep breath.

'Maybe in a couple of months when I'm feeling a bit better.'

'You should do it now, but it's your decision.' Penny's bottom lip was stuck out in a pout.

They flicked through racks and racks of second-hand clothing, but Cassie didn't find anything suitable for a date.

'Maybe I should just cancel. I'm too much of a mess to be dating,' Cassie said as she reached the end of the last row of women's wear.

'Don't you dare cancel this date. I have clothes you could borrow, you know my weight is a bit up and down these days...'

Because you get really skinny when you're into the drugs, Cassie thought.

'That's sweet of you, but your style is uh... I don't know if I could pull it off.'

Penny laughed, 'I'm sure we could find something sedate enough for you.'

Cassie smiled and took her sister's arm, they walked out of the store and down the road to the tiny Greek cake shop where they had very strong coffee and so many baklavas they felt sick.

As Penny ate some of the colour came back into her cheeks. Cassie remembered what it had been like when they were close; before Penny and Kev had started dating and Penny had had her first taste of amphetamines.

'Would it be alright to come have a look at your stuff that doesn't fit you now? My date is only a couple of days away.'

Penny hesitated. 'If you promise not to be horrified by the state of the place, then you can come 'round.'

It wasn't usual for Penny to worry about the cleanliness of her house; Cassie was concerned. 'I can come tomorrow is that's better, you know, you can have a look through what you don't want and uh, then we can go through it.'

'It's okay. It's not that bad. Just give me five minutes to put some stuff away before you come in,' Penny said.

'Okay.'

She and Kev must have had a big weekend. Cassie didn't think Penny would be anxious if the mess was not drug-related.

They drove back to Penny's place in Cassie's car, even though it was only a couple of minutes' walk.

'Okay, I'll stick my head out when it's safe to come in,' Penny said. She jumped out of the car and ran to the front door.

Cassie turned off the engine and pulled out her phone. She looked over the messages between her and Jason. *How could it possibly work?*

Scrolling through their messages Cassie felt warmth and nervousness in her belly. She hadn't had that feeling for a long time. There would always be obstacles to overcome with any relationship. The care he was taking of his brother showed he was willing to do whatever was necessary to help people around him.

Penny came charging out of the front door, she seemed to be much perkier than she had been when she went in. She'd taken the time tidying up her house to have a quick smoke. Her eyes were a little more glazed than they had been.

'Are you high?' Cassie asked.

'No, I just, okay, yes, I had a little toke. I really needed it, and it was only a small one.'

'I wish you wouldn't.'

Anger swept across Penny's face, appearing and disappearing in an instant. 'I know. Do you want to come have a look at my clothes or not?' Penny's voice sounded almost tired.

'That's why I came isn't it?' Cassie said. She followed her sister into the house and closed the front door.

The house was not as bad as she'd imagined. There were dishes piled up in the sink, and a couple of pizza boxes lying on the coffee table, but it didn't smell too stale.

'Okay, why don't you put the kettle on, and I'll get some bits out of the pile. You'll probably need to wash them, I don't know how recently they've been done,' Penny said. She went into the bedroom, 'Some of this stuff I haven't worn for a year or more. Even if it was clean then, it'll be all dusty or whatever now.'

Cassie didn't feel like shouting to her sister in the other room. Penny had a cute little teapot and small china cups that she used for green tea somewhere. Cassie opened a few cupboards; they were mostly empty except for the sets of mismatched crockery.

Penny only had teabags, so the teapot was largely for appearances, but Cassie wanted to make it nice.

'You won't want my clubbing stuff, will you? You know fluoro or leopard print?'

'No. I'm probably looking for something more classic,' Cassie replied.

When the kettle had boiled Cassie still hadn't found the teapot, so she just put teabags into two mugs. It didn't feel as special. She carried the two cups into the lounge room.

'Come in here and look at what I've pulled together,' Penny said.

The house was small, and the bed took up most of the bedroom, not counting the built-in wardrobe which looked as though it had vomited its contents all over the floor and the top of the bed.

Cassie handed Penny her tea, 'I couldn't find the teapot.'

'I broke it weeks ago. I put it down on the corner of the table and it must not have been on properly and it fell and splashed boiling water everywhere. It was horrible. Lucky no one got burned.'

'Didn't Mum buy you that teapot?'

'Yeah. I don't know whether to buy another one. It seems wrong somehow.'

The sisters were silent for a long moment; the weight of their mother's death had come back to sit between them.

'I'll get you another one,' Cassie said. 'What have I got to choose from?'

'Well, there are a couple of cute skirts in here, and one or two pairs of pants. I don't have much in the way of tops, they all too revealing, or too bright, or too patterned for you.'

'You know that classic doesn't have to mean black right?' Cassie smiled.

'I know, but in my wardrobe it kind of does.'

Cassie tried a few of the items, some didn't fit. She put on a skirt that was made of layers of floaty grey silk.

'Oh my God, did I look like that when I wore that skirt?' Penny exclaimed, laughing.

Cassie looked in the mirror on the front of the wardrobe. She looked ridiculous; the skirts layers wafted around her making her look much bigger than she was.

'No! You're taller so it didn't look so blobby on you.' She peeled the skirt off and put it on the reject pile.

'Hey babe, I'm home!' Kevin called as he opened the front door. 'Is your sister here? I saw the car out the front.'

'Cassie's trying on clothes. You can't come in.' Penny giggled before slamming the bedroom door.

'Oh, righto.'

'Do you wanna finish going through the pile? I'm gonna go say hi to Kev.' Penny slipped around the door to save her sister's privacy and Cassie was left alone. It wasn't as much fun without Penny. She picked her way through the piles of clothes until she found a slinky dark green evening dress. Cassie didn't think she'd ever seen her sister wear it, and as she looked, she saw there were still tags on it. She slipped it on, and it was a good fit.

She looked at herself in the mirror, her hair was lank and needed a wash, and her white socks came halfway up her calves, but other than that she thought she looked pretty good. She put her jeans and T-shirt back on and went out.

'Did you ever wear this?' she said, holding the green dress.

'Oh that? It was a present, I never really liked it.'

Penny and Kevin were sitting on the couch together. He was stroking her thigh, she looked suddenly very tired and thin.

'What are you two having for dinner?'

'There's pizza in the fridge. I thought we'd have that. I'm going to have a night off work. I'm not feeling up to it today.'

Kevin squeezed her knee, a reassurance Cassie guessed.

'Well, I should probably leave you to it. I've had a pretty big day myself.' Cassie stood beside the couch, her hands full of clothes, unsure of what to do.

'It was good to see you,' Penny said.

'Yeah, nice to see you,' Kevin added. He didn't look at her.

'Have you got a bag?'

'Yeah, there's one in the kitchen, fourth drawer down is full of plastic bags.'

Cassie shuffled in and got a bag out of the drawer, which almost refused to close it was so full. She rested her hand on the doorknob, hesitating before she left.

'Bye then,' she said.

'Bye,' Kevin said. Penny looked like she might have fallen asleep.

Cassie felt oddly empty walking back to her car. She pulled out her phone and texted Jason.

I went shopping today and I actually have an outfit for Saturday. I can't wait to see you. X

She'd sent the message before she realised that she'd signed it with a kiss. *Oh well, it's done now. I hope he feels the same way.*

***

Saturday night came around quickly and Cassie spent all day getting ready. Since sending that kiss in her text message, she and Jason had exchanged a few more messages—conversational stuff.

He'd insisted on keeping where they were going a surprise, so Cassie was waiting for him at the top of Burke Street, near the Imperial Hotel.

I hope we're not going there, she thought to herself, I've dressed all wrong for that.

'You look nice.'

She turned Jason was wearing a dark blue suit, crisp white shirt and no tie. The suit was tailored to show off his broad shoulders and narrow hips. His sleek brown shoes clip clopped along the footpath as he walked.

'So do you,' she said, giving him another obvious onceover. His cheeks coloured slightly. 'So where are we going? I hope I'm not over-dressed,' she continued.

'Not at all. I thought we could do an evening of cocktails and dinner. It will be hideously expensive probably, and I might regret it tomorrow, but I haven't had the opportunity for a long time.' He smiled, but there was a weariness that remained in his eyes.

'It sounds very hedonistic.' She slid her arm into the crook of his elbow. 'Lead the way.'

Jason had chosen a quaint bar for their first stop, through an unmarked door and up two flights of stairs. Fake grass covered the floor, and a fake brick path through the centre. The furniture was all spindly white metal chairs and obscenely patterned floral couches with white wooden frames; the sort you might see in a garden party in Florida in the 1940s.

'I've booked us a table out on the balcony,' Jason said, leading her outside.

The view over the dark city was excellent, but Cassie didn't spend much time looking at it. She looked at her companion. The worry in his eyes concerned her.

'This is beautiful. I've never been here before,' she said, taking a seat facing back into the bar. There were outdoor heaters which cut through most of the evening chill, but Cassie didn't remove her jacket.

'It's a bit pretentious. Overpriced of course, but you're paying for the experience, not just the drink, aren't you?'

'I'm sure you're right.'

They fell into silence for a moment, broken by the petite waitress who came to offer them menus.

'If we get a jug of something, then we can take our time and have a chance to talk,' he said.

'Sure, do you have one in mind?'

'I thought the gin and fruit one looked good.'

Jason kept tapping his fingers on the table. She reminded herself that it was nerves and tried not to be annoyed by it.

When their drink arrived, Jason poured for both of them.

'Cheers,' she said.

'Cheers.'

They each took a sip and the silence between them descended once more.

'So ho—' Cassie started to say. 'What have you been—' Jason spoke at the same time. 'Sorry, you go.'

'No, no. You go.'

'I was just going to ask what have you been up to this week? Any luck with the job hunt?' he asked.

'I've been applying for this and that but going back to uni is looking like my best option.'

'Yes, you mentioned that.'

'It seemed like the thing to do at the time, drop out. My mum was on her own and my sister was still at school. I felt like I had to pay my own way. I didn't want to keep living off Mum while I finished my degree.'

'That sounds like it was a tough decision.'

'By then I'd decided hospitality was what I wanted to do with my life. I was earning good money, I would stay back late drinking with the other staff, my boyfriend at the time was a bartender too. It was a lifestyle I got used to.'

'What's prompted you to go back to uni now?' Jason asked.

'I guess it's a combination of things. My mum; the fact that she lived her whole life with something burning deep inside of her she never allowed herself to pursue. And the whole saga with my ex. It really makes you reassess what you're doing.'

Jason was quiet, the sound of the ice clinking around in his glass now loud over the lull in the conversation.

'I wish I had your courage,' he said softly.

'What makes you say that?'

'I'm sorry, I don't wanna be a downer.'

'You're not a downer. I'm interested.'

'I just... well, now I'm taking care of Knox, I feel like I can't just quit my job and float around looking for my life's purpose.' He put his glass down on the table with a bang, making Cassie jump 'I'm sorry,' he said.

'There's no progress on the Knox situation? Don't his parents want him back?'

'No. Dad isn't interested. He's crawled into a hole. He lost a lot of money and now he seems to be trying to avoid taking responsibility for his youngest.'

'What about his mother?'

'She's not a cruel woman, but she's not maternal. She knows I'll look after him. She's probably relieved she doesn't have to have a ten-year-old following her around making her look old.'

Cassie reached across the table and took his hand.

'Not all brothers would take it on.'

'What else could I do?' he asked.

'I don't know.'

Jason picked up the jug of cocktail and poured out the little remaining into each of their glasses. 'But that's enough of that.'

Cassie wanted to take the conversation back to something light, to provide a distraction from their worries for a while, but she couldn't think of anything to say.

'Next stop is dinner. Are you ready to eat?' Jason said with a smile, but his eyes were still sad.

'I'm starting to get hungry.' Cassie stood up and felt a wave of warmth spread over her legs. She regretted having had so much to drink on an empty stomach.

She took Jason's arm again as they went down the stairs and out into the street. The Saturday night crowd was starting to pick up.

'Is it far?' she asked. The shoes she'd taken from Penny to go with her outfit were ankle high black leather boots with a wicked stiletto heel. The idea of a long walk to get dinner did not appeal.

'No, it's just down the lane here.'

The laneway posed its own problems, the cobblestones threatened to trap the heel of her shoes with each step.

The restaurant was a swish looking Asian-fusion place. Every spare corner of the tiny space was filled with well-dressed patrons.

'It must have been difficult to get a reservation here,' she said once they were seated in a noisy corner.

'I had booked this a while ago. I hoped you would be interested to come with me.'

Cassie was taken aback. 'How long is a while ago?'

'Well, about three weeks. I know we weren't really, y'know, but if I wanted to impress you, I needed to get this place lined up.'

'I'm impressed, if a little worried.'

Jason laughed. 'I would have asked my friend Lucas to come if you'd turned me down.'

'It's a good thing I'm unemployed now. If I'd still had my old job, I would have had no hope of getting Saturday night off.'

He laughed. 'I didn't factor that in when I made the plan.'

The loud atmosphere of the restaurant made it difficult to maintain a conversation for long.

'I'm not used to this sort of fine dining. Tiny plates with dots of this and that,' Cassie said when the waiter had taken away their dinner plates.

'What did you serve where you used to work?'

'Just regular café stuff – pasta, chicken parma, burgers and chips, sometimes we'd have specials like seared salmon or something, but generally it was the same stuff every week.' She took a sip of the white wine that had been recommended to match their meal, a bouquet of subtle flavours rolled over her tongue.

'I would eat there when I worked, perk of the job, so I got used to that food. I'd worked there for years.'

'And?' Jason prompted.

'Sorry, I was just remembering how much I'd enjoyed working there.'

'It's hard when people don't appreciate the work you've put in.' Jason's fingers started drumming on the table again.

Cassie looked up at him. 'Are you alright?'

'Yeah. Sorry.' The fingers stopped. 'Shall we get dessert? Or go to another bar?'

'Let's go sit somewhere quiet.'

'Alright.' Jason waved the waiter over and settled the bill.

They walked out into the evening; the night chill had settled.

'I don't know anywhere that will be quiet and warm and close by,' Jason said.

'You could, uh—' Cassie hesitated. 'You could come to my place. We could have a hot chocolate or something.'

Jason was silent for a long time. Cassie was sure that she'd said the wrong thing and he thought she was a fool.

'I can't stay the night. I have to take Knox to soccer practise in the morning.'

'I don't want to put you out. It's fine if you want to call it a night—'

Jason cut her off by kissing her on the lips. He was trembling, but his mouth was firm on hers. As the initial surprise ebbed away, Cassie found herself swept up in the exploration of him. She slid her hands inside his jacket and pulled him towards her. She felt the muscles of his back vibrating as he kissed her.

When he pulled away, she stumbled, she had been leaning into him in an effort to pull him closer.

'Let's grab a taxi to your place,' he said.

In the back of the taxi Cassie didn't trust the happy feeling that had come from the kiss. Her mind kept going back to the night she'd found her bed covered in the remnants of her clothes.

'Are you okay?' Jason leaned over to whisper in her ear.

'I'm alright.' She squeezed his hand where it lay on her thigh. 'I haven't dated much since Tony.'

Jason nodded, his hand absently rubbing the inner thigh just above her knee.

'Do you want to do this? I could just drop you off.'

She turned to look at him, his hand was displaced as she twisted in the back seat of the cab.

'I want this.' She leaned forward and planted a fierce kiss on his lips. He seemed surprised, but then he started kissing her back. Their hands wandered over each other.

The taxi driver turned the radio up and Cassie pulled away. 'Sorry,' she said to the back of the driver's head.

'I get it all the time,' he said, he didn't turn the radio down again.

Jason insisted on paying the driver as Cassie searched for her keys in her handbag. Her fingers seemed to be drunker than the rest of her.

'My place is pretty small. It's just me.' She led Jason up the stairs toward her place.

She let go of the breath she hadn't realised she was holding as she saw that the door was still closed, just as she'd left it. Tony probably wouldn't try the same thing again, but Cassie didn't want to assume she was safe.

Inside the apartment, Jason grabbed her around the waist and buried his face in the back of her neck, kissing the sensitive skin there. She giggled as his lips travelled around her hairline.

Once she'd managed to close the front door again, she spun in Jason's arms and met his lips with hers.

'You said you can't stay, does that mean you have to run off quickly?' she breathed.

'No, I can take my time, but I'll need to be back at mine early.'

His hands were trying to find their way into her dress, she giggled again as he tried to find the opening.

'The zipper is here,' she said, indicating to the invisible zip under her left arm. She pulled it down slowly as he watched. 'Now you can slip it over my head.'

He grabbed the hem of the dress and flipped the whole thing over her head in one movement. She shivered as the cool air hit her skin. Jason's eyes were drinking her in.

'Wow,' he said.

'Thanks. Now you.' She ran her hands inside his jacket and slid it over his shoulders. He went for the shirt buttons, pulling at them in his hurry.

As he slid off the shirt a wave of his smell washed over her; he smelled like subtle musky aftershave and a hint of leather. His chest was thinly covered in hair; she ran her fingers over it.

He still had his pants and shoes on, and as they stumbled backwards towards the bed, Cassie wrestled with the buckle of his belt.

'Here,' he said, grabbing the belt with one hand and deftly flicking it open. Jason's pants fell to the floor around his ankles and he tripped, tumbling onto the bed, taking her with him. As they lay there, shaking with laughter, Cassie felt safe with Jason.

His hard cock was against her thighs, the heat of it pushing up against her own hot groin. Jason wriggled on top of her, trying to get his shoes off without moving his mouth away from hers.

'Ah shit,' he said, after struggling with them for a minute or so. He rolled off her body, untied his shoes and slipped them off. He dropped his socks and pants onto the floor beside the bed.

Jason hesitated.

'What is it?' Cassie's eyes flicked down to the bulge now clearly visible through his tight boxers.

'It's just… is this too fast?'

Cassie's arousal cooled. 'I really want you, I have for a while, but if it's too soon we can wait.' She looked away, through the open bedroom door into the lounge room. Her hands moved to cover herself now that she was conscious of being nearly naked.

'I'd really like to just hold you; I don't want to get too carried away. Would that be alright?'

'I guess. It will be a first for me to have snuggles before sex.' She smiled. 'Let's get under the covers, it's pretty cold.'

They crawled into the bed, Jason slipped one arm under her head and curved his body around hers. Cassie's mind kept coming back to his hard cock pressed up against her buttocks.

She adjusted herself, shuffling her arse back against his pelvis and he let out a sigh. His hand that had been resting on her stomach drifted down to her hip and pressed her further into him.

Cassie started to rock her pelvis, rubbing her arse over his groin. Jason has pushed his face into her neck and his hot breath was getting faster.

She took her hand and slipped it between them, and started to rub his cock, up and down through the fabric of his boxers.

'I really want you, Cassie.'

'Say it again.'

'I really want you,' he said, louder.

'Again. Be specific.' Cassie could feel herself getting wetter as she rubbed him.

'I want you; I want to be inside you.'

Cassie took her hand away from his cock and took his hand. She guided him, slipping his fingers around the side of her knickers and into her slick pussy.

'I want you too.'

His fingers dipped in and out, sliding her wetness all along her lips.

She hooked the waistband of her knickers and pulled them down away from her hips. There was an inelegant shuffling under the blankets, and she tried to free her feet from the fabric. She wanted to kiss his lips again, and she turned over, pushing him onto his back and mounting him.

She pushed her wet groin onto his boxers, the heat of him against her.

'Let's get rid of these,' she said. He reached around her and pulled them off, his cock springing free and slapping against the firm skin of his stomach.

'Mmm,' Cassie sighed. She leaned over to kiss him, pushing her breasts against his chest. She snuck a look towards her bedside table and groped around in the top drawer for a condom.

'Here we are,' she said, lifting herself up a little to hand it to him.

'Thanks! I was dreading having to go get my wallet for one of mine.' He smiled before tearing the wrapper with his teeth.

Cassie slid herself along his cock, transferring her wetness onto the condom. The thrill of the anticipation was almost too much, she grabbed him and pushed him into her. He was big enough to make her sigh as he entered her.

They fucked each other for a long time, rolling through several positions and throwing all of the bedclothes off.

'I don't think I can hold off much longer,' Jason panted into her hair.

'If you're ready, that's all good with me.'

Jason thrust a couple more times, the last one was deep, and he let out a shaky moan as he orgasmed.

He lay still on top of her for a moment, his breath slowing. She stroked his back; his skin was smooth under her fingers.

'Thanks' he said, pulling away and curling up beside her.

'Thank you,' she said, stroking his hair.

'If I fall asleep, can you wake me and tell me I have to go home?'

'Sure,' she said. She had no intention of kicking him out yet, but when the moment came, she would let him go. She reached out to pull the covers back over them, the heat of their activity was ebbing away and the chill night air raised goose bumps on her skin.

Jason was nestled into her side; his breathing was slow and steady. Cassie raised her head a little and saw his eyes were closed.

Chapter 18

Jason woke in Cassie's bed and smiled. She was sleeping, the thin morning light falling over her face where it seeped in around the curtains. He had waited so long for this. She stirred and then he heard a soft rumble under the blankets.

He couldn't help but laugh that she had farted in her sleep, and he carefully extracted himself from the bed before his giggling woke her.

He walked out into her kitchen and looked around, hoping to have coffee and possibly breakfast ready when she was up. He felt strange poking his nose into her cupboards, but he was sure she wouldn't mind.

The coffee grounds were in a tin conveniently labelled 'coffee'. Opening the biggest set of doors, he found the pantry. There were three bottles of oil, some packets of pasta and a loaf of bread and some peanut butter on the bottom shelf, which he pulled out.

In the fridge he found eggs and butter, as well as a small amount of milk.

That's everything I need for a good breakfast. He tried to be quiet as he moved around making the breakfast, but every time he picked something up, or put it down it seemed to make a horrendous crash. Once he had the bread toasting and the eggs frying, he turned to the coffee machine. As he brought the milk up to the frother it screamed and spluttered.

'What are you doing out there?' came a voice from the bedroom.

Jason laughed. 'I'm surprising you by making breakfast.'

She emerged from the bedroom pulling a robe around herself. He glimpsed her nakedness underneath it and felt a surge of blood to his groin.

'You made enough noise to wake the dead. But it is very sweet.' She walked over to him and rested her head on his back as he continued to struggle with the milk frother wand on the coffee machine.

'Do you want me to help you?' she said.

'No. I will master this machine if it kills me.'

'Whatever you say.'

He turned to see her smiling, as she turned the gas down under the eggs and started to butter the toast.

He sighed. 'It's just because I'm not used to your kitchen. I'm better at my place.'

'You'll have to show me one day.'

'Deal.'

They sat and ate their breakfast at the kitchen counter, Cassie's apartment was too small for a dining table. He noticed how she allowed her thigh to press against his while they sat side by side. He struggled to keep his mind on his food.

'I'd better be getting back to Knox. I hadn't really planned to stay over. I texted last night but I have to get back.'

'Of course,' she said, putting her hand on his leg. It was so warm, he put his hand over hers and forced himself to stand up, clearing the plates away.

'Leave that for me,' she added, 'I'm not doing anything today.'

Jason felt a tightening in his stomach, although whether it was because he was leaving this beautiful woman or neglecting his brother, he couldn't be sure.

They kissed in her doorway as he said goodbye, her body pressed against his, with only her robe between them. He ran his hand up her back, pulling her close to him, and he could feel himself becoming hard against her. She pushed him away.

'You have to leave remember?' She was smiling.

'I know. I'll see you soon?'

'Very soon.'

He snuck a look back as he started down the stairs, she was still standing at the door and blew him a kiss.

Jason walked towards the gate to her apartment block. He was lightheaded and grinning like a schoolboy. Nothing could spoil his mood now. He stood on the footpath and tried to orient himself.

As he headed towards the train station, a man stepping back behind a tree a little way up the road. Wary, Jason had never been one to shy away from a person just because they seemed homeless, so he kept his stride steady and kept walking.

As he passed, the man leaned against the tree; his hair was scruffy and he had several days' growth of stubble on his face. Jason kept walking but heard footfalls not far behind him.

They came to a cross-street, and Jason decided that was enough, turning to face the man. He was holding his arms rigidly by his sided, his hands in fists.

'Can I help you there, mate?' Jason asked.

'You're a motherfucking dead man,' the man said, his voice low.

'I don't know what you mean.' Jason put his hands up in front of him, gesturing surrender.

'It's too late for that. You should have thought of that before you tried to take my woman—'

'Your what?' Jason knew who it was.

'You think you're so smooth with your nice clothes. You don't know her like I do. She's mine and you can't fucking have her.'

The man lunged at Jason, who leaped backwards to avoid his grasp and the smell of stale alcohol and sweat emanated from him. There would be no reasoning with him. His only option was to try to de-escalate the situation so he could get away.

'I don't know what you mean, mate. I'm not trying to steal anyone's woman.' The phrase felt disgusting on his tongue.

'That's a goddamned lie!' the man bellowed, lunging again towards Jason. 'I saw you slinking out of her bed. You think I can't smell her cunt all over you?'

'Tony! Stop!' Cassie was running towards them; her gown was flapping behind her in the cold morning breeze.

'You two-faced bitch!' he said, turning to her as she caught up to the two men. Before he could stop it, the guy slapped Cassie so hard across the face she fell to the ground. Jason rushed to her, trying to push his way past Tony.

Tony grabbed the back of his jacket as he went past and pulled. He was very strong; Jason was throttled by the front of his jacket.

With Tony's attention back on Jason he hoped Cassie might escape any further injury.

'Let's just take a deep breath. There's no need to get violent.' Jason tried to move away from Tony, to lead him further from Cassie, but he still had hold of his jacket.

'You don't tell me what to do, maggot.'

Tony slammed his fist into Jason's solar plexus. He couldn't breathe. The world was blurred, he couldn't see. He felt panic rising as he tried to inhale, and no air would come. Then the pain came. It spread its fingers from his belly through his body. Jason struggled to stay upright and fell over the curb and into the road.

'Jason!' He heard Cassie screaming, but it seemed far away. He still hadn't drawn breath. He was convinced he would die.

Jason felt a strong pair of hands helping him to his feet and guiding him back onto the footpath. He looked around to see Tony had slid away and a couple had come out of the house nearby to help.

'Just try to relax,' said the man helping Jason. 'You'll be okay.'

Jason was taking tiny gasps of breath, but the man's voice calmed him, he was able to take deeper and deeper breaths.

A woman was standing with Cassie who was shivering and crying.

'I'm sorry, I'm so sorry,' Cassie said over and over.

Jason didn't know what to do. His brain felt full of fog.

'Are you okay?' he asked, going over to Cassie.

'Yes, I think so,' she said between sobs.

'Maybe you should come inside, you're not dressed,' said the woman.

Jason looked at her tear-streaked face and felt his cheeks colouring. He hadn't realised how bad the situation was with her ex but what could he do? Knox needed him home, he didn't want to risk Tony turning up again.

'I need to get home to Knox, but I'm going to wait here until the police arrive. This isn't something you can wave off, Cassie. You can't let him get away with this.'

He called the emergency operator and reported the incident. The three of them waited in the street for fifteen minutes before the police arrived. He gave his details and promised them he would come back to give a statement once he'd taken care of Knox and jumped into a taxi home.

***

When he arrived home, Knox was alone. Lucas had had to leave for a gig ten minutes before Jason returned, he'd texted Jason while he was in the back of the cab. It wasn't long but he never wanted to leave Knox like that again.

'I'm so sorry, buddy, I didn't mean to leave you on your own like that,' he said as he came in the front door. Knox looked up from the couch where he was playing a racing game on the Xbox.

'That's okay. I got my own breakfast, Lucas was sleeping.'

He didn't want Knox to be left to himself like he was with his parents. There was no one else who would do it, and Jason should have made sure he was home last night.

'I won't do that again. I promise I'll be around.'

'I'm not a baby, you know.'

'I know you're not. But it's still not good to leave you on your own.' Jason looked around and sighed. They needed to move. David and Becca weren't going to take Knox back, at least not for a while.

'I'm just gonna have a shower, okay? You need anything?' Jason felt dirty, he could still smell Tony on him—sweat and whiskey.

'No. I'm okay.'

'Have you got homework you're supposed to be doing?'

'Yeah.' Knox rolled his eyes, but he paused the game and got up.

Jason let the hot water run over him. His belly ached and his throat felt raw. It had all seemed so perfect, but he had to think about Knox.

What if Tony had followed him home? He had to keep Knox safe and the best way to do that would be to stay away from Cassie but that meant leaving her alone to deal with her violent ex-boyfriend.

No matter what he did in this situation someone was bound to be hurt in the end. It would be better to end the relationship now and protect his little brother. Maybe in a few months Knox would be back living with his parents and by then Tony would have lost interest.

If Cassie didn't get the restraining order now, she never would, the police had been called and were taking Cassie's statement when he left.

He would have to break it off with her. It would be more painful later. As soon as he made the decision, he was miserable. He'd been thinking he might be happy for once.

'Jason! I can't do this one.' He heard Knox calling through the bathroom door. He turned off the taps and called back. 'Okay, I'll be there in a minute.'

He felt ridiculous. It was only one night after all. He dried himself and dressed, and then went to sit with Knox at the dining table.

'Where are you stuck?' he asked. He heard his phone ringing from the pocket of his jeans, still lying on the floor in the bathroom.

'You gonna answer the phone?' Knox said.

Jason sighed, it was Cassie calling. He would worry about her all day if he didn't answer.

'Hi. Are you okay?'

'Yeah, it's fine,' Cassie said.

'It's not really fine.' Jason sighed again. 'Did you report him?'

'I gave the police a statement, but I don't think I'll press charges.'

'What about me? I'll have to make a statement too. What if I want to press charges?'

'I wish you wouldn't. I know he seems extreme but he'll come around eventually—'

'And what about before then? He doesn't seem to have any qualms about hurting you Cassie. I don't know what he was like before you split up but what he's doing is criminal. He needs to be held to account.'

Cassie's breath hitched. 'I've seen people go through intervention orders. I've seen what it does to people. If you're not going to be supportive then I guess I should let you go.'

'I am being supportive. Please, just… think about it, okay?'

'Goodbye Jason.'

He hung up the phone. Something in the way she said goodbye made him think she would never want to speak to him again. Perhaps she'd made the decision for him.

***

Jason left his phone in his pocket the next day at work. He didn't want to be tempted to call Cassie or check if she'd called him. It would be better for everyone if they held onto the one night together and moved on. But he couldn't get her out of his head.

Both partners were in early and were in particularly belligerent moods.

'Jason! Where are the letters I asked you to write on Friday?' Mr Pierce started yelling as he walked towards Jason's desk.

Jason sighed. 'I sent them. You said they were urgent.'

'You idiot! I need to change them.' Mr Pierce turned away, muttering under his breath. 'Such incompetence.'

'What did you just say?' Jason stood up at his desk.

Mr Pierce stopped, straightened and turned back to Jason. 'I said, "such incompetence". You were never really cut out to be a lawyer. You'd know that if you weren't so dense.'

Jason's thrust his hands into his pockets to hold them still.

'I am not incompetent. I have done exactly what you asked me to do. The fact that you have given bad advice to a client is not my fault. If I were indeed incompetent, the letters would still be here, but now your mistake stands.'

'How dare you!' Pierce was panting.

'Don't make me the scapegoat for your mistake. I have had enough of being your punching bag, Mister Pierce,' Jason said his name deliberately. 'I'm done being blamed for your mistakes, I'm done covering up for you, and having to check everything that goes out of this office.'

'You! You check everything, do you?' Pierce spluttered.

Jason turned his head to the other staff, hoping one of them would back him up, but they sat there, stunned.

'I think I had better take a break now.' Jason started to towards the door.

'You don't get off that easily. You think I'm just going to let you talk to me like that?'

'I shouldn't have said those things. We could both use some time to calm down. I'll be back in shortly. If you're still angry, we can talk, away from the rest of the office.'

Pierce said nothing. He just stood in the middle of the office as Jason walked out. He could feel the adrenalin coursing through him; his fingers were tingly, and he felt light-headed.

Jason had walked out without his coat and he folded his arms, shoving his hands into his armpits in an effort to keep the chill wind out. It didn't really work.

What a nightmare, he thought, as he turned down the hill towards the centre of the city. As he walked, he realised he was angry at Tony. And at Cassie.

He took his phone from his pocket and called her.

'Are you alright?' he asked.

'Yes, I'm fine. I told you that.'

'Did you change your mind about charging him?'

'No, I don't think that will help.'

'Mmm.'

'Is that why you called me?'

'I hoped you'd had a chance to change your mind. I hoped we would be able to salvage what we had...'

'Had?'

'Yeah. We can't see each other again.' He put his hand up and rubbed his forehead, his throat felt so tight.

'What? It's not my fault that Tony's crazy!'

'I never said it was,' Jason sounded tired. 'I have to think about Knox. What if Tony had followed me home to Knox? What about next time? He's just going to get worse. I know you are afraid of the repercussions of reporting him, or of the trauma of going through the courts, I know how hard that can be. I can't to force you to get an intervention order, but if you don't I can't see you anymore.'

Cassie was silent on the other end of the phone. He could hear her breathing.

'Are you still there?' he asked.

'Yes. I don't know what to say. I should have known it was too soon to date. I'm sorry Jason. I wish you all the best.' She hung up.

Cassie had given up very easily. He felt flat, he stared his phone, hoping she'd ring back, but she didn't. The blank face of the phone stared back at him and he remembered how cold he was. He let out a deep sigh and turned back towards the office.

Chapter 19

Cassie sat down on her couch. She had known Tony was not in a good place and had been getting steadily worse and not better. Now she'd lost Jason because of her inaction but she still felt paralysed.

Why can't I just do what I know I need to do?

She wanted to cry, but the tears wouldn't come. Her phone vibrated on the coffee table where it had fallen from her hand. She opened the text, but it wasn't from Jason.

Do you want to come for dinner tonight? Ian and I haven't seen you for a while. X Tessa.

The thought of having dinner with her aunt somehow burst the bubble of numbness around her. Cassie's tears flowed and her face burned. She cried for so long that her head ached.

When her phone rang, she realised that she had never responded to Tessa's invitation.

'Hello,' she said, her voice thick.

'Are you okay?' Tessa asked.

'No.'

'What's happened? Has Tony done something?'

'I'm such a moron.'

'Honey. We all tried to help you, but you weren't ready.' Her aunt's voice was kind. 'Do you want to come for dinner? You don't have to talk if you don't want to,' she added.

'Yes please.'

'Do you want me to pick you up?'

'Yes please.'

'Alright, I'll be there soon. I love you.'

***

Tessa rang the buzzer twenty minutes later, and Cassie had managed to pull herself together enough to put on some clothes and brush her hair.

'I'll come down,' Cassie said through the intercom.

They were silent on the drive. As they pulled up at Tessa's house, she turned off the car.

'Do you want to talk about it?'

'Maybe after we've eaten. I haven't really eaten all day.'

'You just let me know when you're ready.'

'Thank you.' Cassie took her aunt's hand.

'You're welcome, my love.'

Dinner was an eggplant lasagne. 'Ian's going through a vegetarian phase, but if it means he cooks then I don't mind what sort of phase he goes through.' She smiled at

her partner and Cassie was struck by the love in her eyes.
It reminded her of what she'd lost by being afraid.

'I had a date with Jason on Saturday. You know, the
lawyer?'

'How was it?' Her aunt took a sip of her wine, and Ian
was silent except for the clink of dishes as he washed up.

'He, uh, stayed the night—'

'That's wonderful!' Tessa interrupted.

'I hadn't finished. It was wonderful. It was one of the
best night's I've ever had. But in the morning, Tony was
waiting outside my house.' She told them the whole
story. 'And now he says he can't see me.'

'He's got a point.' Ian broke through the quiet.

'I know he does. That's what makes it so terrible. I
should have just done the right thing and then Jason
wouldn't have been attacked.'

'We don't blame you for being scared,' her aunt said,
putting her hand on Cassie's.

'I'm so sick of being scared. What do I have to lose
now? Jason's already gone. I doubt he'll be back even if
I do get the intervention order. And Tony can hardly get
any worse.'

'Don't be like that. If you want to make the report,
then I think that's a good idea.'

'Thanks.'

'And I wouldn't completely give up hope for this new
man. You never know, he might change his mind.'

'I don't think so.' Cassie sighed. 'Can I stay here tonight?'

'Of course you can,' Ian said.

'Will you go to the police in the morning?' Tessa asked.

'I'd better get it over with.'

Tessa set up the foldout couch for her to sleep on before she and Ian disappeared to bed. Cassie lay on the thin mattress staring at the ceiling in the dark. She could hear the other two talking behind their bedroom door. They were keeping their voices down, but Cassie thought they were fighting.

More lives I've ruined, she thought, her mind was filled with darkness. She lay there for what felt like hours. Eventually the sounds of her aunt and Ian talking faded, the sliver of light under their bedroom door went out. The house was silent and dark.

When Tessa woke her in the morning she felt as though she hadn't slept at all.

'This is scary.'

'I'll be there with you. It'll be okay. Tony needs help. To stop drinking and stop threatening you.'

Cassie sighed. 'You're right.' She rolled over and looked at her phone, hoping that something from Jason had come through in the night, but there was nothing.

They chose the police station closest to Cassie's home in Northcote; it was in the carpark behind the supermarket. They waited at the front desk and told the officer there that they needed to make a report of an assault. The two women waited for a constable to be available and were then led into an interview room.

'I'm Constable Weiner,' the young female police officer said to them. 'I understand you have a report to make?'

Tessa looked at Cassie, then nodded her head towards the cop.

'Yes. There are a couple of instances. Do I need to do them separately?'

'Well, let's hear the story first.' Weiner smiled at her, and Cassie tried to take strength from it. She was squeezing her aunt's hand under the table.

'Well, there was a break-in a couple of weeks ago. Some officers came then, but I didn't want to take it any further. And there was the time he hit me, and I ended up in hospital a couple of weeks before that, but yesterday he punched my boyfr—uh, well, he's not my boyfriend, anyway, in the chest.' Cassie started to regret coming in.

'Take your time,' Tessa said quietly.

'I want a restraining order. I've let him get away with it for long enough. Standing outside my house, waiting for me to bring someone home and then attacking him! He's ruined everything.' Cassie's voice had risen in volume as she spoke.

'I can see it's very upsetting for you,' said Weiner, 'I'd like to tell you it will go away on its own, but that's just not how these things work. As for the intervention order, that's done in the courts. The police can apply on your behalf, but—'

'I would like to do this myself,' Cassie said, slipping her hand out from her aunt's.

'Good. This is a difficult process, and you might be feeling like you should have done this earlier-'

'How did you know?' Cassie asked.

'Unfortunately, this isn't the first time I've dealt with this situation. You have nothing to be ashamed about. This is not your fault. You are taking action to make yourself safe. That's what matters.' Weiner looked her straight in the eye for so long Cassie had to look away.

'What did I tell you?' Tessa said softly.

'You need to make the application to the magistrates' court, then the police will serve, that is deliver, the paperwork to the respondent, the person the restraining order is against. You'll have to go to court to present evidence to make the order permanent, but the interim order can be put into effect almost immediately.'

***

I've got an intervention order against Tony. He's not allowed to contact me, or come near me. I'm sorry it took me so long. The process was a nightmare. Cassie sent the text to Jason after spending all the next day in court. She didn't expect him to reply but thought he should know.

She'd been agonising over the content of the text, and whether to send it at all since she got home from the court at six o'clock. She lay on the couch, too exhausted to even go to bed. She switched on the TV.

She was woken the next morning by the sound of her phone ringing. At first, she couldn't find it, but she managed to answer it before it went to voicemail.

'Hello,' she said.

'Hello, is this Cassandra Morton?' the female voice asked.

'Yes,'

'It's Constable Weiner, I'm just calling to let you know that we handed the order to Mister Bryant this morning and explained what it means.'

'How did he react?'

'To say he was upset would be an understatement. However, with two police members in his home he was sensible enough.'

'But?' Cassie could hear something in Weiner's tone.

'But, I'm a little concerned. He seemed quite alcohol-affected, for so early in the morning. Is there somewhere you can stay for a couple of nights?'

'I'm sick of running away from this shit,' Cassie said, she didn't want to feel powerless again.

'I understand. But, statistically speaking, this is a dangerous time for a woman in your situation.'

Cassie felt as though she couldn't breathe. When had she become a "woman in a situation"? She didn't want pity, she wanted Tony to leave her alone.

'So, how long would I need to stay away for?' Cassie asked, her jaw was clenched so tight it was hard to speak.

'Three or four days at a minimum I'd say. I'm sure it will be fine. We'll check the residence every so often, to make sure it's secure.'

'Great.' Cassie couldn't keep the sarcasm out of her voice.

'We're really very restricted in what we can do in these situations, Cassie, you know we can't harass him.'

Cassie sighed. 'I know.'

'I'd advise you to leave soon. We can send someone by to escort you if you like.'

'That isn't necessary. I'll go.'

When Cassie hung up the phone, she felt exhausted. Tony was still calling the shots; he was still able to force her out of her home.

And I thought getting the order would be the end of it.

Tessa would be out at work for the rest of the day, but Cassie knew where her spare key was. She gathered the few clothes had now, her toiletries, phone charger and laptop and was out of the flat in ten minutes.

***

She sat down at Tessa's dining table and looked at her phone. There was still no response from Jason.

As she typed a message to Tessa asking to stay for a few days, her phone vibrated, and a message came through. Cassie's heart was beating so fast she was sure she would faint.

That must have been difficult for you. I'm glad you'll be safe now, Jason had replied.

But what does that mean? Cassie read the text over and over trying to understand whether he meant for her to reply or not. He hadn't asked a question, or invited conversation, but he had still replied. Maybe he was rethinking things.

I'm so sorry you got caught up in my shit. I really didn't think he would be dangerous. I was being naive. I haven't stopped thinking about you. The other night was so special to me. If you'll have me, I'd like to try again.

Her hands trembled as she sent it. A message came through seconds later, but it was just Tessa.

She waited several minutes for Jason to send a reply, but none came. She sighed and went back to looking for jobs. She scrolled through hundreds of jobs which seemed too hard, or too easy, or too permanent. After all she was going back to study in a few months.

Then she saw an ad for a hospitality agency. They wanted casual staff to do events and cover shifts. It would be very last minute, at any sort of venue, any sort of event, any sort of time. But she had plenty of experience and they seemed to pay well.

She sent an application and went to get a cup of tea. Outside the sky was overcast and the house was dark. Looking at her watch she saw it was almost three in the afternoon and she hadn't eaten. It wasn't like her to skip a meal, but her schedule recently had been very disrupted.

Cassie hadn't brought any food with her, she decided to go for a walk and find a bakery. Tessa would be home later, and they would have a big sit-down meal, she'd just get something small and sweet. She wanted to treat herself without guilt for once.

She left her phone at Tessa's place, and went for a stroll through the quiet suburban streets. She went past a school as the kids were getting out, watching the various parents collecting their precious boys and girls reminded her of Knox. It would be better for him to stay with Jason, but she guessed she would never know now.

It wasn't meant to be, that's all, she told herself. As she tried, unsuccessfully, to eat the croissant she'd ordered without getting flakes of pastry all over herself her mind was stuck on Jason. Everyone had problems, couldn't he see they had something worth taking a chance on? She uncurled her fingers from where they were gripping the handle of her coffee cup.

'Do you want another coffee?' The waitress startled her; she was standing right by her elbow.

'No thanks. I'll never sleep again if I do.'

The waitress smiled and went back to wiping down the tabletops. Cassie looked around; she was the last person in the café. She got up, paid, and started the walk back to Tessa's.

By the time she got back Tessa was already home. The light was on outside, probably for Ian, but Cassie was comforted to think it was for her too.

'Hi!' Tessa called as she walked in. 'How was your day?'

'It had its moments. I thought Jason might have forgiven me, but that was wishful thinking on my part.'

'Is that your phone? It's been ringing.' She pointed to the coffee table where Cassie had left it before going out.

Cassie tried not to get excited, but her heart had started jumping inside her ribs like a demented frog. She picked up her phone, there were no texts from Jason, but there were two missed calls and a voicemail.

'I have been thinking about you a lot, Cassie. I know it's a tough time for both of us, but I think maybe that's just how relationships work. They come up when you're not looking for them, and not ready for them. I'm not ready to give up either.'

She listened to the message again, just to make sure she'd heard it right.

'Are you alright, love? You look a bit peaky,' Tessa said. 'It wasn't Tony was it? I'll give him a piece of my mind hassling you.'

Cassie spluttered a laugh that turned into a cough.

'No. It was Jason. He said he wants to see me.' Cassie was grinning. She couldn't stop herself; she didn't want to.

'Jason? Wasn't that the boy Tony punched?' Ian said from the couch.

'Yes.' Tessa flapped her hand at him as though to shut him up. Cassie registered it, but her smile didn't dim.

'Should I call him back?'

'What do you mean? Of course!' Tessa said.

'But,' she faltered. 'What if it doesn't work out? I mean even with Tony out of the picture.'

'I don't know if I've told you this, but you're one of the strongest women I know. You can handle whatever comes your way. But if you let this one get away...' Her aunt was smiling, but Cassie knew she was serious. She'd used her mother's death as an excuse and then she nearly allowed Tony to push him away.

'Okay, I get the message.' Cassie stepped outside the front door into the cold. She wanted to have this conversation away from her aunt.

She dialled the number and it rang for so long she thought he wasn't going to answer.

'Hello? Are you still there?' He sounded out of breath, and Cassie laughed.

'Yes, I'm still here. I—'she didn't know what to say. 'I got your message.'

'Good.' They were silent.

'I was kind of relieved when I got your voicemail,' he said. 'I wasn't sure I could have said all that mushy stuff when I knew you were there. I get a bit shy,' he said.

'I feel like that sometimes. I almost didn't call you back.'

He laughed. 'Really? I thought you liked me.'

'I do! God, I do. With everything that's going on for both of us it's not going to be easy.'

'A wise man once said nothing worth doing is easy.'

'Jason! Help!' she heard Knox's voice in the background.

'Ah, shit.' He put the phone down onto a hard surface. 'How did you manage that? There's milk everywhere.' Jason's voice sounded far away.

'Hi Cassie.' Knox had clearly picked up the phone.

'Hi Knox. What's happening?'

'Jason and I were making a cake. There's a cake stall at school on Saturday and we all have to bring something. He was helping me when you rang.'

'What sort of cake is it?'

'We're making butterfly cupcakes.' Knox sounded proud, and Cassie smiled.

'Hey, give that back.' There was a scuffling sound and Jason was back on the line. 'Sorry, I better go, I don't want him burning his hands off on the oven.'

'I'm not an idiot! I know how to use the oven,' Knox said across the room.

'Let's catch up soon,' Jason said.

'I could come to the cake stall. I'd buy a butterfly cake from you.' As soon as she said it, she felt a fool. *Surely that's too corny for words.*

'That'd be nice. There'll be a lot of parents and I'm not sure I'm very popular with them at the moment. They're a bit snobby.'

'I can imagine.'

'It would be good to have you as moral support against the hordes of Brighton stay-at-home-mums. And,' he laughed, 'at least one person will buy our cakes.'

'I'll buy them all if you like.'

'I'll hold you to that. I'd better go. Knox has the beaters.'

'Okay. I'll see you soon.'

'Love you, bye,' Jason said.

Did really just say he loved me?

Surely, she'd misheard him. There were two days until the cake stall when she hoped they'd be able to start over.

***

Saturday morning was overcast and dreary, not exactly what you'd want for a cake stall, but Cassie knew it wouldn't matter what the weather did, as long as Jason wanted to spend time with her.

'I can't wear the green dress, can I? That's too much?' she asked her aunt at breakfast.

'A bit. Just wear some jeans and something nice on top, it'll be cold so practicality over fashion. There's no point getting pneumonia to impress him.'

Cassie smiled at her aunt and pulled on her jeans and a T-shirt. She put a grey knitted jumper over it and a black coat. There was no telling how windy and cold it would be, but Brighton was near the sea, it was better to be safe than sorry.

She was meeting them there, as Jason had to set up. She had a cold fist of nerves in her belly as she walked up to the school. She'd thought she looked nice until she saw the other women there.

'Cassie!' She heard her name called from her left and turned to see Knox running towards her. 'We're over here. Jason said I had to come get you, coz he's not allowed to leave the stall.'

He grabbed her hand and pulled her along behind him towards a row of tables with an obscene number of cakes covering them. Each table had been draped in heavy looking tablecloths, pristine white and rippling in the breeze.

Jason smiled as they caught each other's eye. Cassie could feel her cheeks colouring.

'Hi,' he said.

'Hi.' She didn't know whether to hug him, shake his hand or kiss him.

Knox broke their moment. 'We made these ones. Do you wanna buy one?'

'Of course! That's what I'm here for isn't it?' She pulled out her wallet.

'We haven't sold any yet. You're our first customer. The other parents seem to have put me down this end, so they don't have to talk to me.'

'I'm sorry.'

'Now you're here, I don't care what they do.' He smiled at her and she imagined kissing him, remembered her skin next to his and feeling safe in his arms.

'Come around this side. I want to give you something,' he said.

'Oh, alright.'

On the other side of the cake stall, Jason was wearing tight black jeans that showed off his bottom.

'What did you want to give me?' she asked.

Jason took her hand and pulled her closer to him. He leant down and kissed her. Cassie's legs momentarily wobbled. When she'd recovered from the initial bliss of it, she wrapped her arms around him and kissed him back. She hoped he knew how much she wanted him.

He pulled away from her and the cold air came between them. Knox was running around with some other boys his age, she and Jason stood quietly, holding hands, waiting for a customer.

'You know the other day, when I said I loved you?' His voice was quiet, there were a few people at the next table down.

'Yeah,' she said.

'I've thought about it, and I mean it. I love you. I know it's too soon, but I just wanted it out there.'

'It is soon. I don't want to go rushing into anything too quickly. You've got Knox to think about and—' She slipped her hand from his grasp.

'I've ruined it, haven't I?' He looked at the ground.

'No, you haven't. I was going to say, I think I might love you too.'

'You don't know how good that is to hear.' He wrapped his arms around her and whispered into her neck. 'Say it again.'

'I love you,' she said.

'Now that I know you're into me, we can take as long as you like.'

'I'm into you. That's for sure.' Cassie pulled him away from her and planted a kiss on his lips. 'Now, hadn't we better behave? There are children present.'

'Alright. I guess we've got plenty of time.' He slipped his hand back into hers and they turned to watch the other parents.

THE END

Epilogue

Dear Kerry

I'm sorry it's taken so long to get back to you, I've been busy since finalising the estate.

In answer to your question, yes, I'm well. I'll tell you all about the family, since you're keen to hear about us. I'm very glad to hear that Junior is settling in well with his new job.

Life has been very different in the year since we lost Mum. I've recently moved in with a lovely guy, Jason. He actually worked for the law firm who handled Mum's will. I seem to have acquired an instant family; his younger half-brother lives with us now too. He's eleven and a really sweet kid. We get some support from his mother although she's still trying to put her life back together after everything his father, David, went sideways. He'd sunk all his money into some terrible stocks and then started gambling to try to recoup his losses. In the end he had started using investors money to cover his losses and it was a miracle he didn't end up in prison. He went bankrupt and plead guilty to embezzlement. It was his first offence so he got a fine and some community service hours, which seems pretty inadequate to me.

Jason hasn't forgiven him yet but tries not to speak badly of David in front of Knox. I've never known someone to be so selfless for a child who isn't even his responsibility. Not really anyway. Jason also has a sister, Tam, the same age as my sister Penny, she's a bit of a wild child but I think the business with David has scared her straight for the time being.

Speaking of, Penny's doing okay. She went through a rough patch with substance abuse, Mum's death didn't help, but it had been an issue before then. She got into ice with her boyfriend and ended up in a bad way. After her third trip to hospital in as many months, he realised that he was enabling her addiction and left. Since then she's went to a rehab facility and has been able to pull herself together. She still drinks far too much, but she's got a new job in a call centre and she comes to hang out with me and Jason and Knox about once a week. It's been nice having her around.

Before Mum died I hadn't spoken to Dad for a long time, you wouldn't have met him, he came along after you and Mum stopped writing. He never knew about you two. It nearly killed him and it's what ended their marriage. I was pretty shocked to realise that he had been so hurt. He's so different to the man I thought he was – fragile. Penny and I have had dinner with him a few times in the last couple of months. We're just taking it slow but it will be nice to have him back in our lives.

It's funny how things go when you start thinking about parents as human beings instead of only as your mum or dad.

As for me, I went back to school to finish the degree in Social Work I dropped out of a few years ago. Losing my restaurant job and seeing how many people around me were just a few disasters away from being in real trouble put a few things in perspective for me. There has to be more to life than just making money.

If you're ever in Melbourne come and visit us and if I ever have the money to come over to see you I'll be sure to drop in.

Lots of love,

Cassie.

www.ingramcontent.com/pod-product-compliance
Lightning Source LLC
Chambersburg PA
CBHW032001130726
47903CB00012B/218